YOUTH

For Sebastien & Fleur

YOUTH

KEVIN CURRAN

First published 2023 by
THE LILLIPUT PRESS
62–63 Arbour Hill
Dublin 7, Ireland
www.lilliputpress.ie

A CIP record for this publication is available from
The British Library.

10 9 8 7 6 5 4 3 2 1

ISBN 978 1 84351 870 9

The Lilliput Press gratefully acknowledges the financial support of the Arts Council / An Chomhairle Ealaíon.

Set in 11pt on 16pt Adobe Garamond Pro by Niall McCormack
Printed in Kerry by Walsh Colour Print

Down Mainstreet

Angel, 18

He speaks in your voice, Dublin, and there's something hopeful in the new edges of his words and phrases that has come through revolutions, generations, and across continents to be witnessed here, on these streets, now.

Angel is shaping down Mainstreet of a Friday afternoon in late March. Traffic is heavy, the footpaths are busy and he is one of three friends bustling through – a blur of hands and fingers at angles making shadow puppets to the uninformed. A simple K for those in the know.

They're all theatrical eyes, aghast mouths.

—That's a bar, Isaac, allow.

—That's a bar? No this is a bar: you Congo boys eat rocks.

—That's a lie, bro, that's a lie. All you Ghana boys eat eggs.

—Don't say nothing bout us Nigerians. Swear down, boys, yous'll be getting hands!

All three of them are on display. Teenagers – roadmen – giving verbals while widening the aperture of this washed-out world.

The rain has stopped and the pavement is bright and slick. And although it's Friday and sunny, they know this spring buzz won't last for long.

Hunger drives them. Luckily, this four-hundred-metre slope of Mainstreet, Balbriggan – from SuperValu to the Square – is the meal-deal capital of County Dublin.

There's Libero's Italian pizzas warming in the oven and shielded by dirty netting in the window; Borza with the blue neon signs saying value, value, value; Macari's high top chrome counter guarding the fryer; SuperValu deli a trek past the fruit and veg, under the always-suspicious eyes of the security guard; Polski Delikatesy hiding its bland meats and sausages behind frosted glass lettering; Deli Burger in its prime location across from the monument, overlooking the Bracken; FLC, Noodle Box, Apache, Domino's, Moti Mahal, Han Lin Palace, Coffee Pot, Supermac's, Papa John's, Mr Wu, the soup kitchen beside the dole office. And Spar.

As tall as the others, Angel is the thinnest of the three. His wide, cat-like eyes are forever scanning for trouble. If he sees it early, he can sidestep it, like a Messi feint. Because that's what he does as he walks, he feints and shuffles.

His nervous energy is a necessity. His black Nike Air Force runners are worn to a woolly grey where the imitation leather meets the sole. It's a low-key embarrassment only evading detection by scaring his feet into constant action.

His school trousers are short, tight above the ankle, unable to keep up with this sprint through adolescence. His jacket, the black puffer North Face uniform of all three, is that bit older and looser on him.

On they go, Pelumi spitting out some new bars he's working on.

—*I love my block.*
That's all that I got.
I love my block.

Isaac and Angel support him with loud shouts of encouragement. But being loud doesn't come natural to Angel. It might seem to fit well, but it weighs heavily, like a wet T-shirt.

Be the collective experience when alone. That's the ambition. That's the shame. The lie under this fluid, confident strut. The aggressive disregard for onlookers is a rebuke to himself: the self-aware, self-conscious bitch boy who worries his way through the town when on his ones.

Why does he always need his boys? Why is he always on sketch, ready to dash, so lacking?

For now, Angel commands the street with his friends and, without pausing for permission, they stop traffic and cross, a mixtape of car horns soundtracking their parade.

They own the path and refuse to make way for some guy in shorts coming through the Spar sliding doors with a six-pack of beer. Pelumi blocks him, knocks into him. This wasteman is hench and still he staggers and his bottles clink – one cracks and suddenly there's a mess of suds.

Pelumi kisses his teeth and sneers:

—What you gonna do?

The lad curses at them but on they go, defiant, without remorse or consequence, striding into encounters Angel would rather dodge.

Tanya, 16

She's lost in her phone and has that hurried, got-to-attend-to-this-message vibe about her as she steps off the path. The screen exposes her squinting eyes and she groans because she can't see anything but herself.

It's the sharp screech of tyres that jolts her out've the reflection. The phone flips from her hand with the shock. The scuffed white toe of her black Converse high-top takes the initial impact. She's full sure she's only gone and cracked the screen on the road.

—Who you think you are? is spat from the window of a supped up red sports car.

—I'm Tanya fucking Guildea, that's who I am, she shouts back, refusing to meet his eyes as she crouches in the road.

The fan from his bonnet whirrs at her head. She's afraid what she'll find when she turns the phone around so she takes her time to pick it up. It's grand but, thank fuck.

He starts revving the engine. He wants her to acknowledge him. Most of them do. She's used to the attention, okay with it. She ignores the taunts, his big boiled head with the oversized Borcrew cap out the car window, shouting:

—*Kurwa mac!*

She strolls to the path, shoulders back, chest out.

—What ye looking at ye muppet?

—*Palant!*

Of course, there's always an audience. Especially now. Always someone passing comment. She's too young, she's showing too much skin, she's a disgrace that one.

She's a kid, only looks older. And so she behaves like she thinks people who are older should behave. With disdain for those giving her the looks, a snarl for tender approaches, a reproachful smile for those who whistle.

She walks with her head high as if she's not really on these streets, as if she should be somewhere more glamorous, a catwalk, a red carpet.

Her hair is blonde and brown, glossy, tied up in a bun. Beyond the huge glue-on lashes that constantly give her red eye, her face is stern, serious, self-conscious, always set into a pout as if someone might be recording her. Her bright pink Nike schoolbag flails from her left hand as if she's about to fling it, underarm style, into the river beside Deli Burger. Her school skirt is short and blows a bit in the wind. She can feel the small gusts travelling up her legs and she sees them looking, random lads, pretending they're not, but always looking.

They're quiet and sneaky, from teenagers to aul lads, staring from the tables of the chipper, coming out of the Medical Centre on the corner, tapping their hands on the counter in the vape shop, or loud and jeering, like Lil Pel and his K3P gang across the road going into Spar. She gives them the finger and they love it, but there's nothing else she can do.

Dean, 17

There's no queue at the deli in Spar. And into this grey tiled space Dean attempts to swagger. He thinks he has perfected the wavy arms, raised chin, gum-chewing march. To everyone but himself though, he's just a lanky teenage cartoon. An anime character in a 3D world.

The hot food counter is practically empty. An uninspiring assortment of dried-out wedges, burnt chicken fillets and a handful of chicken poppers are all that's left. They're already boxed – but still open – a two-euro sticker stuck on the flap under the spotlights.

His hands feel the warmth of the deli-counter glass and immediately jerk away, recognizing the all-too-familiar burn of the everyday on the greasy surface. He rubs his palms on his worn, silky grey school trousers, stained at the crotch by hurried shakes at the Seniors' urinals. Always in the school bathroom he stares ahead with a gamer's determination – until someone steps up, grunts and pisses with a force that both splashes and alarms. And at the end, after the fumble and tuck, Dean turns and catches a glimpse to compare. Always comparing. Because if he's honest, that's really why he left the queue at the deli earlier: in among all the other lads, he felt inadequate. With the jeers of his peers burning his ears, he turned away from the deli and left without lunch.

Now, with no queue, and a two-euro coin moist in his hand, Dean is preparing to be served by the girl. She's out the back, washing utensils. He takes a hairbrush from his school bag and, with practised care, shapes his hair. His right hand brushes right to left while his left pats and buffers.

Without the pressure of the lads at lunchtime, he hopes all redners will stay away and he might have a chance to chat with her. Maybe say something funny. Have her speak to him so he can mould her words into something more for when he's alone with himself.

She arrives with a smile, her braces catching the light.

—For the Taco Fries? she says in that Spanish accent of hers.

—Eh, are there any left?

She disappears behind the hot counter. He doesn't know anything about her. Only that she's going to the Convent as an exchange student and is on work experience for TY. In the gaps between seeing her – using her smile, the way she flicks her hair away from her eyes with her wrist, the way she addresses him – he has started to stare at the ceiling above his bed and begin to know her, or who she might be. And who he might become in her company.

Taco Fries. How does she know that? His brow darkens as he debates with himself the meaning of her remembering his past orders. At least he has made an impression.

—Let me see. Oh, one left. That is a karma.

—Lucky me, Dean says.

—Anything else?

He hesitates. She waits.

—Your name?

She looks into the deli, confused.

—My?

—Name.

—Name?

—Yeah, like, what you're called.

—Oh, name! Ah, okay …

The lads' laughing and shouting only registers when it's on top of him.

—Alright Martina, Lil Pel says, shouldering Dean aside.

Dean stretches out to take the slightly soggy box and she gives him a soft, hopeful smile.

Another lad knocks on the glass.

—Hola Martina babe. Gissa chicken fillet roll there please, yeah?

Dean doesn't say goodbye to Martina. He retreats, not because he's physically afraid of them – even though he is – but because their friendship, their togetherness, lessens him. Makes him realize what he doesn't have.

His redner has taken over. *Your name*, what was he thinking? He was thinking of creeping.

Princess, 17

The library on a Friday afternoon, like most afternoons – and evenings – is her refuge. The soft silence wraps around her as she moves through the electrical doors, clear of the Town Square's white noise.

No phone notifying, no baby crying, no shower running, chores waiting, TV droning, speakers playing, toys chiming, dogs barking, neighbours shouting, doors slamming, footsteps pounding. Just a photocopier sweeping out two black and white counterfeits of a passport, while a lady smiles and whispers and the old man behind the counter silently nods along, stamping her books.

Princess sighs and scans the tables. She smells of the cold. School jackets are an expense her mother wasn't willing to pay for in her final year. Her school jumper is unnecessarily big, lumpy, a bottom-of-the-drawer lost-and-found effort last worn four years ago. Princess has knotted the back with a hair tie to tuck it up and give her some shape. She's done the same with the skirt. Folded it up twice around the waist, hooked it there to provide some semblance of style.

She walks into the library with a slow, heavy-footed scrape as if her feet are magnetized to the carpet. Her black runners pass as shoes in school, and sometimes, if her sister Becky is going somewhere important, she'll take a lend of them too. So they're loose, from two pairs of feet confusing the material. It's not that Princess likes to walk slow. If ever a runner came off, she couldn't be sure her sock wasn't ripped at the heel or a big toe bright with green nail-polish wouldn't be exposed. Crowded school corridors don't ever forget. Or libraries.

For some reason, the library is busier than normal. Princess is already growing weary of the struggle to find a small space for herself in this world. This place is becoming a microcosm of her home life. She flicks her purple braids over her shoulder with a subconscious sudden flap and, with what grace she can, sits across from a quiet-looking guy.

When she whips her head, she feels her braids will establish $A=\pi r^2$ and provide a minimum space to exist in. Basketball taught her this in first year. No matter where she'd turn with the ball, some other girl was crowding her, slapping at her, hassling her. If she had braids, a swift turn of the head would clear the space.

She removes her school bag quietly from her back and places it on the table. A faded Tipp-Ex 'Becky' is scrawled across the front pocket. The corners of textbooks stick out through the frayed material on the bottom of the bag. The thin strands of material get lighter every day. She doubts there's enough thread to get her to June.

Her zip is barely open when she sees the Spar deli box, smells the food.

—Like, seriously? she says, her chin dipping into her chest.

The guy goes so red she nearly feels sorry for him.

He shrugs an embarrassed:

—What? and almost hugs the box.

—That.

The guy holds up a limp, greasy taco fry like an apology.

—You want one?

She bites her lip and grabs her bag.

The next table has two young teenagers. At least one's a girl. That's something.

Princess has half a page of her Chemistry book highlighted in a strong pink when the teenagers start to giggle. And then there's the wet slap and suck of a kiss and she looks up and there's tongues. They're literally giggling into each other's mouths. Princess snaps the highlighter down on the desk and slams her cover shut.

Princess is seething, fuming, not just with them, but the library, the librarian who has gone soft after he was tackled to the ground by some lads a few weeks ago, with the school for closing early on a Friday, with her mam, with her sister, little baby Michael, the architect of the apartment block she lives in for making the walls so fucking thin. Everyone and everything is against her.

Her chair falls over with a clatter when she stands up. She smashes her bag onto the table.

—This is such bullshit, she shouts. Is no one here to actually study?

Silence. A few people look at their laps. The young couple at her desk smile as if she's entertaining them.

—You know he's just gonna break your heart, she says to the girl.

The librarian, the one attacked a few weeks ago, is shuffling over, hands out.

—Excuse me, excuse me, you cannot behave like that in …

—I can't behave like that? I'm the problem? Oh my days.

The librarian shakes his head and mumbles as she passes. The doors swish open. Princess, blinded by tears and refusing to blink, searches out the silver rail to guide her down the steps to Mainstreet.

All at Once

Princess

Don't. Have. Sex.

That's the one definite way not to get pregnant. I am not gonna have a baby like my sister, Becky. You mad? First sign of a man and she dipped. Gone from the house, leaving me alone with mum and our silences. Only to peg it back home after loverman Oisin pumps her and dumps her.

Crying.

—He broke my heart mum.

—It's okay baby.

—He told me he loved me mum.

—Hush now. Sshh, it's okay baby.

—He said he'd be careful.

—Now, come on. It's okay.

—Look after me. He said he wouldn't do it.

—What now?

—Oh mum.

—Do what?

—Mum, please.

—Do what?

—Get me pregnant. I'm pregnant mum.

The silence. Oh. My. Days. The silence.

I've never seen my mum like that before. She put her hands on her head. The stubble from her last close shave scratched under her nails. It was like she was trying to massage her scalp, calm herself.

Me and my friend Iwona got an extra science class a few months ago after school. Miss let us stay back on our own and showed us some supplementary experiments. At the start Miss made us blow up balloons. I was like, I could be at the library studying now instead of being Miss's party planner. Then she gave us goggles, brought us behind the table and told us to throw our balloon at a couple of milligrams of powder on a different table. When that red balloon landed we were nearly knocked off our feet. I never seen a reaction like it.

Until my mum heard about Becky.

My mum got so angry. It was like Becky's words were the balloon floating slowly to its destination and mum was nitrogen triiodide waiting all her life for this contact. Her hands left her head and her fingers spread wide. She just exploded, jumped for Becky in a purple rage. Bam, bam, bam, bam.

Poor Becky goes out into the world, gets pregnant and then her boyfriend Oisin disappears to Limerick to milk the cows on his dad's farm. Now that's tight. See me, I've got two big luminous highlighters and I've made note. Yellow is for general observations: Make sure to get an education before leaving home. Pink is for specific life-advancement threats: Have the cop on to steer clear of farmers looking to pump me and dump me.

To help me get into the world I've printed out three two-page CVs in Tantine's Global supermarket. Why only three? 1) There are three independent pharmacies in Balbriggan. 2) The paper was fifteen cent a page and I only had one euro.

I put my CV and cover letter into a plastic sleeve. Then I tie my hair back and put on the skirt and blouse I wore for baby Michael's dedication. It still fits, so, you know, why not? I take a cardigan from my sister Becky's room. It's not like she'll ever notice. She wears her Nike Tech, like, everywhere she goes. Plus, she takes and ruins enough of my stuff.

The kitten heels hurt my feet. Some of those lads, Pelumi and them, are sitting on the wall at the entrance to my apartment block when I click past. Kids are out on their bikes, some are kicking a ball on the road. Older teenagers are zipping by on electric scooters and there's one lad with a big muscly pit bull being restrained on a leash. I try to walk natural since I only had a few metres to practise from my apartment to the lift, and then a few metres from the lift to the main door. I try hard not to care cause I know I shouldn't.

They whistle and shout like they're Americans and go:

—Mmhh, mmhh, damn gurl, shake that ass.

I can't help it, stop it. I think, forgive me lord and turn around to them and shout:

—Fuck off you paedo bastards.

This makes them nearly fall off the wall in hysterics. They all point at Pelumi.

—Eeey, that's a bar! Burnt!

He doesn't smile, only stares with those heavy lazy eyes, like something interests him behind me. Like I'm in his way. I turn and move off, forgetting about the heels for a second, trip over. It's enough for them. Their jeers bounce around the estate and I hope Becky hasn't given Michael his afternoon nap bottle. They'll wake him up with their Pelumi chanting and howling.

When I look up, Angel, Pelumi's minion, is beside me. He puts his hand out.

—What you doin? I snap.

—Woah, I was only tryin to help you.

—Don't.

—It's calm, it's calm.

—Really? I say, getting up, looking past him to his crew giving each other slaps and pats.

—Well? he says, standing there with a goofy grin.

—What? Quit making me late.

—One question, just one question.

I stop and I'm like, why am I trying to be this angry girl? Those big puppy dog eyes, they disarm me.

—What? I say, losing patience, energy – unable to maintain the fake anger.

He points to his head.

—My durag's fresh, yeah?

—You going bald or something? I say.

I don't have an opinion, really don't. He lifts the durag off, pats his waves. In fairness to him, they're tight.

—My trim's loud, yeah?

I just shrug, but that doesn't keep him quiet.

—And the juice, you know it's fresh, yeah?

I'm in a rush so don't really have time to be talking and then, what does he do only start chatting about my shoes! I tell him what I'm gonna do with my shoes, walk right out of this town as a qualified pharmacist!

—Take me with you, he whispers with those big eyes, genuine face.

—Whatever, I say.

It's hard to tell if he's serious or being sarcastic.

They cheer when he returns. I'm kind of impressed by his endeavour, for sure, though less than enamoured by his academic application and prospects. He's different to them, but not that different.

His mam stopped me once in my school uniform outside the apartments, asked me how much I study, how much should her son study.

—It depends on how well you do in the Mocks, I suppose.

—My Angel got 200 points in his Mocks, that's good, no?

I was lost for words and didn't want to disrespect her, or her son.

—It's a solid start.

—He does maybe four hours study, she added, looking at me with hope.

—That's a good amount to do a day.

—A day? No, a week.

But she wasn't to know his prospects were totally influenced by the people he hangs around with. They set his goals. They'd only let him reach certain levels, no matter how much he studied.

Grey clouds are like a dark, ominous roof on the evening. Small puddles creep up, jump out of nowhere, and I have to keep a sharp eye on the path in case I slip. Drains are overflowing with the afternoon's earlier rain, spilling out from the apartments above Spar, adding an extra layer of chance to my already treacherous expedition.

A dog shit, some blue disposable PPE and an FLC wrapper with some chicken skin stuck to it make up the last of the obstacles. If I fall and ruin my outfit it would be a perfect excuse to go home, give up and try another day. Faint drizzle flecks the pavement. The spinning green cross seeps onto the path like a mirage. The orange streetlamps merge with the green, giving an Instagram filter to the evening. I'm hyper focused, in the zone. Double yellow lines and a massive white YIELD marks the end of my expedition.

I don't yield.

I'm nervous before I enter the pharmacy and then I'm like, wait, why'm I building this up so much?

Because this is the key to getting the course I want.

My pharmacy course is over 500 points. And I need a scholarship.

But if I can't get the points – and I don't know if I will anymore, I'm not as certain as I was a year ago – I've found a scheme: the Higher Education Access Route. It's for people like me, from backgrounds like mine. It could offer me a chance – regardless of results – to get into the course I want. But this scheme is super competitive. And if courses are in demand, like Pharmacy in Trinity where I wanna go, there's interviews. Winner takes all interviews. Like, how am I gonna stand out in an interview? By being proactive, by getting experience in an actual pharmacy.

I'm a scientist. I have three CVs: three opportunities. If nothing else, I can learn from this one.

The hush of the pharmacy, the sense of decorum makes me think of the library. I'm glad I'm here. Classical music is playing low on the radio. Stepping into this place is stepping into another country, one with a deep, lush green carpet.

An old man is talking with the pharmacist in a warm whisper.

—Can I help you?

The voice spins me and an assistant is in my face. It's a girl who used to be in my school. I don't really catch what she says the first time cause I'm trying to listen to the pharmacist chatting with the old man.

—Sorry?

—Can I help you?

I'm put off by her orange tan. It's so loud I can barely gather my thoughts. There's so much make-up. Even the hair round her ears is orange. I giggle like a fool. Nerves I suppose.

—I'm sorry, I say, real polite. I was hoping to speak with the pharmacist.

My voice is new and clean.

—He's busy at the moment, the assistant says, gliding out from behind the counter, her grubby orange hand floating towards me like a paper aeroplane.

She raises her tan fingers to my head.

—I love your hair. God, it's mental, isn't it?

I'm thinking, wait, is this a hairdressers?

She helps herself, weighing a braid the way she would a necklace on display in Penny's. I snort like a pig, nervously, stupidly. It's like I'm a little girl again.

It's no secret I'm shy. I'm kinda embarrassed – I don't know why – and I let her do what she wants to do, put her fingers through my braids.

Feeling like I've made the adult proud by being polite and obedient, I hold up my CV.

—Oh, we don't accept walk-ins, she says.

—I don't want a job.

—We can't. Sorry. Policy.

Her smile is gone. She has this pressed lips, wide-eyes innocent-of-being-a-total-bitch look. I breathe in, compose myself, and think, like, why get thick?

I'm going to wait for the pharmacist. He has a stern, taffy pink face like he's been stressing all his life about exams, or qualifications. This skin tone makes him look as if he has either blood pressure or is on the sunbeds. He's a pharmacist, so I presume he'd have the right tablets for blood pressure. Sunbeds it is. So he's vain. And would like the attention. I'm gonna make a point of putting my CV and my cover letter into his hand. This is my future, my life after all. I'm like, why worry about how you look to this girlo with the blonde hair and Fanta skin? I've been raised to stick up for myself. Fight for everything.

She lets her powdered chin drop, her hands are on her hips now. How bad do I want this? More than anything. I try to be judicious. Practical. Pragmatic. Yellow highlighter: Don't let emotion get in the way of progress.

—Everything okay, Nathalie?

His voice is strong, filled with the weight of his learning. It arrives over her shoulder in a nice reassuring tone.

Nathalie gives her best customer service smile. Her polite manner just barely conceals resentment.

—This young lady here, Mike, is looking for a job. As a *pharmacist.*

There's way too much surprise in the word. She's too impressed by my ambition. He laughs and I laugh with him. Why am I laughing?

—Really? he says, all eyebrows now.

—Not really. I mean, like, it's more of an internship. Work placement kind of thing, without pay of course. And only for a few weeks. Not too long.

—For what exactly?

—Oh, excuse me. Em, college. For interviews. It wouldn't be for long ...

I don't tell him it would need to be long enough for me to impress at an interview for the HEAR scheme. If I have to do one.

His face on closer inspection is an undercooked-chicken lavender blush. Definitely sunbeds. He smiles through his refusal. Says something like he'd love to but they have a policy of not considering internships, for insurance and customer confidentiality reasons. And no, they don't keep CVs on file. And he wishes me all the best in my career as a pharmacist.

—Sure, look at her, Nathalie smiles, relieved now. She'll only do fabulous so she will.

His eyes try and stay steady on mine, but right at the end they relent and go to the top of my head, the colours, the texture.

There are two other independent pharmacies in Balbriggan. This is simply experiment number one.

*

Me and Iwona are meant to be watching Miss at the top of class while she's demonstrating how to determine the percentage of ethanoic acid in vinegar. We're just whispering to each other since we've both seen this experiment about a million times on YouTube already.

—You're doing what? Iwona says.

Miss calls down to us.

—Princess and Iwona, stop talking!

I put on my goggles to look like I'm busy. Iwona's still staring at me.

Normally, I keep things to myself. No one knows my plans, ever. Not even the girls at my old church. They'd be jealous, or if not jealous, suspicious. And then my mum would find out. Iwona is my only real friend in school. She's white, yeah. But Polish. There's a difference. The white Irish girls think I'm stuck up. The Black girls think I'm too quiet. I don't listen to their music. Don't watch their shows.

Iwona is ambitious. I like that about her. To a point.

I told my mum and sister about Iwona. Told them about that drive she has. They were like:

—You can play with them, play with them and other white people, but when it comes to fighting, stuff like that, an argument or something, stay with your own people cause they're gonna stay with their own people.

—Oh, you're just being racist, I said, and Becky was all like:

—I saw it played out, Princess. You'll see it played out. Watch.

—Hardly. I'll let it play out, I said.

So I don't tell them anything more about Iwona. They're too close-minded. Too bitter. The world has been unkind to them. I'm going to be the educated one. The world will have its arms open for me.

Iwona wants to study medicine and be a doctor, and she's a genius. H1s in every test, for every subject, every time. There's no HEAR scheme for her, no interviews or panic about points. So we aren't in competition. Our relationship wouldn't be as open if we were. Wait, we probably wouldn't even have a relationship if we were in competition. Because she'd beat me. I wouldn't be able to cope with that level of stress every day.

Iwona is titrating the sodium hydroxide against the vinegar, the right wrist action quick and strong in the swirling of the flask. The light lemonade pink churns around easily like a candyfloss machine. Consistently whisking, whirling. Her left hand is steady on the stopcock. She sighs and tuts, goes:

—Konrad would probably love this.

She nods without humour to her hand pumping the flask. I play along and laugh uncomfortably. She knows I've never felt the touch of a boy. I think she just says things like this to embarrass me; remind me I don't have a boyfriend.

Grades. Teacher's approval. Boyfriends. Ambition, I suppose, makes you want to be the best at everything. And I'm like, wait, why do I put up with it? I put up with it because she drives me to do better.

—Well, show me, she says, with such enthusiasm I wonder if she's putting it on.

I put down the pipette and pull a CV out of my bag.

—Take over here, she says and nods to the flask.

I take it without stopping the swirl and I'm real self-conscious about how stiff my wrist action is.

Iwona is poring over my CV, and without even looking up she says:

—Wow, Princess ...

I'm delighted until she finishes.

—You've a spelling mistake.

—Where?

—There. Pharmaceuticals. You spell it right here, but wrong there.

I shrug like it's no big deal.

Iwona smiles that pretty smile, blonde like summer, so proper and mainstream, like a Ralph Lauren ad.

—Thanks so much, I say and take it from her and turn back to the experiment.

—The solution is turning brown, she moans.

—You never di-ionised the water, I say.

That wipes the smile off her face.

Angel

I'm not gonna lie, I never thought Pelumi's new track, 'Blazed Boy', would be banging like that. Yeah, he's got bare views on YouTube since that English channel with a million subscribers put up his last video, but shitden, the new track is fire. And hearing it booming out've Isaac's JBL Bluetooth speaker on Mainstreet is next level.

We've all linked up beside the monument to shoot the video. Gregory and Benni are taking small sips from their balloons and creasing up. Isaac, Mo and Harvey are sitting on the wall doing hand signs to a phone. Their trims look fresh in the light. I nod to myself, gassed cause I did that, went to work with my clippers, shears and curl sponge.

It's dark and there's steck elders waiting for their chips in Deli Burger across the road. They're all staring at us like there's gonna be some beef and you can tell they're a bit stressed by the bare heads. I'm not gonna lie, I get high off this. Me with the boys. Owning the streets.

More elders come out've the pub, not the burnt out busted one at the Square end, the other one with the red paint and the mad mural thing. Some yutes were murdered on these streets a hundred years ago. No lie, there's fire painted all over the side of the pub showing how the Briggz was shook when those British boys came and drenched man down on these streets. It's a mad thing.

It's calm with all the boys, but I can't help thinking the feds will be called soon if Pelumi doesn't show and we start recording quick.

There's one oyinbo with us and he's all sweaty and pressured with this HD camera on a small pole thing that must've cost serious bags. He's filming us standing round and chatting shit. He was in my school and he's sound.

Next thing Isaac shouts at him.

—What you doing, Lorcan? Pelumi's not even here yet, or can't ye tell?

All the mandem shout approval and laugh, but Lorcan and his sweaty face keeps the camera up like he's doing a documentary or something.

—I've got to get some casual shots guys, for any fill-ins I might need. Keep talking and don't look at the camera. Pretend I'm not here.

Swear down, this truck roars by and Lorcan balances on his toes on the edge of the path to stop from falling in front of it.

—Stop looking at me! Don't look at the camera, guys, just keep chatting.

This guy. He thinks he can control what we do. Chap, allow, I feel like saying, no one, not even the feds, can control us when we link up like this.

Pelumi arrives finally, in his big Canada Goose jacket, zipping down the street on his electric scooter like he's King Kunta. A bottle of Jack is in one hand and he's dripped in ice his sister got for him in Claire's Accessories.

—Wagwan boys! he salutes before swigging from the whiskey, sunglasses on, hood up like a proper driller bout to drop the coldest verse.

Pelumi makes straight for Lorcan and they chat for a bit and then Pelumi calls us like we're his army or something. Everyone goes quiet.

—Right boys, Pelumi goes. Lorcan says we're gonna get some shots of all of us walking up Mainstreet, yeah?

It's a mad thing seeing Pelumi take advice from Lorcan, but swear down, when it comes to his music and shit, Pelumi always listens to the lads that know best.

Lorcan blazes ahead with the camera and speaker. He plays the music and it bounces down the empty road. No lie, Mainstreet on a Thursday night is dry as fuck.

Lorcan waves across the road from the hotel, up beside the bando barbershop.

—Right boys, play it sharp yeah, Pelumi says.

We all walk towards him like we're roadmen linking up at a scrap. Pelumi's out front and all the boys are trying to make shapes beside him to be seen in the next video, cause everyone knows the next song is going to take Pelumi clear, and this video is gonna be fire.

Some of the boys are so fake trying to walk and act all hard and tough. Obviously yeah, I don't get stressed when there's a camera on cause swear down, I feel like I have to do that shit every time, every day I leave my house and walk through my ends, walk into a shop, walk down these streets. No lie, I am aware, always, of what people see when I walk alone. Only time I never have to act all hench and be Angel the Roadman is when I chat with Princess. She has that effect on me. If yuno, yuno.

When we get to Lorcan he positions us in front of the busted shop fronts, all cracked glass, rotten wooden door frames, black plastic bags in the windows. Pelumi grabs me and moves me right beside him. I am gassed.

—You know the bars, yeah? he says.

I kiss my teeth like I'm vexed he even had to ask.

—Safe, he says. Stay right there, yeah, be my right-hand man. Look to the camera like he's your opp and shout bars in his face like you're gonna ching him in his belly!

The track plays and Lorcan shouts action, and it is activ on these streets! Pelumi's in front of everyone and I'm right by his side.

The two of us start it off:

—*Man don't show, where he go?*

And everyone shouts:

—*Where man go?*

—*Paddy done run.*

—*I fucking know!*

And we all go:

—*Blazed boy! He's blazed boy!*

It's a lethal hype.

Lorcan says we should do another verse and chorus down the beach, but this time, Pelumi's not having it.

—Nah fam, the beach is dry. Mainstreet is popping. Do it here.

Lorcan makes this face.

—Nah, it's so clichéd.

It's a mad thing to see someone go head-to-head with Pelumi and not be scared.

—This guy, allow, Pelumi says and he turns to us and goes:

—Yo Isaac, grab some bricks from the bando pub, and we'll smash this shitty barbershop window and get the feds down and dash. Lorcan, you stall it across the street and record it, yeah?

Swear down, Lorcan's face in the orange light goes white and his lips look all dry.

—Not this window Pelumi, he says, his voice cracking.

—Why not?

—It's my brother's mate's.

—Allow, Lorcan, this gaff's a bando.

—He's not been right the past weeks. He'll open it again soon, just don't smash that window, yeah guys?

Swear down, if Pelumi listens to this white boy again I'll start to wonder. Pelumi turns to the barber's, looks for a few seconds at the big dusty window like it's a whip he's thinking of finessing.

—It's calm, Lorcan, he says with a flick of his hand and we all murmur like we agree and the beat starts up again.

Lorcan is across the street with the camera and we're all doing our hand signs, and next thing Isaac is up the front with a red brick in his hand from the burnt-out pub.

He's holding the brick over his head and no lie, we're all bumping into each other, shouting the bars when Pelumi takes it and launches it at the blue shop window beside the barber's.

Everyone cheers but the window only shatters cause of the massive sticker on the inside: 'The Track, Turf Accountants, Est 1973.'

The music stops. There's an alarm going off like a mad thing now and Pelumi shouts:

—Yo boys, grab some more bricks, we gotta finish the window for the shots, yeah?

From nowhere the boys all have them scorched red bricks and they're lined up and firing them. Last time we were like this we were youngers at the fairground near Tesco tryna knock down cans on a shelf. The feds came then, when Pelumi got thick and gave hands to the guy behind the counter. Basically, the elder wouldn't hand over the big teddy Pelumi wanted for his ma. Pelumi got the teddy, yeah, but we all got barred.

So, obviously, I don't bother grabbing anything to finish the window. I wanna keep my energy for when the feds arrive and we gotta dip.

It's a mad thing.

*

Princess is leng, yeah. Can't remember when we first talked, said alright and that. But now she's all gassed when I give her a shout if she's crossing the street or coming out of the blocks. Pelumi's all:

—She's butters, man.

But Isaac and the boys be all:

—Dassit Angel, her sister's gotta little baby, she's a sket man.

And I'd play along, all shy like I don't wanna say too much, yuno.

I'm not gonna lie, it feels lit, yeah, to be in the centre of the boys for something good for once, not having them takin the piss out of me for lacking.

When me and Princess talk it's calm. Mostly we only talk for a minute or two while she's passing. Cause she's always passing, too busy for me. I like that. If I was her, I wouldn't stop for me neither, yuno. The boys are normally with me, we're hanging out and I haveta dash after her, make a big effort and all to get her to talk.

I skip beside her when she's leaving the block and go:

—You see Pelumi's last track with King Don from London? It's a game changer.

She keeps on walking, looking ahead.

—Yo, you gotta have seen it. It's got like nearly seven hundred K views in three months. Pelumi's the new king of Irish drill, yeah. Pause it on one minute twenty and you'll see this mandem spitting out bars!

—Wow, you're really in his video?

—For real. And wait til ye hear his new track, 'Blazed Boy'. That's next level. I'm in that too, yeah, up the front with Pelumi spitting more bars.

—If you think I'm impressed by someone whose sole ambition is to be a bitch boy for a driller and be seen for like, two seconds, holding a bottle of whiskey and a spliff that looks too big for him, then you're chasing after the wrong girl.

—How'd you know I was holding whiskey if you didn't see it?

—I'm going to the library, she says. Another time, yeah.

—Allow, I say. Please, come on. I just wanna chat.

She's chuffed for sure when I chat with her. She pretends she's not chuffed though, being all, I'm busy, and all that. But I know, yuno. I know.

When I go back to Pelumi and Isaac at the wall, I go:

—Was telling Princess bout me and you, Pelumi, sharing bars on Mainstreet for the new video. Meant to say it to ye bro.

I clasp Pelumi's hand.

—Nice one for putting me up the front, yeah? Appreciate it.

Pelumi looks at me like I'm thick.

—Hardly, bro. You're a nextman, yeah? There was too many light skins there the other night, especially Isaac. I needed Black boys up front, innit. And God knows, you are waaaay too black bro.

He's creased up, but Isaac isn't smiling now and I go:

—Allow.

Pretending it's all good.

*

Me and Isaac and Pelumi and the boys are just chilling about outside the blocks at the Fire Exit. Pelumi has some new bars about the scrap with Paddy and his boys. Swear down, like, Pelumi is getting more outta that fight than my mam does fufu.

Princess comes out of the entrance and ignores me and goes clicking and clacking by in these cute little heels I never seen no girl wear before. So I ask her bout my durag. What does she do only kiss her teeth and then look at my waves under it like they're lacking. She's real sharp like that. And when it comes to my barbering, that hurts. So then I say, just buzzing, yuno:

—Well, what bout them shoes. Oh, my days, they're dead.

What does she do? She just looks at me like I've rocked her and turns and walks off.

—Wait, I call. Wait. Shit, I'm sorry. I'm just playing with ye.

The boys are all laughing behind me. She stops, yeah, but looks over my shoulder back at them like they're fools.

—You can chat your shit, but I'm busy. I've got plans. These shoes and me are dropping a CV into a pharmacy for a work experience role and then I'm gonna do pharmacy studies in college and walk right out of this shithole.

—Allow, I whisper. I've got plans too, yuno. Take me with you.

She laughs a cruel laugh like the thought of me ever getting where she's going is too funny. The wind gets sucked out've my lungs. I try not to deflate like one of Benni's FastGas balloons, especially in front of the boys. She turns away again and I don't follow, yuno. God knows I want to. But, yuno, the boys.

It's calm. It's calm. She's fresh so I'm gonna keep talking to her. And that's what I do, yuno. I just talk to her when I see her. Every time I ask her bout her plans, the CVs and the pharmacy, just so I can talk, even if it's only a few words. And if she's wearing the heels, I say:

—You getting ready to leave us all behind?

And every time she just nods and smiles, and says:

—The only people getting left behind are the roadmen with no plans. I know one of these pharmacies are gonna take me on. God guides me, he's kind.

Amen.

Dean

—Condoms? Cian says, looking at me like I'm speaking French or something.

The escalator in Millfield goes on forever, feels like we'll never get to the top. The glass ceiling is so high.

—Condoms, I repeat.

—You gonna have a posh wank?

—No. We're both gonna need them.

—Wooaahh, he says, digging at his braces with his little finger. I'm not into that shit.

—No, ye dope. We're going clubbing on Saturday. The Home. I've decided.

Cian squirms. His face squints at his runners as if he'll find an answer there. He shakes his head and his hairspray-curled fringe sways in a panic. And I get it, I do. I get why he's worried.

—Nah man, he says, the elastic from his braces stretching. Nah. Can't see it. I'm not going up those steps to be embarrassed in front of half the town.

—That's the thing, we won't be.

—Ah, we will. I barely look seventeen. Them bouncers will make a show of us.

—Only if we let them.

—What we gonna do, bribe them with condoms? he says.

The black rubber rail shudders in my fist.

—Don't be an eejit.

—Then what we gonna do with condoms?

I join my index finger and thumb in my left hand together, make a circle, then put my right index finger through the hole. Repeatedly. Cian bursts his shite laughing. I have him on side.

—Yes man! I say. I'm in training, I'm fit, I'm fighting. I'm ready for this.

He arches an eyebrow and looks closely at me.

—You taking some of yer da's steroids again?

—No, I laugh. I'm a new man is all.

We step off the escalator. Walk towards the red doors of CeX beside Tesco.

Being a new man is mostly about getting back to my old self again.

I was a cool and confident cheeky pup of a twelve-year-old. Been with a few girls down the bandstand. We'd sit on the cold concrete and there'd be so much saliva from our mouths washing round I'd feel like I was drowning. The girl's make-up would be all mushed around her lips and I'd swallow and secretly retch.

But once the redners started, the girls and all that lark stopped.

The redners scorched my face like a blow torch.

—Ourlad, yer cheeks are absolutely cooking so they are.

—Ourlad, yer da giving ye a few slaps again, wha?

The laughter, so much laughter.

Then, this Friday after school, I went to the library – talked to a girl – and didn't go red.

I was eating my Taco Fries at a table and, cool as ye like, offered some to her.

She kind of snarled with disgust and said:

—Are you for real?

She tutted so loud everyone else in the library heard. She had beautiful eyes, but they narrowed and she shook her head, grabbed her books and went to another table.

Now, under normal circumstances, such a burn like that, in public too, would make my head explode. I'd have instantly combusted. Only my runners and some ash would've been left. Not so this time. For some mad reason, I just nodded to myself, took the knock-back.

—Fair enough, I shrugged and started to gobble the fries.

I offered her a chip, she declined – a bit too vocally if you ask me – but that was it. Nothing more. Her rejection didn't go deep and stop my heart. It was just that, a simple rejection and nothing more. I sat there and thought, wow, I'm still here. She said no, and everyone saw her say no, and I didn't pull a redner.

It may have taken five years to get comfortable with girls again, but I was back.

*

After the carnage of buying the condoms, we go for food. We sit on the high stools near the balloons eating our Big Mac meals off the red plastic trays.

I open the internet browser on the phone and go to the proxy site: the Spacer Murray's brother in sixth year says it isn't blocked by the firewall. He works in McDonald's and knows what he's talking about. I put in the full URL – I have it learned off – and start the download. Straightforward, easy.

—Your ma and da still haven't put the internet back on? Cian says.

—Nah, they're sticking at it. They only gave my phone back this morning. Keeping the WiFi off. It was alright for a while without it – I did my homework and stuff – but then I heard them saying, 'It'll get him out of the house,' so I decided, fuck it, I won't leave the house. Just to piss them off.

—That's why ye haven't been out, ye mad thing.

—Yeah, but they're wrecking my head now fighting all the time. Me da's gone up to sleep in the attic. I had to get out.

Cian laughs, takes out his phone and starts to scroll.

—Man, what did ye wank to without yer phone? he says.

—That's the thing. I used me imagination.

He spits out a bit of his burger, looks for food in his braces through his camera.

—Your imagination?

A birthday party comes in and charges the counter like a midnight opening at GameStop. They order a million Happy Meals and scatter to our right, sliding over the seats with short slippery squeaks, knocking their knees off the tables. I don't mind because we're sitting above them and my phone is definitely out of their eyeline.

—I don't like porn like that no more, Cian says, motioning to my phone. I prefer the amateur stuff. Like, closer to home. That Tanya Guildea thing. Her down on her knees in the carpark. That sorta thing's the real deal now.

—Do you know her?

—Nah. Never spoke to her, but I brushed off her in the corridor last week, got a good sniff of her hair for some me time later. The smell of her hair, man. It stays with ye for ages.

—Ye dirt bird, I say, but I'm actually well ahead of him when it comes to imagining Tanya.

I mightn't have seen her video, but I have my ways.

—I don't need an MP3 when I have an MP Me, I say.

—A what? You're some man. MP Me! Get a grip Dean and watch her video.

—Nah, I don't need to.

Of course I've cracked one off to Tanya. All the lads in school are talking about her, and her video. There's like a Mexican wave of boners when she walks down the corridor these days. She's our very own Mia Khalifa. A porn star – in the same fucking school as me!! Tanya is my go-to face. I don't need a clip of her to make it real. Boxing gloves do the job.

The manager lad brings out a cake and all the kids behind us start singing 'Happy Birthday'. The download is almost done.

—Here, I say to Cian. Get this on your phone so I can post it.

It takes a second for Cian to cop what I mean.

—The McPorn challenge? he says as if the words themselves have a rank taste.

I shrug it off like it's no big deal.

I'm killing two birds with one stone. Looking cool and mad into porn for all the lads in school, and actually getting a bit for my phone.

Cian removes a gherkin from his burger, slops it on the table.

—They're losers, those lads. They won't even watch your clip.

—Just start recording, will ye?

I ease the phone up a few degrees to create a tiny angle and ensure Cian can record the last percentage of the download. I position myself right so there can be no doubting it's me who did it.

—The noise of these fucking kids, Cian says.

He looks around with disgust at the red cheeks gobbling and screaming, then stands up and claps his hands:

—Right, kids, enough. My friend's da is an Olympic boxing champion, and if yis don't shut up, he'll knock yis all out!

Their faces are stunned and all eyes look to me. Even the adults there don't know if Cian is joking or not. The whole place plunges into silence.

For a second – two max – the calls from the workstation melt into brief concentration on the job of sliding the cheeseburgers from out back to out front, the hand-dryer in the toilets wheezes down, every mouth is either full with food or sucking in some air. And into this silence an unmistakable sex moan rips through the place. The frantic slapping of balls is next and everyone's heads snap to our table.

I go to grab the phone and flick it off the table. It falls to the ground near three little boys and, of course, it lands screen up.

Cian's off his chair, still recording. I duck down to grab my phone and the porno star is moaning for everyone to hear.

Some kid's eyes are wide with horror as he bites his finger, another is crying. The screen is locked so I can't turn it off. I have to just grab it and run. The electric doors won't open quick enough and the security guard's coming from behind a self-service depot, arms out to grab me.

I glance up at the window as I leg it by. The manager is standing over the kids and they're all pointing at me out the window. Cian is in stitches miles away up on the hill, phone still out, laughing.

—You absolute loser.

*

The tap is running in the bathroom. A little trickle that can be heard when I close the front door behind me. I go upstairs, turn the water off. Check the back bedroom for my sister, and the front bedroom for my ma. No one is in. I call out:

—Hello.

Just to make sure. Seagulls squawk a reply from the roof across the road.

I ease onto my bed and whip down my kacks. Take out my phone and press play. It starts off tame enough, all bad sound in a bright mansion kitchen. The woman has long blonde hair, big lips, flower dress. He's jeans and a tight white vest top. A tool belt around his waist. They talk for too long and I fast forward it, land on a close-up of his hairy ball sack. I think of the finger thing I did to make Cian laugh earlier: the circle and the in and out. I see Cian laughing, food gone syrupy in his braces. I fast forward again and her eyes are nearly popping out've her head and she's choking, about to puke. His hairy ball sack is in full rhythm now like a speed bag back in the gym.

The video's just not doing anything for me. Nothing is happening.

I've got used to life without the internet. I've got used to lying in my bedroom after waking up from a dream, staring at the ceiling and thinking up the most mental scenarios and just going with it. Concentrating on the scene, the girl in my mind and lashing away from there. No video needed.

I turn off the phone and reach under the bed for my old boxing gloves.

The thought of Tanya stirs me – her hair tied back, wearing tight boxing shorts, boxing boots, a blue singlet, lips swollen over a gumshield, her hands in the red leather and the soft smack and slap of the gloves as they're clapped together. She looks at me with disgust, as if she wants to fight.

It's Tanya, with her fake tan and sweet perfume. That snarl of hers does the job and I drift off into the rhythmical tugging. It's her face I stretch towards. My eyes closed, it's her groans from the start of the clip I've heard the lads play that I sample. There was her brief, oh so brief look in my direction last week. That's when I heard her voice – the one time she's ever directed her attention to me – when she caught me staring at her while she ate her lunch in the canteen.

—What the fuck you looking at, freak?

Somehow I can morph her words, the sound of her voice, into some sort of pleading, breathless, urge to get myself in her. I use the sound of her syllables and rearrange them into:

—Want to fuck? You look like a freak!

Oh, yeah.

Drenched in sweat and ripping each other's boxing gear off, Tanya jumps on me. It's like I've been in training with Apollo in LA. Eyes closed, I'm a finely tuned, lean, mean, wanking machine.

—Want to fuck? You look like a freak!

I reach towards her, the boxing gloves on my stomach as if she's leaning on me for support.

—You look like a freak!

—You there?

Tanya. I'm almost there, Tanya.

—Dean, you there?

Then the attic stairs creak and heavy footsteps descend. My da's voice comes through.

—Dean, you there?

The bottom of the attic stairs is at my door.

The door's pushed open. His face is flushed, some sweat on his forehead. He's out of breath himself.

—Answer me when I call you.

—Sorry Da.

—What you doing in bed?

He edges into the room.

—I've got a headache, I moan, my hands holding the blanket tight around my neck.

—I'll give ye a headache, he says and swings from his standing position in the doorway and catches me on the side of the head with a slap.

—Now get up the fuck and answer me when I call ye in future.

Tanya

Bad & bored asf

♫ WAP – @Cardi B (feat. Megan Thee Stallion)

Tanya holds the phone on front pov at a full-length mirror in a bathroom. She's dressed in a light T-shirt and pyjama shorts. White splashes of toothpaste dot the reflection. She sways slowly to the song, singing the lyrics before laughing.

>135

Open the door, Tanya. I wanna talk to ye.

I'm busy.

I don't care if you're busy. You've been in there for ages.

I'm on the toilet, Ma.

If yer on the toilet that long you've got issues.

Stop Ma.

Open it, she says and bangs on the door.

The little lock finally gives and she barges in, her phone in her hand, the screen real bright.

See this? she says, backing me towards the toilet bowl.

What?

I swear to ye, Tanya. I swear to ye, she says, shaking her head.

What now Ma?

She looks around the bathroom as if I've hidden something in here. She takes a breath and holds out her phone for me.

It's been forwarded around now, she says.

Getting checked out take out

♫ Bulletproof – @La Roux

Tanya drops her head to the side and smiles into the camera. A neon green sign flashes behind her. She's leaning against a dark

window. Between patches of condensation on the glass, the reflection of a chipper counter can be seen.
>29

Me ma and her chips. She's so tight she sends me down to get them instead of paying the one euro delivery. All sorts do be in the queue.

Alright Tanya! Brian Quinn says.

Brian fucking Quinn with his little sneaky fucking eyes. He never said alright to me before. Never would've had the balls. He's with another two lads and they're huddling into themselves in the corner at the high table, sniggering like thicks. They keep on lookin down at their phones.

Yup Tanya, his little mate says and they giggle again.

Eh, who are you? I say, loud, so the heads behind the counter, and the others in front of me hear.

The little lad looks shocked.

PJ, he says.

PJ, ye little dope. I don't even know ye, so why the fuck ye calling me name?

Just was.

Don't.

Fair enough.

Good.

The fat head behind the counter shouts, Salt and vinegar?

He looks at me like he recognizes me. Of course he does, the paedo. I take the chips and tut at him like he's a weirdo.

Gissa chip Tanya, the other friend of Brian says.

Fuck off.

It's head she gives, Brian says. Not chips.

Im famous

♫ Bump It – @Kenzo B

Tanya appears in selfie pov walking down the street. She exhales vape smoke into the screen before sticking her tongue out and sticking the finger up.

>521

So I'm a celebrity now. How? I got drunk on a naggin of vodka and Red Bull last week and gave a lad a blow job. Why is this news? Not because it was bright out. Not because it was during the day, not because it was down a lane, not because I'm sixteen, not because it was caught on some dope's phone. Isn't there always someone watching? Nope. None of that mattered. But some eejit put it up on Facebook, and then WhatsApp and then all the old bitches on Balbriggan Connected went mad. Including my ma. Not a word from me da, but.

Me granny's media were all over it. But she never knew it was me. There was a front page in the paper she reads, and it was on a phone-in on some FM104 radio thing she listens to. I mean, have they nothing else to be talking about? I swear, if they think that clip is bad, they'd wanna see the stuff that does be on everyone else's timelines.

The only thing that makes me different from half the girls in the town is someone was brain-dead enough to share what I did on WhatsApp. I mean, who puts stuff up there?

I'm bollixt these days catching everyone taking a secret second look at me. But it's nothing new really. When I was thirteen some aul lad stopped his car outside SuperValu and gave me twenty quid. 'You're looking well,' he said, leaning out the window. He winked, licked his bottom lip like I was a kebab and just handed me the note. I bought a six-pack of Hunky Dorys, a four pack of Monster, this mad expensive green tea and a new Dove deodorant. Never told me ma nothing.

Gran cant smell for shit

♫ Ghost – @Ella Henderson

An old woman, crouched shoulders, short hair, purple rinse, is over Tanya's shoulder making tea in a small kitchen. Tanya vapes into the screen on a couch. A long exhale clouds the shot.
>107

I love my gran. I love my gran's flat. She's mad. It's ancient. Hasn't changed in years. Old blue carpet with little black scorch marks near the fireplace. The old yellow wallpaper. Me and me da and me ma would call over every Saturday and one Saturday, when I was like nine or something, I remember my gran being thick with me for the first time ever.

Football? me gran goes.

And some Gaelic too, I say, all proud of meself.

GAA? Do they have teams for girls?

Me gran squinting through her smoke while she holds the cigarette in the corner of her mouth. Her lip dragged down like a melted candle to hold the thing in place.

Not for the football yet, but they do for the Gaelic, I say.

Me gran only goes and looks at me ma, And you let her run around with these lads?

Amn't I trying to get her to join Street Dance my mate Gemma is running at the Community Centre, but she wants to follow her da, me ma says.

Me da's munching on the sausage sandwich me gran made him.

She's doing great so she is, he mumbles though his full mouth.

A football pitch is no place for a young one like you, Tanya, me gran says.

Me da played when he was my age.

Exactly! My da goes.

And look where it got him, Gran says. You didn't get a look in with that one, Derek, and then she decides to play ball like some mad young one!

Leave her enjoy her sport. Ye should see her. She's some goer, aren't ye love? me da says.

I love sport, Gran.

A girl like you isn't made for a rough sport like that, my gran says.

A girl like me is made to do whatever the fuck I want.

Jesus Christ Tanya! I'll redden yer arse for ye ye speak like that to me again! Well, she's getting a mouth like her da now anyhow.

I love my gran.

My block is such a kip

♫ As It Was – @Harry Styles

Tanya walks onto a housing estate, flipping from selfie to front pov. A football pitch is in the centre of the estate. The houses, in various states of upkeep, surround the pitch on all sides. The picture reverts to selfie and she sings along, flutters her long eyelashes and gives the peace sign.

>94

When I was younger, my da would take me out to the green and we'd knock one of those real light Cup Final plastic balls about. He'd boot the ball up and tell me to catch it. Sometimes he'd kick it so high he'd have the time to pick me up and fire me into the sky like those rugby players at a throw in. He'd catch me in his arms and we'd bundle over in a big mess of laughing. His head would rest on the grass, his mouth open wide, his fillings black and deep. Sometimes I'd put my head on his chest and feel his heartbeat.

Pov I used be a baller
♫ Cornfield Chase – @Dorian Marko
The shot wobbles: a football pitch with no nets up. Young players, an array of tracksuits on, kick a ball about. Tanya flips the phone to selfie every couple of seconds. She blows smoke in the camera, sticks out her tongue and smiles.
>85

I'm fourteen when I play my last game. It's a Sunday like any other Sunday. We're at home and we're winning, as usual. My da is there like always, cheering me on from the sideline.

We're two up. I'm on the edge of the D when, in the corner of my eye, a large, dark figure goes legging it by. It's too big to be a player – and the ref is near the peno spot so it can't be him. I look over and it's my da! Only storming across the pitch he is.

At first I'm totally scarlet. Like, there's loads on the sideline and they're shouting at him to get off the fucking pitch. The ref blows the whistle. Everyone now is looking at me da. He crosses the field and just barges some parents out've the way. In the gap in the crowd, I see him throw a dig at a random lad sitting on a garden wall away from the pitch! And they're struggling and fighting with each other near the corner flag!

My da left home that day. Never turned up to a game again.

Old business, never in my feelings now
♫ New New – @Inayah

'4:06 am' is over half the screen. Tanya sits at a kitchen table in a light T-shirt, hair tied up. Green eyes filter is on giving her pupils a new sparkle and intensity. She sways the camera in a selfie and circles around the empty kitchen before giving the peace sign.
>92

I had to have it out with my ma. I needed to know what was going on.

She was in the kitchen on her phone, sitting up against the radiator for heat, wearing her pyjamas already for bed like a waster.

We fell out of love, she says, not even bothering to look up from her phone.

I don't sit down.

That's not what everyone's saying though, is it? Did that lad Da beat the shit out've tell yis to finish? I'm fourteen, but I'm not a kid Ma.

Don't be silly, Tanya. No one thinks you're a kid.

Everyone's saying you had an affair.

I swear to ye love, she whispers.

She puts down the phone, drags her hands down her face. Her eyes are red raw under the eyeballs.

I did not have an affair. I wouldn't do that to you, or your da.

Then who was that lad Da beat up?

An old friend of your da's.

No wonder he doesn't have many.

Don't be like that.

Like what?

Harsh on your da.

He's left us Ma! What do ye want me to do, give him a hug and say good luck!

No.

Then why's he gone?

I told ye. We just fell out've love.

Her fingers push up her cheeks, as if the drama of the last few days has made them collapse. Her nails are normally clear and polished. There's dirt under them now.

And has he fallen out've love with me? Cause he's been gone ages and he hasn't called.

You'll have to ask him that yourself, she whispers.

She goes back to scrolling.

It's been two years now. No matter how many times I call, or ask, he won't answer.

Princess

We first arrived in Balbriggan just before the Covid lockdown. My mum had one of her migraines and she sent me down the town to get her some medication.

Mainstreet was real quiet. Eerie. One side of the street had shutters up where an old shopping centre was. Paint flaked from the brickwork, and big weeds swayed on the roof. I was like, wait, this place needs new life, like now. A hotel imposed itself on the skyline up from the old mall and gave the only bit of warm golden light to the whole street.

The other side was dilapidated and depressing for about fifty metres. Every shopfront had wooden boards in the windows and every building and wooden board was painted a uniform pale, pastel turquoise as if they were trying to camouflage the fact the street was a failure. I went down the hill past the shuttered SuperValu and the monument for Sean Gibbons and Seamus

Lawless killed in 1920. They died in the Sack of Balbriggan. The town was gutted by the British one hundred years ago. I had no idea about any of this stuff until my too eager History teacher tried to make me do my Special Topic on it. All I did was ask what the monument was for and she literally threw an armful of local history books in my direction. I didn't read them.

It was dark and a drone buzzed by overhead delivering fast food to a far-off estate. I traced my fingers along the names of the men on the monument and looked at the Sack of Balbriggan mural on the side of the pub. Large painted flames of red and pink gave a manic note of colour to the scene. I was only new in town, but this place was mental.

I moved on and had to pass a gang of lads standing around outside Spar. I didn't look up to see their faces, not that I would've known anyone. But they were loud and intimidating. I walked towards them and got real tense, and I was like, wait, if they do anything I'm just gonna scream. But then I saw the neon lights of a late-night pharmacy up from it. The green cross was flashing and spinning like pixels from an old-school video game and I dunno, but I felt relief, kind of safe when I saw it.

I walked in. It was as if this place was insulated from the world. And I said to myself, wait one minute, what are all these African faces doing on the walls? Posters and framed pictures of Black faces were displayed prominently everywhere. Proud and smiling. This was more like it. The same Black man was smiling in all of them. I went over and inspected the pictures. Tried to feel the sealed wax stamp behind the glass. His name was Tunde. I was like, okay, that's nice and then, right there, standing in the most brightest white doctor's coat was Tunde himself, his eyes shining proudly down on me.

—Hello, he said, in the freshest, clearest Nigerian tone.

I felt so special and happy to see someone like him in a place of prestige like that.

That pharmacy isn't there anymore. Boots opened in Millfield shopping centre on the edge of town soon after and Tunde's pharmacy disappeared. The Noodle Box has expanded into the empty space Tunde left behind.

Tunde, I heard, packed up his business and family and left for Tullamore. There he will be the only Black man in the town and they will love him. And his pharmacy will do well because of it.

When I qualify, I will drive down to him in my car. If my mum will let me take them off the wall, I will bring my own framed qualifications with the wax seals. I will hold them up for Tunde and say:

—Hello Tunde, you inspired me. I'm a pharmacist like you now too. Thank You.

Mine will be a family one. On the main street. Like Tunde's used to be. Adedokun Pharmacy. And the flashing green light will be a beacon for all. A sign to say I will look after you. I will accept you. If you are sick (and you have money) I will serve you, care for you, no matter who you are. And I will wear the white coat with the name tag: Princess Adedokun, Pharmacist.

Of course, my mum kissed her teeth when I came back with the story about Tunde. Maybe she was just coping with her migraine.

—Why you want to be a pharmacist when you can be a doctor!

I tried to explain but she just waved me away and told me to do my chores. Me and Becky looked at each other and held in our laughter. Mum always feels the need to improve on our ideas, or dismiss them with an order to stop delaying and do our chores.

I did consider being a doctor, after Mum said it: until I got sick in this town. I always thought doctors' surgeries would be buzzing with community spirit and be bastions of equality, places of mutual care and respect. Everyone would be treated the same. Then I experienced the Medical Centre near Deli Burger. Me, my mum and Becky and Michael, masked up, had to sit there for hours.

The waiting area is real small, with paintings of the Lion King and Snow White and glossy, ripped posters stuck over older ones asking patients if they've travelled to West Africa lately. There's a kid's abacus nailed to the floor, with one ring of wood remaining. Chewing gum shines trodden on the carpet. Frosted glass hides the interior mess from pedestrians. The doctors don't even wear white coats. They seem bored when they are examining you. Like you're a hassle.

So, I suppose, becoming a pharmacist is a natural progression after the disappointment of seeing behind the curtain of a doctor's life in this town.

*

We're preparing a solution of ammonium iron sulphate and using this to standardize a solution of $KMnO_4$ by titration. Sorcha O'Neill, of all people, has been put with us. And she is ruining me and Iwona's modus operandi.

—I'm going on the pill, she announces.

I nearly choke on the top of my pen. But Iwona, as casual as anything, nods, as if Sorcha just said she is going to hold the burette.

—Where'd you get it? Iwona asks.

—Eh, my doctor! Duh! Sorcha laughs, snorting a little.

—Which one? Iwona continues.

—Doctor Reid, she says.

—Is she on the second floor? I say.

—Where? she says with an impatient exhale, looking at me like I've asked her for a fiver.

—The second floor of the Medical Centre.

She brings her neat little lips into a discreet O.

—Oh, no, not the Medical Centre. I don't go *there.*

—But you live just up from it.

She shakes her head, to kind of dodge the question, and answers me like it's an inconvenience.

—They accept medical cards there and like, all sorts go there.

Her lips dress the words with disgust. It's as if she's just smelt ammonium. Iwona, who was eager at the start, is quiet now. Her family go to the Medical Centre too.

—We go there, I say.

Sorcha snorts again, nervously.

—Who does?

Iwona starts to doodle in her writing pad.

—Me and Iwona.

I always wondered why I never saw any white Irish there. I mean, we all bleed red. What's the difference?

—It's just handier, she says.

—You literally live two seconds from the Medical Centre.

Sorcha puts up her hand.

—Miss, Iwona and Princess are distracting me. Can I move?

And I'm like, what a bitch. She gives me a big wide smile and shuffles away. I'm happy. Without her annoying us, me and Iwona can get back to our usual Chemistry class routine. I love Chemistry. But seriously, what a bitch.

Why do I love Chemistry class so much?

The teacher? Of course not.

The other students? Of course not. Other than Iwona, they're all like Sorcha.

The subject itself? Yes. And, I'm not gonna lie, I get a thrill when I hear about Iwona's life. What she gets up to with her forty-year-old boyfriend, Konrad. Joke. He's not forty. Even though he looks it. He's in his twenties. Which is still weird.

Iwona somehow does all this crazy shit on the weekends with him – all the sex and all the trips to Nando's and Eddie Rocket's – it's so exotic and exciting. Still she manages to come in on Monday morning smelling of roses, literally, with all her homework done and study complete.

I admire her because of that. Sometimes I even think, like, wait – why don't I give it a try? The whole work hard, party hard thing. Only Michael cries for his bottle and I see Becky pad past me and I realize I'm not going to be a hard luck story of promise and unfulfilled potential. Besides, I don't have the same level of academic ability as Iwona anyway.

Me and Iwona have started already when Miss tells the class to remember to put on lab coats and safety glasses. If she'd paid attention to us instead of scrolling through her phone when we came into the room, she'd know that's the first thing me and Iwona always do.

I'm pipetting out the diluted acid and Iwona is gripping the conical flask. Only this time, instead of putting her tongue out and panting with effort, she's just holding it as if it disappoints her.

—Just like a big cock, isn't it? she says in a real bored voice.

I keep an eye on the paring and shrug, attempt a silent laugh. I prefer when she smiles telling jokes.

—Where to next then, with your CVs? she says before yawning.

—Bracken on The Square, I suppose.

—I hope you fixed the spelling. You'll need all the help you can get.

—What's that meant to mean?

—Nothing. It's a great idea, but I'd hate to see you waste it.

I scoff and look at her closely, see if she's alright. She seems down.

We continue as before and Iwona doesn't even notice when I finish pipetting.

—Hello? You alive?

—Yeah, course, she says before sighing.

I'm looking for my pen to take down our notes.

—Hey, Princess, how'd you feel, if you got the job, about getting me, like, the morning after pill?

—Huh? I say, missing it the first time.

—The morning after pill.

—Oh my days, Iwona. You're not that thick are ye?

She looks at me like I've slapped her and she sits up straight on her stool, blushing a bit.

—No. Course not.

—Good. Because that'd be the stupidest thing I've ever heard coming out of your mouth.

—No, course not. It's just Konrad's asking. Saying it doesn't feel as good.

In my head I'm like, wait, that wasteman Konrad's running the show? But to Iwona, I don't know what to say. What can I say? I know nothing about this kind of stuff. She's been seeing Konrad these past two months. I don't know if that's the time to start thinking about sex, condoms, getting rid of condoms, or what.

He looks a bit thick, if you ask me. I've only seen him from a distance with his head out the window of his car, baseball cap and big stupid droopy eyes like he's constantly stoned. He drives a souped-up sports car. I never thought someone like Iwona would be impressed by that kind of stuff.

He roared into the school last week to collect her. The exhaust growled and sighed as he did a 180 in the carpark. The tyres screeched and skidded. The windows were down and the Polish hip-hop was so loud. I thought he was being ironic. It felt like the whole school stopped to watch him skid to a halt and nod in Iwona's direction. She played it cool, but you could tell she was loving every second of it. She gave me this real casual wave and almost skipped over to him. One of the cleaners, in her yellow apron, was wheeling her trolley across the yard. Konrad revved away in a cloud of dust, leaving the poor cleaner coughing behind him in his wake. When the cloud cleared, I saw it was Iwona's mum.

I don't think anyone other than me knows that Iwona's mum is a cleaner in our school. She normally comes in after four, when most of the students are gone home. If you look hard, like really study her face – get past the lank, short, dyed black hair, the deep dark rings around the puffy eyes, the lines on the face, the sagging cheeks, the blackening teeth – you'll find a slight resemblance to her daughter.

The glamour of Konrad's car I suppose, isn't something I'd begrudge Iwona.

My silence must give me away because Iwona's staring at me now, like she's waiting for me to say something. Her cheeks are still flushed.

—What Princess? What's your problem?

I hold my hands up, whisper:

—Nothing. Really Iwona, you're taking me up wrong.

—It's not the same with it on he says. I'm not stupid you know. There's no need to call me stupid.

I really don't know what to say.

—See what you'd do if you ever got a boyfriend. Quit judging me.

—I wasn't judging you.

—Whatever, she says, looking to the conical flask like she's never seen one before.

Dean

—Yer meant to change hands, Cian says, miming the action. Otherwise it'll get lobsided. That's what happened the Bop Byrne.

I make a face like I can smell his bullshit. It's not bullshit I'm smelling really, it's this strange bang of boiling potatoes you only get in Cian's house – especially his kitchen. I know it's weird, but I kind of like the smell.

—The Bop. You know him, Dean. From the Drogheda Road. He got caught showing little kiddies his dick cause they could tell the cops what it looked like and all. It was bent to one side from the pulling.

—So, you're afraid kids will tell the cops about your lobsided dick?

He doesn't respond, only squishes up his mush like he's gone and tasted his own bullshit.

—I've started to write with me left hand as practise – Cian's not finished yet – to get used to having control, you know, of the muscles and direction and all that.

—Is it not weird?

He slurps from his second can of Dutch Gold like a pro. Like he does this at eleven o'clock every Saturday night when his ma's out.

—That's the best part. If I close my eyes hard enough and really, like, ye need to really concentrate, it almost starts to feel like it's another person. There's a different action to it. Motion like. Direction nearly. It's hard to describe. Ye have to try it.

I do the action under the kitchen table with my good hand, discreetly, and then try it with my left hand.

—Fucking hell, I say, impressed.

—Have you really never done it before? I thought you broke yer hand boxing in first year?

—I did, but I could still do it with the tip of me finger and thumb through the cast.

—Like holding a pencil.

—Or a big fat permanent marker.

—Me da's bookie's pen more like, Cian laughs and slobbers his lips over the can like he's trying to kiss it.

Our little giggles are silenced by the wild laughter of women coming through the wall. Cian's next-door neighbour is a few years older than us, and a bit of a ride.

—Maybe we'll see them at the Home tonight, I say and we cheers each other, but Cian doesn't smile.

Cian's sister comes in and fills up her plastic bottle with water. She's fifteen and a real pain in the arse.

—You two losers better have all this shit cleared away cause ma is only gone the pub. She said she'll be back tonight.

—She says that every Saturday night, Cian replies and the sister tuts him and says:

—You're such a loser, Cian.

—Want a can? I say.

—Fuck off, weirdo, she replies and shakes her head as she leaves the room.

Cian shrugs and smiles, takes out the one skinner he got from his cousin.

*

With the squishy blue squares of Durex loaded into our pockets, we stroll down the Home via the harbour. I'm wearing these gammy brown leather shoes Cian robbed from his da's press. It's dark and every step is a potential disaster.

—I look drunk cause of these shoes, I say.

—You look drunk cause you are drunk.

—Nah, sure we only had two cans each.

—Exactly.

—What if the cops stop us, breathalyse us?

—Breathalyse pedestrians?

—Drug test us even? Me da would kill me.

The boxing club sign has changed, but the mural of the young lad boxer who killed himself years ago is still there. The lad's massive wide smile and open arms greet everyone who darkens the gym door. We haven't been down this way in ages. I haven't been to the gym in five years myself. Of course Cian has to say:

—You miss it?

—Fuck off, I say.

—I'm only asking. I heard you were good.

—Whatever.

—I wish my da was a boxing legend so I could get his fighting genes. If my da's genes were jeans he'd give me Penneys. Your da's would be Levi's.

—Second-hand Levi's.

—At least your da isn't a fucking loser who fucked off on his family.

—Yet, I say.

But he doesn't notice.

We take a few steps in silence, but I can't get the boxing club out of my head.

—You don't have to live with it, I say.

—Live with me da fucking up on the horses every week? Eh, yeah I do. That's why me ma kicked him out.

—No, not your da. My da. Everywhere I fucking go.

—Everywhere you go you're treated like a celebrity, man.

—Everywhere I go people whisper about me. And I pull redners because of it.

—You love the attention, Cian says.

I know he doesn't mean it.

When we come out from under the viaduct, the beat of dance music is only massive. The laughter and noise of the crowd out in the smoking area overlooking the harbour is so loud too. The three bouncers are on their phones at the top of the steps, their faces like white anarchist masks.

The top of the steps might as well be a mountain. HOME sizzles, the pink neon M blacking out and popping back like a fly catcher in a chipper. The beat comes through the walls. HO E strobes out to the town and this brings a smile to my heavy lips. The three bouncers put away their phones. My lips are so fucking dry it feels like if I talk, they'll crack.

—Stay cool, Cian mutters out the side of his mouth. I'll sort this.

—Don't say it.

—Say what? Cian says.

—You know what.

—Relax.

A blast of music escapes from behind them when the doors open.

—Don't say it, I say again as we take the steps, me walking with huge lifts of my leg to make sure I don't clip an extended leather brown toe off the edge of the stone.

Shouting and laughing bursts out to us. We make it to the top and the big M sizzles on and lights us in pink. Cian says, real high pitched:

—Can we come in, please?

My head just bobs down in defeat.

The small bouncer, the older looking of the three, sniggers and doesn't even bother turning our way when he says:

—Not a hope lads. Fuck off.

The music goes dull again. The laughter and noise disappears too.

—His da's real famous.

Cian said it.

The small bouncer looks at me and smirks, interested.

—Yeah?

—Yeah, Cian continues, delighted he has their attention.

The other two shuffle in, like massive fucking collapsing pillars.

—He's a real famous boxer, Cian chirps.

The small bouncer smiles.

—Yeah?

—Yeah. An Olympic champion.

—Cian, I whisper, putting my hand out to stop him.

—Really? the smaller bouncer says.

My greener means my redner can't break through.

—Who?

Cian licks his lips, savouring the words:

—The Jock.

The three bouncers look at each other with wide eyes and burst out laughing. Cian doesn't get the joke. I do, of course.

And I shrink into myself.

—Joe O'Connor? the small bouncer says – still smiling – In that case, go ahead boys.

—Nice one, Cian says.

A leather glove – fingers spread wide – lands on Cian's chest.

—He's taking the piss, ourlad. Not a hope. Fuck off.

Their laughter is nothing new to me. I'm glad the big M has zapped off so my cheeks can sizzle under the cover of darkness.

—But his da?

—What's he gonna do, come down here and knock us out?

—If it's the Jock – the small bouncer says – He'll miss.

—Or try for a kiss!

They all laugh big meat-hacking laughs. And I stand there, like a slow spinning, sweaty doner kebab on a skewer.

To make it worse we get an audience when these three lads with baseball caps and these young girls arrive at the bottom of the steps. The girls are all legs and tits in luminous skintight dresses. Eyelashes you could hang your coat on. I nearly get a horn just glancing down at them. The bouncers turn their attention to them too. They look so young, the girls, but even they'll be getting in, shaking their arses in faces that should be mine and Cian's.

—Alright Paddy, the bouncer calls down, and from the bottom of the steps a voice comes back up:

—Story horse. Good for five passes, yeah?

If only life could be so simple.

Two lads clatter through the door behind us. Everything is a mess of grunting and shouting and black overcoats and gloves and bootcut jeans and brown shoes and chequered shirts and girls trying to keep their dresses from riding up their arses. The lads' shirts are ripped open, exposing lean, muscley six-packs.

The bouncers are saying:

—Out, out, out! in this mad rush.

We move aside and let the blur of bodies rumble by.

I grab Cian and pull him back up. Our path is suddenly obstacle-free and on we saunter, like the big aul lads, up to the ticket desk. We pay in and shape on like the new men we are.

—See, Cian says. Told ye I'd get us in.

Angel

From nowhere, a Monday, she calls. I mean an actual phone call. I'm so gassed.

No cap, she wants to come meet. Why? I dunno, but she sounds upset, yuno. So I'm like, yeah, cool.

So basically, we're sitting in the Angola woman's front room while she's in the hall giving some other guy a trim. Normally I stand with her when she's barbering, cause I got my own clippers at home and I'm interested in that shit, barbering and all that. She's cool, Delfina, and she lets me stall it there and watch her work.

This time though, I'm waiting for Princess. Swear down, if barbering in your hallway gets you a front room like this, I wanna barber for life. The floor is all white tiles with the black Versace medusa head in the middle of them. The coffee table is gold legs and glass with the Versace crest in a white design on it. There's steck Versace glasses, I swear to God, Versace glasses on the shelf in the room and her couch is a mad thing, bright red leather, real hard to sit on, get comfortable on, and there's about four or five cushions, black and gold, no lie, with Versace Medusa heads on them too. And then there's three framed pictures of Delfina with her big smiley head, big jumbo jet gap between her front teeth, big afro like a Versace Medusa herself. The gaff is bare leng.

The doorbell rings and I'm not gonna lie, I'm kinda shook and I fumble with my phone. I'm feeling stupid for thinking this was a fresh plan, yuno.

Anyways, the Angola woman comes into us, stands in the door and has this vexed face on her. She points her shears at me, her red nails nearly longer than the blade. Her jewellery jangles like change in Isaac's Nike Tech pockets.

—Hey, she says, calling for my attention.

Swear down like, she's scary, like she's ready to shank me.

—This place is not a café, you hear?

—Yes, Delfina, the three of us, me, Isaac and Pelumi, whisper.

She bare stares at me like I've disrespected her.

—We clear, Angel?

Pelumi kisses his teeth. The silence is so awkward.

Then Princess steps in from the hall when Delfina leaves. Shitden, her hair, yeah. It's a proper wig. Straight big black hair. No braids like the other day or nothing. God knows she's beautiful. None of those click-clack heels no more, but a busted-ass pair of black Nike Air Max and real tight jeans and a puffer jacket. But, my days, the hair. She's fresh. I feel so proud, yuno, for her visiting me, here, now, in front of the boys.

Obviously, I thought it'd be calm to bring her here, let the boys meet her, see me with her, and all that, yeah. But having Princess in the room, the silence, all four of us together, it's like I'm seeing Isaac and Pelumi clear for the first time. Like, Pelumi, yeah, that guy's a sicko. People are scared of him. Especially the white boys and that's calm. God knows he disses everyone in his tracks, and if you spit bars back at him, he goes mad and gives you hands.

Pelumi's bars are violent – vicious even. Some of the shit he says is on point, but cold. Even if all of his lyrics are about his scraps with his opps, he makes the most of them. God knows, in small things too though, Pelumi is bad out. You gotta be on edge around him, 24/7. This drill thing he has going on, is sixty percent bars, and forty percent reputation. More than anyone, Pelumi knows he's gotta stay sharp and sound fresh, have a few banging tunes and maintain a few opps.

Me and the boys, Isaac and another few lads, we're called the K3P Crew. But all we do is pretend to be tuff yutes in the music videos, fake knowing his bars and look like we're mean from wet ends.

Anyone, anytime is game ball to enhance Pelumi's street cred. Any opportunity to add more bars about scraps to a new track, he'll take it.

Everyone, apart from Isaac, has got bet one time by Pelumi. Even me. Badly. And obviously, Isaac isn't gonna get bet cause he's hench. Pelumi knows Isaac'd rock him if he gave him too much shit. Yeah, he gives bars about Isaac being a light skin, but Pelumi knows when to quit. Isaac is quieter. Not as mad. I like Isaac. He's not as unpredictable as Pelumi. Yeah, he loves being Pelumi's plug in all the YouTube videos, but he's not relying on bars and tracks to enhance his rep. So he's more relaxed.

Princess dips to the toilet.

—What the fuck you bring her here for? Pelumi says. She's frigid man.

—Nah man, I say. She's leng. Her hair's fresh.

Pelumi twists his lips, shakes his head.

—Nah man.

—He's right, Isaac says. She's butters. What you doing? Her hair's like Lego or something.

—Her hair's too big for her head man, and she's waaay too black, Pelumi laughs.

They slap each other's leg.

—That's her ma's wig, Isaac says.

—That's a bar, Pelumi adds and they nearly hug each other they're so hyped.

So then I say it. Just to shut them up, yuno.

—Job is job, though.

Pelumi sucks his teeth.

—Hardly, she's never gonna twap.

—All I'm saying is job is job.

Isaac shakes his head:

—No way, no way.

Then Pelumi whispers:

—You're chattin shit, that's what I say.

He squeaks forward on his seat, getting interested, leaning in.

—There's no way she's gonna jeet.

God only knows why I have to prove myself to them. Him. Why now, why this is important. So I don't stop. Obviously, yeah, a yute like me needs them. A yute like me feels on point when my face is in them YouTube videos. 760K views is amazing. All the salty people chattin shit about Pelumi. His crew. Me. Making us real tight.

—You wait, I say.

Pelumi dismisses with a flick of his hand.

—Nah, you're fake as fuck. She's butters man and you still won't get uck.

—Yeah I will.

—Nah man.

—Allow, Isaac says, seeing me and Pelumi are getting into it.

—Nah fam, this little bitch is fake. You're fake and you aint a man like us big boys, wha?

Him and Isaac laugh. The door opens and the Angola woman comes in.

—Who's next?

Pelumi goes to the door, only Princess arrives back from the toilet at the same time and they meet. Pelumi moves against the doorframe to let her slide through. She kind of hunches into herself and lowers her head like she's trying to tip-toe past him without being seen. But Pelumi, swear down, he looks like he wants to either rock her or lips her the way he stares as she goes by. His chin is out like he wants to go head-to-head. It's a mad thing.

So, basically, yeah, once Pelumi's gone, and Princess is back, the room feels bigger. Everything's calm. Isaac even puts away his phone.

—How come you're here? he says.

She goes:

—Huh?

—Like why you meeting up with Angel all of a sudden?

I go:

—Allow, Isaac.

I never even asked the question myself. God knows, there must be something up.

—I needed to get out. See this? she says, pointing to her hair. I got it done for a big interview today.

—Fresh, I say.

She shakes her head.

—Nah. I didn't get it.

—There's gotta be steck jobs, though, yeah?

She starts nodding, a sob.

—That was the last one. It's my only hope of getting into college. Getting outta this town. Making something of myself. I gotta get extra credits for an interview for a college course. I need references.

I put my arm on her shoulder. She sniffles. Swear to God, she smells bare fresh, yeah. While she's rubbing her eyes and looking down at the Medusa head on the tiles, Isaac is staring at me, gassed, his eyes wide and excited. And then he pretends to suck something in his fist and he mouths, Job is job, and raises his eyebrows and gives the thumbs up. Allow man, is all I think to myself. Allow.

*

I'm down town Saturday night for some FLC and mango juice from Bossman – with Princess. Swear down like, I just messaged her and she agreed to link up. We meet at the blocks and I'm not gonna lie, I'm stressed. Like we're hooking up or something, yuno. Even though we aren't, we kinda are.

We get our food and sit in. No one saying much, just eating and sucking on our straws in the corner.

—This is cool, she says.

I look around with new eyes at the stiff plastic chairs bolted to the ground, salt stuck to the greasy tables, dead flies on the window ledge under the flashing sign. The calls of Bossman out back while his chicken fries and sizzles. The smell of grease bangs.

I nod, keep on eating.

—I've never been here before, she says, all delicate with her chicken skin like it's got feelings or something.

Those lips of hers all greasy and polite and sexy.

I nod again, like it's no big deal – but swear down like, I'm thinking, where has this girl been?

She goes:

—You're very quiet when you're on your own.

I just laugh.

—Am I?

—With all your boys you're different.

—Nah.

—I'm serious. You're all like, Hey, look at me, I'm hench. I'm a roadman.

—Hardly.

She leans across the table and pushes my arm. My drink spills from my straw a bit. She puts on this deep voice and goes:

—Hardly. Hey, I'm Angel and I'm a driller.

—That's a bar.

—A bar? Yeah it is. Cause I'm getting to know you. And you know what?

—What?

—You aren't a tuff guy. You're sweet. And cool. And that's fresh.

I'm done out here. My chest is buzzing and all I can think of is a Kendrick track, and I wanna sing it. I love myself. I. Love. Myself.

—So why do you hang out with those guys? she says.

—Wow! Allow, I say, holding my hands up like she's gonna shank me. They're my boys!

—My boys, she says, in that voice that's meant to be me. You gonna hang around with your boys for the rest of your life?

I laugh through my nose and shrug at such a thought. This girl.

—Hardly. Soon as I can, I'm outta here.

—How? she says, like a challenge.

Swear down, a girl like her I've never met before. I shrug, eat some more of the peppery skin.

—Easy. I got it all planned out.

I don't.

—Wait, Angel, you do know your face is all over them YouTube tracks. And you're not even saying anything. Making any money from them or anything. But you'll be associated with all Pelumi's drill lyrics – splashing opps, shanking feds – forever. You're all like Pelumi's little bitches, making him look as if he's got a crew, so he can impress the record industry people, so he can get out of here. You think he's gonna take all of you K boys with him?

—Allow, I say, sucking my teeth, taking a sup of mango juice. I thought you said you liked me and you're roasting me instead.

She laughs.

—I never said I liked you. I said you're nice. There's a big difference.

—That is a bar. I'm not gonna lie, that's a bar. Nice. Nice boy like me, nice enough to hang out with.

—That you are.

Some yutes sit across from us, caps high on their heads, faces in their phones, waiting on their food. Something sizzles furiously behind the counter before Bossman Franco shouts and dampens it.

—What about you then? I whisper across to her. Any change to your big plan to dash out've these ends?

She blows a breath and I'm shook by how amazing her eyes are, how she sucks her cheeks like she has a grape in her mouth. Her lips squish together and make her look so leng. She's really rocked me with them questions.

—Dunno. I really don't know anymore. It's just so hard. It's really hard when you get knockback after knockback. I'm like, wait, maybe I'm getting these knockbacks for a reason. I just wish I had someone who was like me, yuno, looking to the future. Making plans. Someone I could look to for inspiration.

—Me, I say.

I say it before I even know I've said it.

—You?

—Yeah, me.

—Are you even going to finish school?

—Yeah, course. My ma would bate me if I didn't.

Princess puts her hand across the table. I reach out and take it. Her hand, her fingers feel so, so soft. I can't lie, she's too wavy.

—Thanks, she says.

—For what?

—For answering the phone to me last Monday. For hanging out with me this week. I needed someone I could lean on, depend on. And you've been that.

I shrug, like, whatever.

So basically, yeah, Princess has me floating when we step out of FLC into the cold Saturday night, our breath white and thick. Everything is popping, and this town is the only place in the world I wanna be right now.

Then who comes round the corner with a massive crew only Paddy Mac and Mart O. BAM! There's me back down to earth and I'm thinking, shiten.

—Alright Angel, Paddy says, all smiles like I'm his plug. Who's this bitch?

—Allow, I say.

All his crew, must be five of them, laugh at me. They're all freckly white boys with chains round their necks and hands down their jocks. One of them I remember finessed my Nike cap when I was ten walking down town on my ones.

—What time is it? Paddy says.

—Allow, I go, knowing well what's gonna happen here.

—Take out yer phone there, Angel, and tell us the time.

—Hardly, I go and he's in my face, forcing me back against the neon in the window.

Finger, Licken, Chicken, blue, pink, green, blue, pink, green.

—Leave him alone, Princess calls from behind them and there's giggles and I get rocked from nowhere.

I'm on the ground, swear down like, it didn't really hurt – more the shock, yuno?

—Where's your boys now?

But then, basically yeah, a load of legs surrounds me and I'm getting jumped, kicks coming in from everywhere. No lie, I have my hands over my face and I don't see nothing until the boots suddenly stop and there's creps scraping and skidding and I'm pulled to my feet and Pelumi has a hold of me, his eyes are wide as golf balls and he's like a mad thing.

—You alright? he says, out of breath, looking over my shoulder, but still holding me up.

Swear down, I am so happy to see that guy. What a driller. My head's still all over the shop.

—They've dashed to the train station, Benni shouts, grabbing Pelumi by the arm like he's reporting to his boss.

Pelumi lets go of me and I check around for Princess. She's across the road, arms folded, biting her bottom lip.

—Right boys, Pelumi shouts. These wastemen tried to hop Angel. Don't back down now, come on, come on!

He's shouting like he's an army sergeant blazin over the top of the trenches. Swear to God, it feels like we're soldiers in Wakanda – not Black Panther himself, but some boys lacking in the background. And then they all sprint, and Princess is across the road, alone, and I swear, I'm fucked, but mans gotta do what the boys do too, yuno? So I dash to the train station with Pelumi and them and obviously, yeah, like all the boys, when I get there I blaze into the scrap too.

Noise, the noise. Boys shouting and grunting and then I get banged again and I'm on the ground and the throb under my eye – where I got whooshed earlier – is only massive. Then a fucking helicopter noise and someone shouts, feds! And blue lights flash through legs across the carpark and the sirens are getting louder. But still the boys are battering the white lads and Pelumi is destroying some chap. I'm up on my feet, dodging opps and staggering over to the lane, out to the beach to hide til it blows over. Fuck that.

I hide down the beach on my ones for hours til all the blue lights from the feds disappear and the helicopter is gone and all the shit dies down. It's cold down there and I see some heads link up at the lifeguard hut, but I don't go over, just in case. If yuno, yuno. I've fuck all battery on my phone so I have to sit there shivering for ages. My arse is getting cold. I watch the fishing boats on the horizon in front of me and listen to the Please stand back behind the yellow line, from the train station.

Everyone's gone from the car park so I walk up through town to get to Princess's gaff. I've only three percent battery. I turn the phone off til I get to the block.

Princess comes to the door, vexed I left her and I'm calling so late. She's looking back into the hall in case her ma hears her or something. But then she sees my face. I can't smile with the pain, so all good, the swelling must still be big. Swear to God but, she's looking bare leng – even with her wig off and her bandana on.

—Your face, she says in a kind of concerned gasp.

I am chuffed.

—It's nothin, I say, being all like I don't wanna talk about it tuff.

—Take a selfie with me? I ask.

She's off her step, her soft hand so warm on my face, touching the tight skin, looking hard at the bulge under my eye. She doesn't hear me the first time. So I say it again:

—Take a selfie with me.

—What? she says like I'm talking another language. Why?

—Please, it's just a thing. Please, for me.

There's like, 2 percent battery left.

She tuts and rolls her eyes like I'm such a kid, but I can tell she's gassed to be asked, to have me calling to her so late, to have me at her door.

So, obviously, yeah, she leans in and there's the double flash.

1 percent battery.

I just manage to get the picture up on my story and walk home, chuffed, like I finally got the yams. My mam's gonna kill me but that's for another day.

Tanya

Got no ca$$ got to hustle gran

♫ Ambition for Cash – @Key Glock

Tanya is sitting back on an old patterned couch of thick, faded corduroy, with her head at an angle, pouting. She lifts her hand to the screen, rubs her index finger and thumb together and starts to mouth the lyrics.

>521

Did ye say ye want tea? Gran says, sitting onto her armchair, eyes on the TV.

No thanks Gran, I say, looking around the room for a sign of me da's presence.

Gran's been different with me since my da left. Almost as if she's embarrassed by what he's done. So many people are bullied by embarrassment. Like, what a waste.

Gran sits down with a muffled groan and nods to me.

I'm flattered you've decided to grace me with your company since you're always out and about with all your friends and not bothering to answer your Instagram.

Instagram?

Ye don't answer your Friend Requests.

Who's asking to be my friend?

I am!

And that, Gran, is why I don't go on Instagram. Me ma set it up for me when I was like seven or something.

You do go on it. Your ma is friends with ye. I've seen your pictures with all them girls.

I'm not really out with them much these days.

You look like you have fun in them pictures.

We did. Some of them are from the team.

Football was never for you.

Well me da thought it was.

Sure what does that eejit know?

I wouldn't know. I never see him no more.

I haven't seen him in ages myself, she mumbles, a fresh cigarette dripping now from her bottom lip.

He's always in the gym with this Barry character, she exhales. Or busy with his new taxi.

Whatever he's doing he's too busy to call me, I say. Or give me a lend of a fiver if I need it.

I used to sleep on this couch when I was younger. Holding Da's hand down the Dublin Road, my overnight bag on his shoulder. As soon as we turned into the cul-de-sac Granny'd be waiting at the door for me, arms folded, squinting, fag in the corner of her mouth.

Sure, you're too busy with boys by the looks of your pictures to be playing sports and talking to yer da. Too many boys if ye ask me.

No one's asking ye Gran! Ye sound like me ma. And she has some cheek talking to me about boys.

If you're courting, ye should be courting only one boy at a time.

I should be doing whatever I want.

And that's why ye need to friend me on your Instagram. I'd keep a close eye on ye.

Instagram's dead, Gran.

You're right. Facebook's better. I get all me gossip from Balbriggan Connected now.

Mainstreet is dead

♫ Memories – @David Guetta (feat. Kid Cudi)
Tanya looks into the camera while walking down a street. Street lights are glowing bright orange above her and flaring off the screen. She blows vape smoke into the screen and flips the pov to looking out on the empty road. A green Paddy Power sign glows through the murk. Rain is falling and some splatters on the screen as she zooms in on a window above the PP sign.
>122

I was never invited up there.

One night a while back I just arrived at the door and buzzed myself in. My da was hotboxing the gaff, stoned off his face. Barry Rooney's there too, this new mate of me da's, twenty-six he is, panned out on the couch, his eyes like Kermit the Frog's.

Barry has this weird smile on him and he's barely able to lift his big muscley arm. I wave back with a smile because it's nice that he notices me.

I'm drunk. My da is standing in the doorway, hasn't a breeze, pretending to be sober: You alright?

Can I stay here?

Tonight?

No, tomorrow. I'm pre-booking a room just in case yer sold out.

Ye wha?

Yeah Da, tonight.

Hold on Tanya, yer not making much sense.

I wait there for a second to see if he remembers me birthday now that I'm in front of him. He blinks at me so I don't bother saying anything and go into his room to get some kip. I haven't seen him in months, but we can talk in the morning, when I'm sober and I've calmed down and he's not stoned.

All I can hear is Barry and me da's goofy laughter coming down the hall and me head's not great at all so I get up. I grope my way along the wall. Me da and Barry are oohhing down the hall in the front room. I hear these noises from the laptop. The moans of a woman, the grunts of a man, the woman calling out, and me da and Barry are laughing.

Mother of Jaysus … go on ye good thing, Barry is saying.

Me da is all, Now that's a good girl if ever I saw one. Fair play to her.

Weirdos. Me da especially. That's more than he's ever fucking said to me this last year. As if an ability to suck dick is what impresses him most.

Barry snaps the laptop shut. Da turns around as if his neck is stiff.

Go back to bed, love. Just having a bit of banter here, yeah.

This party is popping tho

♫ Savage – @Megan Thee Stallion

Tanya is in a busy shopping centre. She sticks her tongue out on selfie pov and places the phone at her feet on an escalator. The phone glides up smoothly, starting on her Converse, then her shins, knees, waist and chest. Tanya steps on and starts moving up with the picture. She dances and sings the lyrics into the camera. A delayed filter appears and sways three versions of her across the screen.

>97

Sorry there, love, this aul lad says to me.

Were you creeping on me dancing? I say, pausing the phone as I step off the escalator

No.

I saw ye watching me.

I just thought I recognized ye.

Wonder why. Weirdo.

He's your typical creep. Long hair, in his thirties, green parka jacket, tan shoes. I just brush past him. He stinks of cigarettes.

You Tanya?

No, I say looking at him like he's a freak.

You're not?

No.

Sorry. I'm a friend of your ma's.

Does me ma have more than one?

One what?

Daughter?

What? No.

Then why'd ye pretend not to know me.

He keeps up with me and he only goes and holds out his hand and says, I'm …

A paedo.

No need for that.

Well then leave me alone.

He watches me for a weird second and then he shrugs and says, Fair enough.

That's what I get all the time these days.

Paddy Power for de sesh!

♫Scream & Shout – @Will.i.am

It's night and Tanya shakes her head, her hair covering the shot momentarily as she dances to the music while exhaling smoke. The shot goes to front pov and we see a drunk passed out in the doorway under the Paddy Power sign. The picture zooms in and out on him.
>89

Only a few weeks before the viral yoke happens, I stall it up there again. Barry answers. He's always wearing real tight tops to show off his muscles. Ye can tell he fancies himself the way he goes round the town with his hair styled to the max all the time. His beard looks like it's drawn on and he's always in shorts with this mad confident walk.

He says my da isn't in cause he's bringing a punter to the airport. Barry smells so good in the doorway. Fresh and clean. He's wearing this tight white T-shirt as usual with a pair of shorts and his huge tattoo on his leg is all Celtic swirls and shit and real sexy. I say I'll wait for me da inside.

There's an opened packet of cigarettes on the table.

Wanna smoke? Shot of vodka? Barry says, his head leaning out to me from the kitchen.

It's the first time we've been alone. What else am I gonna say?

Bit of vodka and Red Bull. We should down it together. For the buzz, wha? he says.

He shows me how to link arms and drink facing each other, tangled up like. Up close his face seems massive. His eyes are bloodshot, the skin under them scaly like a fish, his eyelids all red. There's stray hairs, small clippings that must've floated onto his face in work, stuck to his pristine cheeks.

Sitting on a couch drunk is new to me. Normally I'd be getting wasted on a jacket over the stones down the beach, or on the wall by the canal. The couch is so comfortable, the room so nice, like a nice warm hug almost.

Why ye calling up for yer da?

I need a dress for clubbing.

You've a body could make any dress look sexy.

I close my eyes and giggle, and when I open them again he's on Google images. He has pictures up of models in tight dresses.

He keeps nudging my hip. Pretending to annoy me and tickle me. He says those dresses on the screen would suit me cause I'm so beautiful and sexy.

It feels strange hearing him talk like that. Say those kind of things to me. The words are lovely and all, but they still feel weird.

The last time someone complimented me was when I scored a goal on the pitch outside my gaff. Me da had hugged me real tight and cheered, You're some fucking goer!

Barry lifts the laptop onto his knees and puts on a clip I've seen already that's everywhere. This young one at a gig off her face, locked. He plays the clip. Doesn't say a word.

The wind makes a dirty sound on the recording and distorts the speakers. You can tell straight away it's a gig because of the crowd noise and the lights. Then the shaky camera slows down and autofocuses on the star of the thing, that young one. I feel uncomfortable cause I know what's coming.

She's on her knees, in the shadows, but lit every second by a different coloured light, sucking off some random lad in these baggy ripped denim jeans and brown elf shoes, a checked shirt opened to his waist.

D'ye like that? Barry whispers, eyes on the screen.

I dunno, Barry. What would your girlfriend say you showing me this?

Never mind her. Course you don't like that. You're too innocent for that lark.

I'm sixteen Barry.

Yeah, innocent. I'm not slagging ye. It's a good thing. You're classier than that slut, aren't ye?

The room is swaying. The smell of vodka off his breath makes me feel a bit ill.

You're not like that. You're classier than them, he says, turning to me with this lift of one cheek like a half-arsed smile.

And then he leans in. My legs are hitched up under me arse and he squishes over my knees. He brings his hand to my face and I can hear his breath kind of shaking. The cigarettes mixed with the Red Bull is rank.

You're not like them others, you're a good girl, he whispers, his warm breath on my cheek.

And I don't stop him. I can't. I just sit there like, I dunno, paralysed, like totally freaked. Course he's hench, and normally smells real fresh and he's hot, but it feels weird. I let him lean on my legs and his red sweaty cheeks, his cigarette lips, slobber all over me. The hair clippings rub off my face, making me itch. His fingers fumble under my jumper, his nails catch my skin as he searches under my bra. It's like I zoom out from it all. The hands are massive, cold things. I don't know what to do, what to say. The fingers are long and stiff and swamp me. The stubble is rough and thick and prickly.

And then I gag, and retch, and puke a bit in his mouth.

I laugh. There's nothing else to do but laugh.

Bestie vibes

♬ So Pretty – @Reyanna Maria

Tanya has the phone on selfie, with a girl on either side of her. One girl looks similar to Tanya. Her hair is tied up in a ponytail. She has big eyelashes, a thin nose and pouting lips, but is shorter than the other girl, who has long black hair draped over her wide shoulders. She is larger than Tanya and takes up most space in the shot. A housing estate is in the background. The girls are leaning in to sing the words of the song. They are smiling and holding up their hands, pointing their fingers and making gang signs.

>443

Rihanna spits out a stream of her coke.

The lads asked us to go on a sesh with them Saturday, she says.

Nice one, I say, not showing any emotion cause I wanna play it cool.

They ask you? Britney says, hopping off the wall.

She's shaking her hips and clicking her fingers like she's some sort of star.

Think Marto might have said something, I go.

Britney stops dancing, fixes her ponytail and looks at me. A big smile's on her face and she says, Oh my God, I'm scarlet for ye. They never said nothing to ye.

Doesn't matter, they know I'd be up for it so they didn't need to ask.

You haven't been up for anything in ages, Britney says.

And then Rihanna goes, Yeah, whatever. Callum gave us a shout out the other day. Never heard your name.

So.

And Paddy was saying to Marto you're a dry shite these days, Britney adds.

They're starting to annoy me now.

No I'm not. He wouldn't have said that anyway. He's not like that. I'll say it to him and see what he says.

Needy much? Britney says.

Don't be a thick. He's always on to me messaging all night. He wouldn't say that.

This gives them a laugh and then Rihanna puts on my voice and goes, Here Paddy, do you think I'm a dry shite?

I just tut. Don't want to give them anything.

Then Britney goes, Don't go running to him telling him what we said. I'm just saying what he said. Don't cause hassle. It's what we heard. You're as dry as your ma's fanny these days.

You've been dead this past ages Tanya. The lads haven't invited ye cause you're zero buzz. You don't do nothing no more, Rihanna says, looking into her phone.

Yeah, and yous are the fucking stars now I suppose.

They both smile. Rihanna steps towards me and puts her phone up to my face.

Paddy, Rihanna says.

It's hard to see anything with the shine off the yoke.

Yeah right, I say.

That's Paddy. Swear to God, Britney says.

They both laugh and bump into each other.

It's Rihanna's stupid face, her eyes staring up while she gags on a dick. And this is daytime again, and this is closer, clearer. And when you add to that I've not been invited on the sesh, I'm devastated. I thought he liked me.

How doesn't that end up on WhatsApp? I say.

And they both giggle and shrug, smug, like it's not their problem.

They're right though. I've been zero craic this ages. Especially the last few weeks since the video.

And every morning these days I just lie in my bed til my ma comes up and literally has to pull the blankets off me. And in the shower she has to bang on the door to get me out of it cause I'm checking where there might be spots of psoriasis. And when I see the girls these days I'm always worried how I look, minding what I say. I never laugh no more. But they're all I've got now that I'm not playing sport. And the last thing I want is to be a loner.

Princess

Every day holds a new lesson, every lesson is a new opportunity. Some days these lessons are right there in front of you in your schoolbooks. A simple yellow highlighter and I've convinced myself I've learned. Other days you have to open your eyes, ears, mind and really try and search for the lesson. That's the trick. It's so easy to be lazy and close your eyes and forget to search.

After a few days, it hits me. I'm like, how naïve was I to go in with blue and purple braids? To go in and think they wouldn't notice. The braids took me hours to get in. Hours with all Tantine's talking and tugging and pulling. She needed a model and she said she'd give me a fiver for it. A fiver. Do you think I ever got it? The braids stayed for longer than they should have, because I didn't want to upset her.

Other people's thoughts – again – ruling my head. My head then deciding how I behave. Ambition is singular. Other people's feelings are plural. Both can't work alongside each other. Something's got to change. I've got to become ruthless. Like, I have too much empathy, and not enough drive. Drive is selfish. It has to be. No one is going to hand me what I want because it makes them feel good. If I want to better myself, make something of myself, I really need to look out for myself.

An hour to take out the braids and two hours to get my head back in shape. My hair's all dry, and my scalp is real itchy and flaky. I manage to smooth over the mess after I brush it through with my shea butter conditioner, shampoo and condition again and then cover it up with one of Becky's cool headwraps. I need to look stylish and elegant and I need to take their eyes and hands away from my hair. If I'm being selfish, I gotta be honest and say my eyes are one of my best features. So it makes sense I pick colours for a wrap that highlight this. Soft pink and baby blue African print, done in a neat low bun, finished with my cool hoop earrings. I get my side curls under control and everything feels great, the wrap comforts me like a helmet. I feel ready to go again.

My outfit is the same as the last time – not that anyone would notice. A respectable and formidable cream cardigan and navy knee-length skirt. The kitten heels have moulded into the shape of my foot as well, praise Jesus.

Angel and Pelumi and the others are there as usual, whispering. They're playing a drill beat on their little Bluetooth speaker and it's booming off the buildings. They stare as I approach.

Pelumi hops off the wall and starts getting shifty. I skip down onto the road to circle around him. There are sniggers. The beat is real strong on the little speaker but I can hear someone grunt, groan with pleasure when I go past. I think, wait, why am I putting up with this shit? But I can't do anything.

They laugh and I can see Pelumi begin to shadow me in the corner of my eye. He starts rapping, making a joke of me. I feel him close, catch a sly glimpse of him grinding away right behind me. So I turn into him, stop him in his tracks, and even in my heels and skirt, face up to him, like, what? What you gonna do?

He's face to face, biting his bottom lip. He gyrates so close to me: I feel the heat from his body, see a tiny blemish of pale skin like a birthmark under his left eye. And then Angel arrives between us.

—Hey, hey, it's calm, it's calm, yeah? Angel says.

He knows Pelumi looks angry too.

I'm a bit shaken, and Angel walks with me. Calms me. And comments on how my outfit is looking even better this time. Despite the slight tremor in my voice, I manage a thank you. He is different. I'm beginning to see that now.

*

No music playing this time. No braids either. The pharmacist is another man and he stops what he is doing to watch me approach from the door. His chin is raised and his eyes move slowly, from my unsteady walk in the heels, up my body to my headwrap. He smiles approvingly. As if I've pleased him in some way. Our eyes meet, his don't go any further up, and I know the hoops and the colours worked. But before I can say hello, an old woman appears from behind the sunglasses stand and hobbles between us, her light brown tights bunched and wrinkled at her ankles. He bends down to hear what she's saying.

The bell chimes and a gust of wind blows through the shop as another woman rushes in. I take a second look at her short, tight afro and her black, fitted uniform, highlighted at the edges by a purple trim. She charges towards the counter with a paper Spar bag and coffee. Her lipstick is too bright for her skin tone. The eyeshadow way too extreme. It's like an oil slick over deep water. She drops the items on the counter and turns to me with a friendly smile.

—Hello, my love, can I help you?

Her accent puts me at ease. I feel calm, as if I can be myself.

—Yeah, yes, thank you.

I hold up my CV in the plastic sleeve.

—I'm hoping to speak with the pharmacist.

—About a summer job? I'm sorry, but my daughter Damilola has ...

—No, not a ...

Her name tag flashes as she moves closer. Kind of smothers me, forces me to take a step backwards. RAYO. The smile is gone.

—I'm sorry, but my daughter has already asked about a summer position.

—Not a job, you see ...

Over her shoulder the pharmacist leads the old woman down the shop away from us.

—I'm so sorry, Rayo whispers, her eyelids flickering like a hummingbird's wings. Now, if you will excuse me.

—Can you hand him this, please? I ask weakly.

She sucks her teeth and looks at the plastic I'm holding out. This time I'm not going to go so easily, so readily. I will stand my ground and be selfish. Forget empathy or worrying about embarrassing this woman and making a scene.

—I'll see what I can do, she says.

She accepts my offering.

—Thank you, thank you so much.

The bell chimes when I open the door. The sound of the street mixes with the small sound of the tall metal bin beside the counter creaking open. I see Rayo has her leg extended, foot pressing down on the pedal. She waves at me with her fingers. Whatever she was putting in the bin is gone. I think, wait, no? She couldn't? Could she?

She watches me watching her. Dares me. A scene is the last thing that will get me selected, but I'm like, wait, she wouldn't do me like that, surely?

*

Iwona holds my hand while I try and talk through my sobs down the back of class. We're meant to be calculating a grade based on our short question answers from Section B on the 2017 past paper.

My cowardice, in that moment outside the pharmacy, watching Rayo at the bin, convinced me into thinking she hadn't discarded my CV. Another opportunity wasted. Another time I've let myself down by being so weak. So much for being a fighter. If I don't get the college place I want, I know what Miss will say, how she'll look. That poor-you smile of hers, and the soft pat on my arm to comfort me in defeat, her: There's always other less stressful options, Princess. That reassuring whisper. She never says it, but our silences in her guidance office are filled with all the obvious excuses around me – my background, my home life. But I'll know, it'll be my lack of effort, my lack of true, steel determination, my lack of fight that will have cost me my place.

—It was never going to be easy, Iwona whispers.

—Yeah, I know. I just thought. The lady … It felt, for once, you know. I was like, wait, this place is meant for me. Solidarity, you know?

—Something will work out.

I sniff, dab my nose with the stiff school toilet paper. Iwona continues to add up all the ticks on her questions.

—There's only one more left.

Miss starts calling out names.

We go quiet until girls at the front start announcing their results.

—Where's next then? Iwona says.

—Gogan's, I suppose.

—Don't be down. We're scientists, remember. We have to make mistakes before we find our solution.

—I know, I know, but we change our approach after every negative outcome. And I never did that. Other than the headwrap, I've been lazy in my methods.

I nearly don't say it, but then I just jump right in.

—So I'm making a change now. I sound Irish, right? So, I'm gonna ring ahead and call myself Paula or Pauline or something.

Iwona's eyebrows raise. She watches me for a second.

—You sneaky bitch, Princess. If you get it, remember what I asked for.

I let out a laugh of relief and in trying to suppress it end up snorting, snotting my face.

—You dirty mess, Iwona adds, and we laugh again.

Then her smile dissolves like ammonium chloride in water, and suddenly she seems real cold with me.

—I wish I was as smart as you.

She has never said anything like this before. And I'm like, wait, is she looking for something from me? Then Miss calls my name and I reply with:

—Seventy-five percent, Miss.

—Iwona? she calls.

I spy the total percentage on her page.

—Ninety-nine, Iwona replies.

I'm like, wait, am I shocked because Iwona just lied about her grade, or because Iwona just got fifty-two percent on a test?

Dean

Everything. All at once. Wham! Smoke gushes with a hiss from a machine over my head. It feels like I'm floating. The music volume is insane. The heat. The smell of feet. A massive fucking disco ball. Cian shouts something in my ear and starts to dance. The beat shakes my chest. I put my tongue out to taste the dry ice. Cian spins ahead of me, arm in the air, pointing to the ceiling, whooping. Green lasers whirl like lightsabers, a strobe goes off and the clouds clear away. Cian is holding on to a barrier, head bouncing to the beat, looking down into the dance floor and smiling back to me.

Real life flesh comes into focus. I start to move. Go with the beat. Cian taps my arm. A girl is on the steps beside the dance floor. High heels. Side boob. Bent over. Shaking her ass. This is the IMF of wank banks and my account can't process all the payments. Another girl glides by. I lift my head to try and take in her smell. It's a sweet-scented aura of something I haven't got close to before. She turns and sticks her tongue out, a stud catching the light and flashing like a pearl. It's the smell of sex.

I reach out and try to touch her. She laughs and disappears into the smoke. Everything is mashed together and washing through me. Cian is cheering like a lunatic.

Another girl stands in front of us. Her eyes are a mental see-through blue and her teeth are an extra sharp white. I realize, after a moment of staring, we're standing under one of those glow lights. I immediately brush my shoulder to clear away signs of dandruff.

—You guys want shots? she says.

—Fuck yeah, Cian shouts, swaying.

I can't believe we're about to do shots in the Home.

We dink our little plastic glasses. A tiny bit of splash dribbles onto my finger and I say:

—Here's to getting our hole.

Cian takes out his phone and puts the flash on and starts recording me before counting down, Three, two …

The two young girls from outside with the luminous stretched-tight dresses brush past. Their arses are the most perfect things I've ever seen. The stench of the Aftershock reaches my nose. Before my lips get to taste it, I'm reefed backwards. The shot flips out've my grasp. Cian's flash cuts across the smoke and I watch the spray of my drink falling in slow motion, like something from a lava lamp. The smoke swallows me up and leather gloved hands drag me out through the double doors. I'm marched down the steps with Cian. The queue is massive and it cheers when we're thrown onto the ground at the bottom.

*

Cian holds up his can for me to do a cheers. I leave him hanging. The kitchen clock ticks onto half one.

—You shouldn't have said anything to them about my da, I say, with a sigh.

I'm feeling a little less angry after having a quick wank into a condom in his toilet. So much for a posh wank. It was a mess.

He shrugs, sucks on the suds.

—Why not?

My knee is grazed from being thrown on the ground. I groan as I sit on one of his rickety kitchen chairs.

—Because. I'm sick of people only being interested in me cause of my da. Ye made a show of me.

—At least I tried to get us in.

—I got us in, without my da's name. You were halfway home before I saw the opportunity.

—At least I put up a fight, he says, shrugging again. You talk a lot, but never actually do anything. If it wasn't for me you'd be a grade-A loser, Dean.

Our eyes meet and I look away immediately. In the bright lights of the kitchen, at this time of night, I'm embarrassed he'll realize he's more right than he knows.

He looks tired. His skin is all different shades of pink. His fringe has lost its bounce and is flat on his forehead.

—I asked ye not to say anything. And you didn't listen. And I get made a show of. Next time I say something like that, Cian, listen to me. I'm not me da and I'm sick of people thinking I am and taking the piss.

He slugs some more on his can and looks at the ceiling like something important is up there.

—Okay, okay, Jesus. Newsflash, Dean O'Connor is not an Olympic bronze medal boxer.

I stretch my leg to try and shift the denim off the cut on my knee. My chair creaks like it's going to break. The light above the sink flickers.

Cian sighs:

—The little bouncer was a prick alright.

—They all were. But I'm used to that kind of shite at this stage. That's why I don't box no more.

Cian nods along. I think he finally cops why I didn't want him to mention my da to the bouncers. That stuff never works. Never even worked when I was a kid running around bragging about it myself.

In this town people never forget. They love lording it over you with something. Having something to put you down with. Control the sense of who you are. You think you're good at boxing:

—No you're not, sure your da was an Olympian.

You think you're cool for once:

—No you're not, your da's a loser who embarrasses the town with his carry on these days.

You think you're becoming who you want to be:

—That's the Jock's son, who does he think he is?

Begrudgery, yeah. But something else. Control and an ability to define you. People in this town want power over you.

Angel

Pelumi storms into my gaff, big vexed head on him. Isaac's with him, only he walks down the hall in Pelumi's shadow, all quiet and shy. No lie, but then Isaac looks into the kitchen and says:

—Alright Gloria.

And my mam flicks the dishcloth over her shoulder and gives a big wave back like she's hyped the lads are stalling it up here. She's not. She never is.

We go into the front room and I don't even get a chance to say thanks to Pelumi for saving me.

—Where'd you dip last night pussy? he says.

Isaac sighs and sits down into the chair at the window, supping on a bottle of Power Malt.

—I got rocked. I didn't dash, I say, keeping things low-key so my mam can't hear.

I close over the door.

—Yeah you did, Pelumi says.

—Keep it down, bro. I didn't.

—Say mums, he hisses.

—I got whooshed. Swear to God. Look.

I point at my eye, turn to the window, so him and Isaac can see what's left of the blood. Isaac leans in, kisses his teeth.

—He got battered alright.

—See, I say – chuffed to finally shut Pelumi up – I didn't dash. I wouldn't back out, bro. Not on you. The feds tried grab me so I legged it to the beach.

—You're such a pussy, Pelumi says. You got hands and you dipped like a bitch. We stayed.

—Yeah and you got grabbed by the feds.

My mam looks into the room, big smile.

—You boys want some baked plantain chips?

Isaac gives a gassed thumbs up. But I stare at him.

—No thanks mam, I say.

—No thanks, Gloria, Isaac says, bottom lip out like he's gonna cry.

Pelumi, still standing in the middle of the room, just shakes his head, eyes on the rug.

My mam's eyebrows nearly lift into her headwrap and she looks at me like it's my fault and I'm gonna get it later. She closes the door behind her without saying anything.

—Least I didn't run, Pelumi says, eyes back to me.

—I didn't run. And at least I was there. Where was Isaac?

—You did run. All the mandem come to save you, innit, and you dip. Bitch, Pelumi says.

Isaac laughs, bounces up from the chair, dodging my question, brushing off his Nike Tech.

It hurts, like a pinch, a little nettle sting maybe, yuno, when he calls me a bitch. I try not to look vexed, react, but it's hard when he says it steck times. Do I look like a bitch? Do I act like one? Is that why he only calls me one?

—Don't call me that, man, I say, staring Pelumi straight in the face, pissed now.

I've had enough, yuno. Isaac looks up, big smile, eyes shocked and eager and all that.

So, basically, yeah, Pelumi stands up straight, goes head-to-head, looking down his nose at me, nostrils flaring.

—You are what I say you are.

You are what I say you are.

Isaac always stirring it up, says:

—That's a bar.

—Yeah, and you're chatting shit, Pelumi, I say.

No lie, I glance at the room, see it for like the first time ever. There's waaay too many picture frames of me and my mam, or my nana with me when I was a little baby and steck little stupid china figures above the fireplace. The coffee table is even made of glass.

—Oh, shitden, Isaac says, slapping his leg. Angel's a driller now droppin bars.

Pelumi steps closer, flicks his nose with his thumb, sniffles. There's gonna be beef. The room is gonna get smashed up. My mam's gonna come in screaming, batter me in front of the boys. I don't wanna be this, do this, but mans gotta do what mans gotta do, so I take out my phone.

—Yeah, well, how come I'm twapping while you're getting locked up?

—Twapping? Hardly.

—That's what I said. Look.

I hold up the phone, the selfie with Princess.

—See the time, I say. Half eleven. She's so gassed, man.

—Hardly, Pelumi says.

But him and Isaac take a closer look. Pelumi grabs the phone and inspects it, all shook. Isaac has to lean down into the screen to see it clear too.

Isaac sees what he needed to see and jumps back, laughing, screaming.

—Oh my days, Angel.

But Pelumi just looks up, like this is long. Leaves the phone out for me to take.

—You're full of shit, he says.

—Nah fam, Isaac says, slapping his shoulder. It's legit. Look at the time.

—Hardly. He's a fraud.

This guy, swear to God. I wanna rock him, yuno. Just not here. But what do I do? I just shake my head and nod to Isaac, relieved he believes me.

—Nah fam, Isaac goes. Lookit, she's a sket, yeah, if yuno you know. I knew she'd twap. Dassit Angel.

And he fist pumps me. But Pelumi's face doesn't change.

—Prove it.

—Prove it?

—I've got a free gaff Tuesday. Bring her in and jeet, or get uck, and then I'll believe you.

—Tuesday?

—Tuesday.

My little younger self smiles back in a frame on the wall, only delighted with life.

—This Tuesday, in two days?

—Two days.

—Okay. Calm.

Isaac pats us both on the shoulders, chuffed.

—Dassit boys.

*

Yuno, it's hardly love, but when I'm with her I feel amazing. So hyped. Before, when she came out on the street, I'd get off the wall. Feel a buzz, yeah, like I just had to talk to her. Even if Pelumi was jarring. And if I did, man, if I did talk to her, swear down like, I'd feel better than I do when beating Isaac at FIFA. I'd actually feel better than anytime I was with the boys. And now that we're friends, it's solid.

Knowing that she rates me and actually wants to talk to me, that's fresh. She's bare leng, and sound too. She talks, yuno, about things the boys don't talk about. Doing things, and getting out of this town. Once she said:

—Pelumi and that crew, they're gonna bring you down. You gotta be a man and do your own thing.

I was just like, whatever, she's chatting shit. But later I did a lot of thinking about it. God knows she's smart, yeah. Says she's not gonna be making the mistakes her sister made. Which – I can't lie – makes me happy. Obviously yeah, she doesn't want to get pregnant. That means she's not a sket. Which is fresh. But I wanna twap. Mans gotta twap. This is the problem. Cause we haven't even kissed yet.

Basically, yeah, I'm dead.

Tanya

When you go for a 2am walk and all there is is a taxi and a fox
♫ See You Again – @Tyler, The Creator
The camera shakes. A fox moves past a hotel, through an empty street, and speeds up. The animal is thin, its tail huge, and it keeps low to the ground before disappearing down a lane. All the shops are shuttered. A lone taxi, yellow light on, is parked at a rank.
>73

The fumes are streaming out of the exhaust. I take a breath and try get my head together before I go over.

We don't see each other anymore even though we live in the same town. I sometimes wonder if he even cares I exist anymore, my da. I'd say he does now. And that's what worries me.

I knock on the glass. Can't see anything but me own depressed reflection pouting back. The electric window zooms down and I catch my breath.

Ye alright there, love?

Sorry, wrong car, I say, and turn for home.

Ye sure ye don't need a lift? he calls after me.

The only way I ever recognized my da's taxi was when he parked it outside Paddy Power. Now every taxi I see I nearly wave down to check if it's him. Me da has moved to a three-bed house in an estate at the top of town. Barry is his housemate now. They must be getting close.

Old men in my mentions nasty asf!!
♫ Original sound (milkyshat) – @zack
Screenshots of Tanya's messages with the names blocked out by

thick blue lines. The profile pictures can be seen and they're all middle-aged men. Some of them with wives, some with their kids.
>1227

Das are the ones who DM me the most.

Every time I see one it makes me think of my da.

When there's a ping I hope it's a message from him telling me not to worry about what people are saying. I'm still his little girl.

But what do I get from my da?

The same I've got from him these past months.

Nothing.

Barry messages me though. All the time.

Everyone says Barry's girlfriend broke up with him and he had a full-on melt-down in his shop and closed it up. Barry's never off his phone. He doesn't stop posting stuff up on his socials. If he's not in the gym making mad faces while he does these crazy lifts, he's giving out about the government and refugees and how Balbriggan needs to be given back to Balbriggan people. He's even making videos going into Global and Polski Delikatesy and The African Store and shouting at the staff to give the shops back. Balbriggan shops for Balbriggan people! Weirdo.

Stallin it up with the forest fruit juice!!
♫ Friends – @Ella Henderson
Tanya and a young lad of about fourteen are laughing and posing on her bed for a selfie. He has acne on his cheeks and chin, and looks directly at the camera and away again, embarrassed. Tanya has her arm around the lad's shoulder and exhales into the screen, fogging it up.
>229

Sam's only after coming up into me room and he's trying to ruin my buzz altogether. Sitting on the edge of my bed, big serious head on him like he's here to help me. Why did my ma even let him into the house?

I just wanted to make sure you're alright, he says. I saw what it did to my brother.

This lad Sam's real cute with his dropping of his shoulders like there's a weight on them and then his long sighs. But I can't be having him come in here like this.

I'm a fucking celebrity now. Look at the number of new followers and friends I got. Don't be worrying about me, Sam. I'm grand so I am.

Sorry, he goes, I just thought, like, ye know, depression and all that.

I do a long, slow exhale of the Forest Fruits to get my thoughts together.

How could I be depressed?

Oh, right. Sorry. Just, ye know …

What?

Nothing. I just thought, like … once you're alright, that's cool.

Of course I'm alright. It's just a clip. There's loads going round like that. Only this is on WhatsApp and everyone in the town thinks they know me now. You don't know me, and here you are in my room.

Suppose, yeah. I just. I dunno. I never copped my brother was depressed and I never helped him.

It's cool. You wanted to see me since I'm famous. I get it.

Yeah, that's probably it alright. Sorry.

It's okay. I'm sorry about your brother too.

Thanks. He was cool.

You must miss him?

Everyone misses him.

The poor lad doesn't know what to do with himself now. He squirms there on the bed, so I get him in a selfie with me and we do a small piece for a laugh.

Here, take my number, he says, like he's my friend now.

What?

I'm not allowed on social media anymore, cause of my ma. Ring me if you ever need to talk to anyone.

Eh, you're grand, I say. I don't be ringing numbers.

He looks so sad when I refuse, so I let him ring me to get his number and he leaves. He smells so fresh and pure. It lingers in the room when he's gone. I go back to my phone. But the smell is so nice I can't help but think about him. I feel for him, coming in and being all sad and serious. I heard about his brother a year ago. But I'm the wrong person to be trying to talk to about that shit. I'm one of the ones who's doing well out of social media. I thought lads like him would see that. The fact he doesn't makes me wonder.

*

I'm walking down the street and don't hear what this aul lad says so then I take out my earphones and he goes, Hey Tanya!

He's up in my face and talking to me. I just go, Jesus Christ. Stalker much?

Hey, we met before, he says, ignoring my whole, weirdo, get away from me, vibe.

Good for you, I say.

Yeah, in Millfield, at the top of the escalator a while back.

So? Get away from me, I'm going home.

Wait. You wanna go somewhere for a chat? I'd really love to chat to ye.

I look around real quick, see if there's anyone there to help if I scream. I'm sixteen. Unless you've got twenty euro for me, go away, I say.

Easy there. I tried to contact ye on Instagram.

Touch me again and I'll scream. I don't reply to paedos.

He laughs at me like I'm a kid.

I'm not a paedo, he says.

Okay Boomer, that's exactly what a paedo would say. Look at them shoes. They're paedo shoes.

They're Wallabees. They're cool. I'm Chris. I know your ma. I told ye this already.

Whatever, paedo, I say and move to get clear of him.

But he won't give up and he walks a step with me and goes, I'm Chris. Remember to ask your ma about me.

And then I stop and he keeps on walking so I take out my phone and warn people.

The problem with fame in this town, is everyone thinks they know you. Wants a piece of you. Everyone wants to tell me I'm either beautiful or disgusting. That I'm the worst thing to happen to Balbriggan, or the best thing. Some want to be my friend. Even paedos like this Chris think they deserve a chance.

POV: Briggs got 2 many weirdos on these streets
♫ Original sound – @Tanyeah2
Daytime and Tanya is standing outside SuperValu in selfie pov. She talks into the camera, 'I'm going home from school and old creepy weirdos are following me again. Sick of this shit.' She flips the shot to a man in a long, green parka jacket walking away in a hurry.
>876

Princess

You don't walk away from an argument in African culture.

In Church, Pastor Akimiy was always giving out about this. He said we needed to be reasonable in the face of antagonism, obstacles. See the argument and ask yourself, do I need to stand up, or can I walk away?

This might not even classify as an argument, but it definitely feels like a fight.

—Hiya, how are you?

That sounds the right level of Balbriggan accent, so I keep going.

—My name is Shauna Gibbons and I'm hoping to undertake pharmaceutical studies in Trinity in September … I'd love the chance, over the next few weeks, to observe you and your pharmacy in action in order to gather information on the day-to-day workings of your operation. For experience in the field.

She pauses and I can almost hear her lips purse.

—Okay. Where do you currently study?

—I'm actually a Leaving Cert in the Convent.

—Okay. Do you live in Balbriggan?

—I do, I do.

—That's great. Would I know the place?

I think of all the boys hanging outside the apartment block. The chaos of Castle Apartments.

—I'm up in the estate, Fancourt Heights, at the old end of town.

—Oh, lovely. That's lovely. I know a few people up there. Well, let me see…

The line goes quiet and I hold my breath.

I miss church. Not Pastor Akimiy, or the sermons or talk of God and stuff. I miss the people. The place. The sense of happiness in the RCCG hall. The serenity and feeling of contentment in a place where I knew who I was. I belonged and was always welcome.

*

It's Friday, last class, and normally Iwona' s smelling fresh for Konrad and in great form for the weekend. She usually lists the places they're going to drive, all the restaurants they're going to eat in, all the love she's going to have. Only she's sitting there, looking into space, quiet, reserved, no new spray of perfume for home time. She hasn't said anything to me since I arrived. I look up to see if Miss is watching, close over my notes. Everyone else is writing.

—You alright with me? I say.

She stretches her lips like there's something itching on the inside of her cheek.

—Yeah, why wouldn't I be?

—I dunno. You not taking down the notes?

—No, I'm too stupid to do that.

There's an accusation there that I can't understand. But then, I remember.

—Wait, are you angry about me telling you not to be a thick and get pregnant?

—No, she says as if such an idea is absurd, which makes me think it's not.

—I'm just stressed about the exams, Princess. That's all.

—Why would you be stressed? You got 600 points in the Mocks. Like, you could do the exams tomorrow and be grand.

Iwona nibbles her lip.

—I didn't get 600 points. I lied. I only got 400 and I can't see how I'm gonna do much better.

—Oh, is all I can say.

—Yeah. I'm running around now looking into the HEAR scheme and thinking about interviews and getting references from teachers, or thinking about doing a different course that I just put down on the CAO but never thought I'd actually do. And you're all relaxed and all organized already.

—You're still going for medicine, right? I say.

Her head snaps round like I just tried to touch her hair. She stands, looks at me for a second and without another word, walks out. Writing pad, pen, pencil case, books, bag, all left behind. I'm too afraid to follow her in case I get in trouble.

She doesn't come back.

*

After I finish mopping the kitchen floor with mum's dusty Squeegee, I take my History book off the kitchen table and sit with a sigh on the couch. Becky has RTÉ on mute in the background since we don't have any other channels. The TV gives off good light. That Beaker-looking fool is laughing behind his dark wood desk while he talks to some Z-list Irish celebrity. Becky's holding her phone up to her face, squinting at the screen. Her cheeks, so round and fulsome, make her look like she's smiling. She's not. Michael broke her glasses. The strong lemon scent drifts into us and I know mum will be pleased with me when she gets back.

I rest the book on my lap. I can't study in the bedroom where Michael is because the reading light disturbs him, and the kitchen is freezing because the boiler is gone and the landlord refuses to fix it. Makes no difference where I am, I can't study regardless. Black Panthers. Black power. Black out.

Becky hasn't said anything since she came back from putting Michael in his cot. Mum is at Muiz's mum's house.

—Becky, I say, without looking up from the book.

—Yeah.

—Were you shocked when you found out you were pregnant?

—Mmhh?

—Like, when you found out you were pregnant. Like, how did you find out?

The glow leaves her face and she strains at me across the room.

—I didn't get my period.

The phone comes to her face again.

—Why didn't you get the morning-after pill?

The phone drops to her lap.

—Wait, are you pregnant?

—No.

Her neck extends and she stares across the room to me and says, in a mixture of wonder and disgust:

—Are you having sex?

—No, I reply, a bit too loud.

—Then why all the questions? It's a Friday night, I shouldn't be in here chattin shit with you Princess, specially not bout morning-after pills and being pregnant.

—I was just asking.

—Well don't.

She brings her phone back to her face. The TV flickers. I return to my book. I have literally painted the whole page luminous yellow. Every. Single. Line.

—Oisin didn't have the money for it, she whispers, almost as if she's on speaker phone with someone.

Her voice is disappointed, tired.

—Oh. Did you love him? I hear myself say.

She nods.

—He was so smooth. Fresh, yuno? He said nothing would happen. I believed him. We were just young.

—You could've used mum's medical card.

She laughs without smiling.

—That's why you're gonna go to college and I'm stuck in here on a Friday night.

I don't know if I should laugh with her.

Angel is fresh. And charming. And persistent.

*

She makes us call her Tantine. I think it's so we look on her as family – and don't go anywhere else for our styles. Whenever me or Becky or mum come in she's always real kind to us. Maybe that's because we're buying things, not asking for things. We've never asked for anything. I'm unsure how she'll react.

She's talking with big bald Gideon, the guy who owns the supermarket part of the store. He's the pastor in the church near the Square. Tantine insists he has a wonderful voice. Gideon says we really should go to his church, if only to hear him sing.

One side of the supermarket is a hair salon, one side has computers and printing – 15 cent a page – one side has jewellery, another side has all nails, and another side has all food. Gideon likes to joke there are so many sides to the store it's a sphere, and that's why he called it Global.

Tantine sees me come in the door. She stops talking with Gideon and points.

—What you do to my beautiful braids?

There's mock annoyance in her voice.

—I needed a change, I say.

She smiles and wags her finger.

—No, no, no, she says, making a face like I've just told her a dirty joke.

She looks to Gideon who smiles in solidarity with her.

—I needed a change, and I was thinking: you still owe me a fiver for letting you put the braids in.

—Oh, excuse me. The taxman is here.

—Capitalist! Gideon adds with a chuckle.

—No, I don't want money. Maybe you can do me a favour instead?

She puts her hands on her hips, big surprised eyes. I'm normally real shy and quiet when I'm here.

—Go on, she says, a smile of interest crawling up her face.

I look back to the window display. The silver mannequin heads stare out to Mainstreet, still and lifeless, the wigs on them, soft and shiny, sleek and straight. Glamorous. Serious. Professional.

Tanya

Dollar bills, dollar bill$$$$$$$ at my grans

♫ Money – @Lisa

Selfie pov of Tanya sitting on an old patterned couch of thick, faded corduroy. She has a can of 7Up in her lap. The shot changes to front pov: an old lady on a chair, watching TV, a cigarette hanging from her mouth and a cup of tea in her hand. The camera zooms in on a twenty euro note on the coffee table.
>104

Sure, I never even see him myself these days, Gran says.

No?

No. He's all over Dublin with that taxi.

Yeah right, I say, but Gran doesn't hear.

She takes a pull on her cigarette, peers through the smoke and goes, I see you've changed your profile picture from your old birthday to a new one. You look lovely in it so ye do.

Thanks so much, Gran. Have you been on Facebook much?

A bit. Not as much now. The girls do be only moaning about this one or that one. It does get terrible boring after a while. They should go boil their heads – or get a life!

So you've seen nothing these past weeks on it?

Nothing I haven't seen before.

Like what?

Ah ye know, everyone moaning and commenting on stuff that doesn't concern them. I ignore them. I don't care what they think. You'd swear everyone's lives are perfect outside that yoke.

Gran puts down her cigarette, brushes off her lap and opens out her arms.

Come here to me, you. Give yer gran a hug. Don't be upset. Fuck them love. Whoever has ye upset, fuck them. Here's twenty quid for ye, get yourself something nice.

Thanks, I manage, feeling the crisp blue note in my hand.

Don't cry love. The worst thing ye can do is go on that Facebook if you're feeling down. Balbriggan Connected? Brains Disconnected more like. Ye fart at the church and by the time the story gets on Balbriggan Connected they're saying you've shit yourself.

I wish you could tell my ma that, I say.

Sure your ma's one of the block capital moaners on the thing. Giving out about queues in Tesco and getting the large portion of chicken wings from the Milestone when she only ordered a small. She was a moany hole when she started going out with yer da, and she's still a moany hole. God forgive me.

To be in Gran's smoky arms, feeling her warmth, is something else. She's right, my gran. Fuck them.

Tag your best friend #bestfriendcheck
♫ Big Gangsta – @Kevin Gates
The camera zooms in on two girls walking away from Tanya up past a Spar before flipping to selfie. Tanya mouths the words to the song in a blaze of vape smoke.
>283

I bump into Rihanna and Britney as they come out of FLC. State of them. It's awkward for a sec cause we literally knocked into each other.

Alright Tanya. Any craic? Rihanna says, stepping onto the edge of the path to get space between us.

Nah. Didn't know yis were going to FLC.

Britney holds up her paper cup and says, Just had a coke for the hangover. What ye up to?

Where were yis last night? I go.

The Home, Britney says. It was class. All the lads and me and Rihanna went down.

Rihanna says through a yawn, I'm in bits now. Deadly buzz though.

Didn't know yis were going, I say.

The two of them look at each other and shrug.

We put it up on our story, Britney says.

I didn't look at me phone when I got home.

Ye didn't look at yer phone? Rihanna says.

Nah. These aul lads keep on messaging me cause of the video.

The two of them shake their heads like I'm after boring them already.

Don't look at us, Rihanna says. We told ye, it must've been someone else put it up there.

Whatever. All ye do is go on about it. Get over it, Britney moans before sipping from her straw.

I am, I am. Here. Stall it, I've to go the shop for me ma. I'll walk up with yis.

A woman with a buggy walks between us and they wait for her to pass before Rihanna goes, You're alright. We've to head.

Yeah, we're meant to be at a gaff half an hour ago.

Ah, here, wait for me, I say.

Rihanna looks at her phone and goes, Did Paddy invite ye to the sesh?

Dunno. Left me phone at home.

Check yer phone then when ye get home and we might see ye later, Britney says and with that they turn and walk together up the road without me.

Well Im a lucky daughter and I just gotta tell her ...
♫ Original sound – alayna grace – @Alayna
Tanya sings the words to the song in a selfie while walking between the clothes aisles in a busy, brightly lit shop. The camera flips to front pov and a woman, heavy make-up and long black hair, is close by, looking through clothes on a rack.
>376

What do ye think of this Ma?

Maybe you should think of something not as tight and less bright, she says.

Why?

If ye have to ask, then Jesus, Tanya, I don't know what to say to ye.

What ye saying?

Look, wearing something like that, bet onto ye with bright colours and bringing attention to yourself is the last thing you should be doing now.

I thought you said I should forget about it and get on with my life.

Forget about it, fair enough, but Jesus, Tanya, learn from it.

I put the hanger back on the rail. Try not to get thick with her. It's been ages since we did something like this.

I told you I didn't know I was being filmed, I say real soft, to try and get her back on side.

Let's not talk about it here, Tanya.

But we can talk about not wearing bright colours, though, yeah?

She takes a breath and sniffs as if she's got a snot in her nose.

Lookit, she says, ye know it's not about the colours.

I like bright colours.

Don't start Tanya. Not here.

You brought me here.

To get you out of the house.

And now you're telling me what to wear.

I'm telling you what not to wear. There's a difference. Don't be such a child.

Oh, I'm a child now too.

Lower your voice for fuck's sake.

Afraid I'll embarrass ye?

It's a bit late for that.

What's that supposed to mean?

Do ye really need me to explain it here?

Maybe ye do since I'm such a child.

Me ma puffs out her cheeks and lets the air flow through her lips like a slow puncture.

Alright then, she says, ye have to stop thinking what ye did was alright cause it's common. It's not common. Especially for a sixteen-year-old. Despite what ye think, you're only a child. You're not an adult. And everyone's not doing it. Ye need to accept what ye did was wrong, a mistake, and just move on. Learn from it, like.

But everyone is doing it. Only theirs doesn't go fucking viral on WhatsApp for all the old biddies to see, I say.

She steps back to look at me, hands on her hips now. She looks left then right before going on.

Tanya, please. Listen to me. That sorta shit isn't normal. And everyone doesn't do it. If there's one thing ye gotta get your head around it's what ye did wasn't normal, and it's something ye shouldn't be proud of.

But it is normal, Ma. I know loads of girls and lads recording themselves. Do you have any idea how many blow-job memes I've seen this week? Or I've-just-had-sex memes? Or the walk-of-shame memes? Or how much-can-you-swallow memes? You know how many views they get? Do you know how many private messages I get, that everyone my age gets, from old men asking for shit? You don't even know about what messages are sent by fourteen-year-old lads to fourteen-year-old girls. Or lads looking for girls' sex CVs to be posted online so they can pick them to be part of their crew. Do the Stitch and Bitch club on the estate know about that? And ye know what else, there's loads of girls posting shit to get on that crew. I'm sixteen, Ma. I was born in 2006, I'm not a kid. It's fucking everywhere, only this time it came up on old people social media.

Well then, if it's everywhere, we're moving town, she says.

I laugh.

Are you that thick, Ma? It's not this town. It's every town. It's every piece of social media. It's everywhere. Sure Kylie Jenner's sister got rich because of one clip like mine. The whole family is rich now cause of that shit.

Jesus Christ, Tanya. The fucking Kardashians? Really? I'm trying to be patient with ye here. Have ye no shame?

A teenager, bout my age, don't know her, is across the aisle. She's trying to pretend she hasn't noticed us arguing, but I can see her going to hold up her phone on the sly.

Princess

I have to separate the components of food dyes using thin layer chromatography. Iwona's not in today. She's been missing the odd day lately. Considering how she stormed out on Friday, I'm not surprised though. She's been weird with me these past few weeks. Stressed to the max. These exams, the pressure isn't easy. It affects people differently when there's so much riding on them.

Since I've no partner I get a chance to do an experiment on my own for once. Which isn't necessarily a bad thing. Only, without her there, I lose focus. I start to look out the window. Think about my mum wanting to go back to Nigeria to my gran. I'm not bad, but I've no wish to go back to Africa. I don't even know my grandmother. I've seen pictures and said, oh, she looks lovely. Because I'd never say anything to displease my mum. I've been brought up well. So much respect for my mum. But I'm like, wait, when will be the time I finally put my foot down and have some respect for myself? My feelings? My wishes?

I take the paper from the solution. The colour spots drain away leaving a soft watercolour imprint and I'm like, so relaxed for a second, just a second now, looking at this soon-to-be colourless flower bloom and then fade in front of me.

I'm glad in a way Iwona's not here. It gives me a chance to compose myself before my interview today at the pharmacy. Get in the zone. Get into a positive mental head space. Get ready for the rest of my life.

*

Angel's on his own, which is rare – and nice. Only, I can't stop and talk as I'm in a hurry. My hair took me longer to get right than anticipated.

He lifts himself off the wall.

—Hey, your hair looks fresh.

I give him a smile, instinctively bring my hand to the false weight of it. The exotic give and bounce. I place my hand around it to check if it's still in shape.

—Thanks, I say.

—Where you going? I can walk with you.

—No, it's okay. I'm fine by myself.

I really need to concentrate. I haveta have a clear mind before I get there.

—I get it, it's calm. Those shoes. You're leaving us all behind.

I just smile.

—Well, before you do leave, we should hang out, he says.

—I can't. I'm studying.

—Not all the time, he moans.

I stop walking, give him a smile.

—You hardly study all the time, Princess. So, whenever you're not, gimme a call and we'll hang out.

—Okay. Maybe, I say.

I turn and click away in my heels.

—Safe. It's all good. You gotta live a little, Princess. We'll only share all this once you know.

I turn and walk backwards slowly, taking in the apartment blocks, the short balconies filled with plastic boxes and flowerpots, satellite dishes, the red streaks of fungus scarring once white paint.

—These blocks?

—Our youth, he laughs. Before you know it, it'll dash and you'll always wonder what it would've been like to hang with Angel.

I don't have a reply. I nod and smile in appreciation. Wave to him and turn back towards the town. The future.

*

I stop outside Gogan's and take a deep breath. I fix my hair at the back, brush the fringe away from my eyes, take the plastic sleeve out of my bag. My heart's beating nearly up into my mouth, and I'm like, wait, this is not the end of the world, Princess. But no matter what I say, it sure feels like it could be.

The shop floor is empty. A soft opera fills up the carpeted space and dampens my heels. I move towards the counter at the rear of the building. There's shelves all around, colours and products everywhere. I feel claustrophobic already. I'm literally shaking.

I get up on my tiptoes, try and see over into the back, to where all the prescriptions are. And just before I knock on the counter, lightly of course, a voice, low, near the floor, goes:

—Sorry, can I help you?

I spin round. At first I only see a figure in a white lab coat, on her knees and surrounded by nappies.

I think we both don't recognize each other immediately.

—Princess? she says.

—Iwona?

—Your hair looks ... I didn't reali...

She gets to her feet and comes close to me, suddenly serious and stressed looking.

—I'm so sorry Princess, I had to...

I take in the lab coat and only a nano second is needed for the equation to be solved.

No logbook. No theorems.

Iwona puts out her hands.

—I can explain.

But another voice arrives from behind the counter.

—Everything okay here, Shauna?

It's the one from the phone call. The pharmacist.

Iwona's eyes go deep, implore me, try to say what she can't now say: Be quiet.

—Sure, all good, Iwona says, her voice raised to a chirpy customer-friendly pitch. This girl was just asking for directions.

I'm like a mute, closing Becky's cardigan tight on my chest as I go, the tears blurring my escape.

I pull the heavy door and turn and get one last look at Iwona in the white lab coat. I am ashamed. I'm like, wait, how'd I not see this coming? How naïve was I to think all this work would pay off?

Angel

Princess agrees to meet me after school, and swear down, it takes me ages to convince her to stall it to Pelumi's instead of the library.

—Everyone needs a break, yuno? I say, but I feel fake.

It's not right taking her away from her study. For bringing her to the boys like some sort of entertainment.

Pelumi's gaff is lacking. Like, him and Isaac are after getting some green and they're flaked out on the couch, big smiles and goofy laughing. Pelumi asks Princess if she wants a smoke and I know she's not feeling it. She kinda squirms, flattens out that long green school skirt of hers.

—Nah, I say for her. It's fresh.

—Why don't you go upstairs to my sister's room?

Isaac pauses the game, the crowd stops cheering.

—Allow, I say, just to say something.

Break the silence.

—What? Pelumi says all innocent. If you're bored go on upstairs. It's calm.

I whisper to Princess:

—What ye think?

Pelumi goes:

—You wanna go, don't ye Angel?

I shrug.

—It's grand chap.

—Hardly, Pelumi says.

Isaac is looking at us like we're the game, his finger extended over the trigger button – paused.

—Well, I say. It'd be fresh upstairs I suppose.

Isaac's smile widens, he nods and goes:

—Dassit Angel, my man.

The crowd noise starts up again, and the plastic tapping drills away. Pelumi says:

—Go then.

But what do ye know, Princess says:

—Yeah, come on Angel, let's go, and she stands up and no lie, her warm fingers reach out, lift my hand off my lap and pull me up!

The sister's room is a bando. There are no curtains and the walls and ceiling are covered in black spotted shite. Her bed has a blanket on it but, and that's alright.

We stall it on the bed, sitting beside each other, facing the door I just closed over. The room is at the end of the landing, the opposite end to the jacks and stairs, which is calm. So basically, if Pelumi or Isaac try and sneak up I should hear them, yuno.

Anyways, we sit there, my hands back on my legs, looking ahead, yeah, like there's a view and that. But, I can't lie, this room is dead.

And then, finally, Princess says:

—I should really be studying.

Talk about a buzz kill.

—Yeah?

—Yeah, I mean, I need to be studying.

—You're head's gotta be rinsed with study. Ten minutes, yeah?

She lets a long breath out her nose.

—You're stressed Princess. I can tell.

—I am. I do need to relax. But, I dunno. This just doesn't feel right.

She says nothing then, but after a minute of the worst silence ever, she starts to shake, not shake, kind of shudder, her shoulders start to move and then, swear to God, she sobs, and I turn to her and she's crying secretly. Shitden. I. Am. Lacking.

God knows, I want to dash, but I put my arm over her shoulder and kind of pull her into me.

—I'm feeling so much pressure.

I shush her and say:

—It's calm. It's calm.

I don't think she's listening cause she goes:

—Every day counts. Every class counts. I can't ... I need to ...

And I turn to her, without thinking or nothing and lift her chin, so she can see me, look me in the eyes, yeah. Her eyes are full of tears, and she goes:

—I need to impress ...

And I swear to God, I don't even plan it when I say:

—You're amazing Princess. You're gonna make something of yourself. Don't stress.

And what does she do? Basically, she leans in.

She tastes salty with all them tears dripping down on my lips. Things. Start. To. Get. Hot. Yuno?

I am into it. God knows, the way she is kissing and breathing through her blocked nose, she is into it too.

In. A. Big. Way.

I just get lost in it, yuno. I just get lost in it all.

Her hands go under my jumper, lift up my shirt, and I'm thinking, dassit babe, mans gonna twap. But next thing she just puts one hand on my stomach and one back on my lap.

Obviously, yeah, if she does that, I'm gonna do that. So I move my hands under her shirt, and feel the heat of her stomach. It sucks back in when I touch it and she gasps. So what do I do? Mans gotta do what mans gotta do. I move my hands up her stomach and feel the fabric of her bra too. Hard lace and all that. God knows I'm gonna pop. And her breathing yeah, is so heavy now.

And then I hear the stairs creak. Obviously, yeah, that's Pelumi the freak. But I don't think Princess hears nothing and then the landing rustles and basically it's them preds looking for a charge sheet outside the bedroom door, and when Princess stops, I think, shitden, that's it, we're done. But she just sits up to undo her bra and she giggles and then puts her hands on my head and we start kissing again.

She moans a bit too and I know the boys are outside listening in. I think a bit of spunk leaks out. I can't lie though, I'm about to pop. This. Is. It. Her moaning, her bra on the floor. But if they walk in, I'll have to stop.

And then her leg starts to vibrate. Not shake, like. Vibrate. Princess pulls away and all out of breath, her chest rising and falling in big gulps, she goes:

—Sorry, my phone, I'll turn it off.

Obviously, I'm like:

—It's cool.

But when she pulls it out of her skirt pocket, she looks at the number like it's after dissin her and she kisses her teeth and says:

—One sec.

I can't lie, I'm about to blow. I am so vexed.

—Hello?

—

—Yeah. That's me.

—

—I did yes.

—

—You did?

She kind of brushes me aside, and sits up, pulls her shirt over her chest, the skin of her stomach creased, her chest still rising and falling, this new voice coming out of her mouth.

I can feel the cold bit of jizz in my boxers when I move. Her eyes go wide.

—

—Yes. Sure. Today?

—

—Yes. I can be down in ten.

—

—Okay. Great. Thanks. Bye. Bye.

She doesn't say anything for a second then. Just sits there, yuno, staring ahead, her phone in her hand. Quiet. Just staring ahead at them walls. Me, I'm still flat out, like a thick, hoping.

—That was a pharmacy.

I try not to sound vexed:

—So?

—I thought they'd thrown out my CV. I never heard nothing back.

—Yeah?

She stops, shakes her head like she can't believe what she's saying.

The lads mumble outside.

—We'll link up again. This is really important for me, Angel. I gotta go.

I look at her, see the new smile on her face. She's buzzing. I feel my dick twitch. I swear down like, I am so ready to twap.

—You after getting a job? I say.

—Not a job, she says, looking round for her bra. A placement. Work experience, like. He wants to meet. I thought she'd binned it. Rayo was her name. This is amazing – he would've seen my name on the CV above my phone number.

I don't get it.

—And he still called. He even asked, Is this Princess? He'd know I'm African and he still called.

Then the door opens.

Pelumi – this guy's a sicko – stands there. Isaac's hiding behind him, his plug, like a pred, eyes on the floor. Princess obviously goes to grab her bra, but Pelumi puts his foot on it and says:

—Where you going?

She looks at me like, what the fuck? Kind of scared, yuno. Isaac's mouth is open like he's not even sure what's going on. She goes to move but Pelumi grabs her arm.

—Let go, she says and struggles to free herself.

I'm still on the bed like a wasteman.

Pelumi holds her arm up as if she's a puppet and goes:

—Job is job. You're not gonna prick tease Angel like that.

—Allow, I say, not getting up off the bed, my dick still hard. It's calm, Pelumi. Me and Princess are cool. Allow.

Pelumi is thick.

—You didn't finesse nothing.

And he shakes her arm like it's his. She looks scared, yuno. A small patch of jizz is warm and sticky in my boxers when I move.

—Let go of me you freak, she says.

—Allow, I say again. It's calm, bro. Me and Princess are fresh.

—You not gonna twap? he says.

—It's calm. Allow.

—He doesn't wanna twap, Pelumi says to Isaac, big pretend shocked face. Told ye this guy's a bitch.

—Allow, just let her go, man. It's calm, I say, not wanting to settle this out.

Trying to play it smart, yuno.

—You really gonna let this sket prick tease you?

He looks again to Isaac:

—This bitch is letting this ting prick tease him.

Isaac shakes his head, like he's trying to hold in his laughter. Princess struggles with Pelumi again and tries to shoulder charge free. She hurts herself and kind of whimpers a bit. This. Is. Bad. Out.

She looks all wrong now on the floor, fixing herself up, weak, lost, yuno.

—You tryin to rock me? You looking for hands?

And he pushes her onto the bed.

—Allow Pelumi, is all I say.

My voice is lacking. I am lacking, trying to play it sharp.

—Allow? She's friendzoning you when you're about to get uck. That's a bar Angel. She's disgracing you and you don't give a fuck man.

I look to Isaac for help, yuno. In the bedroom. In this moment. To say something. But what does Isaac do only shrug his shoulders like, hey, he's not jarring.

Princess is shook. I'm shook.

—Please, she says, starting to cry now. I gotta go. I really gotta be somewhere. What you doing Pelumi?

—Angel, Pelumi calls, like he knows I'm not really there no more. Job is job. Be a man and do what ye gotta do, yeah?

My. Head. Is. Wrecked. *Be a man.* The streets will be dead to me. All white faces my enemy. My crew, gone from me. YouTube fame just a memory.

I dunno.

This is a mad thing.

Tanya

Back to this block

♫ I Love My Block – @Lil Pel

Tanya sings the words from Lil Pel's track into the screen before flipping the pov to the front doors of two identical houses.

>52

Hanging out with my fam

🎵 I Ain't Worried – @OneRepublic

A laptop is opened on a coffee table. The bright white and blue screen of OnlyFans lights the couch. The yellow of Snapchat is showing on a phone beside it. A clippers and a scissors is on the table too, beside two cans of Red Bull. The TV is on, flashing colours onto the rug. Everything else is dark. The silhouette of a figure in shorts and a T-shirt goes across the shot.
>47

Bit dark in here. You up to something? I say.

Barry tuts and goes into the kitchen where he calls back in, Cup of tea?

I'm sixteen Barry, I say.

Juice then?

I'm sixteen Barry, not six.

Red Bull and vodka then?

Me da'll only give out when he comes back.

He won't be back for a while yet.

Where is he?

On a run out to the airport.

Barry shuffles into the living room with two glasses of Redbull, looking delighted with himself. He leaves the lights off.

Get this into ye, he says and reaches across to put the glass beside the laptop on the coffee table.

Of course, he only goes and brushes off me chest when he leans over. He apologizes and I feel weird that he had to mention it.

Barry plumps himself down beside me on the couch with a sigh and then holds up his glass for me to do a cheers with him. The little clink from our golden glasses is the only sound in the room.

Put the sound on the TV for fuck's sake, Barry. This place is depressing.

How can it be depressing now you're here? Sure, we'll see what's on this.

He leans over the laptop and guides his finger along the mouse pad.

I'm not gonna creep on OnlyFans and Facebook with ye or join one of your racist rants.

I take a sip of the drink. It burns a bit.

Get up the yard, Barry laughs, and looks at me like I've reminded him of something.

The laptop screen lights up under his touch and he says, Sure, we won't have to do much creeping to find your video, now, will we?

Not you too, Barry, I moan.

What? What did I say?

Barry starts to scroll. I'm not afraid of him. Or embarrassed by what he's looking for. Fuck that. I'm snapping cause he's trying to make a show of me. That he thinks I'm old and shamed by this sort of shit. But I'm delighted too though, when I think about it, that he thinks I'm old like my ma and I might be afraid of this sorta video. I'm not afraid. Just unsure. Is he disgusted by me? Well, if puking in his mouth wasn't enough to put him off, the clip should definitely have done it.

He looks down his nose at the endless bullshit of old people talking shite, and then his eyes light up.

You're a star now, he says. Is that why you're not answering me messages?

What's it to you?

Everyone's talking about ye.

There's old perverts pestering me with messages an all. Like, I dunno, you! And this other weirdo from the town called Chris.

Barry stops scrolling, but his eyes stay on the screen and he goes, Chris?

Yeah, with them weird Indian shoes, you know him?

Not really. Your da does.

He says me ma does too.

Did he say anything else?

Only that he's a paedo.

His face is still interested in the screen and he laughs to himself.

He's not a paedo, he says. Don't be stupid. And I'm not an old pervert. I'm only twenty-six and I'm just looking out for you.

I'm surprised you're talking to me. What did you call yer one there a while back who had the video from the gig, 'a dirty slut'?

What?

That night you got me locked and we ki …

I didn't get you locked, and I didn't say that, he whispers.

He turns to me now, confused, with a hint of a smile being licked off the corner of his mouth.

I tut and smile back and say, Don't lie Barry. You said anyone who does this type of thing is a dirty slut.

He nearly spits out his drink. No I didn't, he says.

Yeah, ye did. And look it, there I am, doing the same thing. Am I a dirty slut?

Of course not, you're different. I said you were too innocent for that stuff.

What? How?

His hand searches for my knee. His fingers are warm. I can feel them through my leggings.

Look, he says, his eyes wide. I'm not fighting with ye. I'm just worried you're all right after it.

Should I be depressed over it? I say.

Depressed? Who said that?

Should I?

No. Of course not. Are you? It's just surprising it's you on the screen there.

Surprising?

He lifts his hand and starts scrolling again, like he's looking for another clip.

Yeah. That's all. Ye seem older in it, he says. You surprised me. It's not every day ye see a local. It's not what I expected of ye.

A sex tape never hurt no one.

But it could hurt you.

I'm not a kid, Barry.

Ye think? he says. I'm worried about you. You're safe here, on the couch, keeping things relaxed with me. Ye don't need to be out there, doing that.

There's nothing else to be doing round here. They're my friends.

His hand comes out again and his fingers tap on my knee.

Friends? Am I not your friend?

I don't say nothing for ages.

You're upset because of what happened. I want to look after you, he says.

I laugh. There's nothing else to do but laugh.

You? Look after me?

Barry reaches out over the laptop and whispers, I can look after ye. I can get ye things. Buy ye things. If I don't look after ye, and you're running from yer ma's, who will?

Eh, me fucking da.

The first time I know something might be wrong is when he gives this smile, a calm, relaxed, smug fucking grin. The front door lock sounds, me da's finally back. Barry's smile disappears quick smart.

The front door closes over and Barry pockets his phone and stands up, his too tight vest leaving his abs and the snail trail of hair to his dick exposed. Me da strolls in, his eyes straining to see in the darkness. He looks around the room, like he's seeing it for the first time. Barry is suddenly all on edge and taking his hands in and out of his shorts pockets.

We wait for my da to break the silence. He seems weird. In fairness, I get why. One, the room's dark, two, there's no music or nothing on, three, there's cans of Red Bull on the table near where I'm standing, four, me and Barry are standing up to meet him and five, well, I'm there. He hasn't seen me in ages.

What's she doin here?

Me da doesn't even look at me. I nearly fall back onto the couch I'm so disappointed.

He shrugs, waiting on an answer from Barry.

Eh, I tried to tell her not to come in, Barry says.

Da! I call but he just looks at Barry still.

I'm going for a shit. Sort it out Barry, he says.

There, without even a glance in my direction, he's gone. The bathroom light comes into the hall and the toilet seat clanks down and the door closes.

Barry turns to me real sharp and goes, Listen Tanya, go out and come back in an hour. You can stay in my room.

Wha?

I wasn't sure how yer da would react. I probably shouldn't have let ye in. He was disgusted with yer video. Absolutely raging with it. And then there's the other hassle too.

What? Why didn't ye tell me this earlier?

I didn't know how he'd react to seeing ye.

What? But I'm his daughter …

Barry tilts his head as if he's trying to understand me better. And before speaking he checks the hall is clear.

Look Tanya. Ye should know something. I'm a friend, yeah?

What?

Am I a friend or not?

Okay, yeah, you are.

Good. Cause I'm a friend I'm gonna tell ye. Ye should know by now. I mean, your ma should have told ye, or your da. You're not to tell anyone I told ye this, okay?

Whatever.

Okay? he repeats.

I nod.

Right then, he says. That lad Chris. That's the lad your da bet the shite out've at your match ages ago …

Who?

The lad with the Indian shoes, Oasis haircut, that's been following ye.

Him? What about him?

Only cause we're close I'm gonna tell ye this. But that lad, Chris, yeah? He's yer da. Chris is. He's your biological da. And he's been hassling your ma and da these past few months saying he's gonna tell ye if they don't. Your da only found out a few years ago. That's why he left. And then he's been stressed these past months cause yer ma said Chris was gonna meet ye.

The toilet flushes. The tap starts up. I have to go.

Me thinking Im all sober going home
♫ Original sound – @Tanyeah2
Tanya, eyes big and red, vapes into the camera as she leaves a house. She laughs 'wooo!' as she exhales. The screen goes to black.
>49

The bonnet of me da's car is warm to touch. The engine's ticking down like a dying heart. My phone says it's half one in the morning. I look around, shift the bag on my shoulder and sigh and shiver. A packet of Tayto flies past my feet.

Shapes appear under an orange street light and then I hear someone screaming. Three girls are bumping into each other, staggering up the road, their hair blowing all over the place. I know one of them, Linda – used to be in my school. She sways to a stop in her high heels and goes, Alright Tanya, where ye heading?

Nowhere, I say.

The other two giggle into their hair, swaying too.

Wanna come back to me gaff for a drink? Me ma's on shift, she won't be back til later.

I look to me da's house.

What ye doin round here ye mad bitch? one of the girls says. She's locked.

Nothin, I say.

Ye comin in for the sesh? the other girl shouts and they all laugh.

Yeah, sure I've nothin better to be doing. They think it's funny, but it's the truth.

Yup Tanya! Linda shouts.

Yup da sesh

♫ Blazed Boy – @Lil Pel

Tanya and three other girls jump into a selfie and sing along to the words of the song before stumbling out of shot in a hail of laughter. A dark housing estate is all that's left on the screen for a second.
>425

After everyone falls around bursting their shite laughing, we stall it towards the gaff and one of them goes, That's yer one, isn't it? Scarlet for her.

She thinks she's whispering, but she's locked and obviously I can hear her.

What ye say? I call after her.

What? she says, her eyes spinning in her head.

Ye said you were scarlet for me.

No I didn't.

Linda comes over to me, all arms out like she's breaking up a fight.

It's grand, Tanya. She's locked. Don't mind her.

Linda staggers, her heel catches on something and she puts her arm round me shoulder. The other two walk off.

I'll burst yer one. Saying I should be embarrassed about the video.

What video? Linda slurs. She didn't mean nothing …

Why'd she say scarlet for me then?

Ah here, it's near two in the morning. I dunno. Like, it coulda been for anything.

Why's she saying I should be embarrassed then.

I dunno, maybe cause she thought you were on yer lonesome.

Lonesome?

Ye, like walking through the streets at this hour on your tod. Lonely like.

Lonely?

The wind throws Linda's hair over her face. She struggles to clear it away.

Ye right? I'm not standing round here all night, she finally says, pulling strands from her mouth.

Is that why ye asked me to yer gaff, cause yis were embarrassed for me with no mates?

Jesus Tanya. Relax like. I dunno. Ye coming in or what?

Dean

The clock above the sink ticks onto one and Cian says through a sigh:

—This time last week we were …

—Yeah, whatever, I say, scrolling through my phone, angry he has to highlight the fact we're in his kitchen on a Saturday night, again, with nothing to look forward to, and on the last of our cans.

—I was gonna say we were having a spliff.

—Oh.

—And look what I have.

He holds up another neat little one skinner, nodding his head, proud of it.

—Ye could've told me this earlier.

—I wanted to surprise ye before the fight.

—Fair enough.

Cian's da left his dodgy box behind, so we're set for all three showdowns.

—Spark it up then, I say. Let's get a buzz going.

—In the back garden. My ma said she could smell cigarettes when she got home on Sunday morning.

—Sunday morning! Your ma on the pull?

—Fuck off, Cian says, spraying me with the end of his can as he gets up.

The wind in the garden keeps on blowing out his matches, but Cian refuses to light the blunt inside. I've only got my hands on the thing when the neighbour's kitchen door bursts open and we hear the cackles of all those young ones. I pull easy, a faint red glow, don't let it go deep into my lungs. A hot rock shivers off the top and burns a small hole in my T-shirt before

I can brush it off. I'm fuming because I've no other good tops. My ma will go mad.

It's quiet for a second and then a head pops over the wall.

—Yis having a sneaky spliff and ye didn't even invite us in?

Within seconds there's a knock on the front door. Loads of voices and shapes bustle through into the kitchen. Cian's sister is moaning from the stairs:

—Who are these Cian? You're not having a party!

A party? I can't see into the kitchen properly from the garden, but there's at least three shapes other than Cian's in there. A party would be amazing.

A rough looking girl, bout eighteen I'd say, comes into the garden and heads straight for me. She's in a white vest top and shiny black leggings.

—Jesus, you're tall. Who are you anyway? she says, brushing the hair away from her face.

Cian gives me a look like he's about to say something smart, so I announce myself:

—Dean O'Connor.

She shrugs.

—Nice to meet ye, Dean, give us a pull off tha, yeah?

I take one long cool drag and let it ease out like in the movies.

She staggers into me when she tries to take it. Her forehead touches my chin and I get the briefest brush off her chest. It's surprisingly squishy and solid all at once and I'm buzzing. There's two other silhouettes in the garden now and one of them slurs:

—You're in bits, Sharon, take it easy.

Sharon tells them to fuck off and grabs the spliff. She takes two massive tokes and leaves the end of it all wet. I take a quick pull, feel her thick saliva on the roach, retch a bit, and flick it away into the darkness.

It's only then that I notice a glow from the kitchen door. There's a fourth girl in their gang hanging back beside the fridge. It's Tanya Guildea! At our gaff party! I've no idea why she's there, or how she's friends with these brutes, but there she is. All quiet and reserved and not angry looking.

—If those yokes from the Home follow us to me gaff, there'll be war, one of the girls says.

—They coming after you, Linda?

There's a wobble of terror in Cian's voice.

Sharon shrugs.

—Might do. Any you lads good in a scrap?

Cian points at me and starts to speak, but I cut him off.

—Nah, not really. We're lovers, not fighters.

I nod to him and he nods back, like we've settled something.

—Lovers? I like the sound of that, Sharon drawls, her chin morphing into her neck, her bloodshot eyes swimming about.

Her tits squash up on my chest and I wonder can she feel it too.

—I'd love another drink, she hiccups, bits of her hair stuck to her lips.

I hand her my last can without hesitation.

Her lips part and shape into a soft O as she brings the can to them. Thick, red lipstick is slathered all over them, shiny and luscious like a well-polished apple. Her tongue appears, glistening, when she goes to drink and I nearly fall into her. Only after she finishes taking a few sloppy, sexy gulps do I notice everyone has gone inside.

—You eh, you want to go in the front room with me? I say.

All the lights are off in there. Except for the TV and the American accent commentating on an undercard's arrival into the octagon, everything is black and silent. Tanya and the other girls and Cian have pulled up the couch in front of the flatscreen. Cian has a demented smile on his face, staring at Tanya and laughing too loud whenever she says something. I can't hear what she's saying. And it kills me. Tanya is on the end of the couch. Silhouetted against the colours from the TV. Her vape smoke gives a mad fuzzy dreamy feel to everything, and I have to blink a few times to make sure this is real.

The TV lights Tanya's face in a lovely soft wash. She looks so fresh compared to the others, detached in a way. Maybe even sad. Sharon drags my arm towards the armchair in the corner. Her hand is soft and warm and I have a horn in my jeans. Her breath is on my neck, her lips almost touching skin. She sits on my lap, her full, warm weight, with her arse squished into the side of the armrest.

—Cheers for the can, she belches in my ear.

My boner is only dying to get out. I shouldn't have worn tight jeans. I've never been so excited and in so much agony all at once.

I try to concentrate on the telly. The lad in black shorts starts with a few jabs. The crowd are mad into it. So are the girls – apart from Tanya – shouting and all. Cian is quiet enough. The hash has hit me and I'm feeling a heavy greener start to weigh me down.

The touch of her hand through my jeans brings me back. It begins to move up to my crotch.

—That feel guh?

I can only groan in reply. I'm freaking out under the weight of everything. I'm scared. From all the porn I've watched, I know a fair bit about horny women, and what makes them feel good. But I feel daunted, unprepared. There's a lot to consider, deal with, deliver. The crowd roars. She probably wants me to smack her a few times to make her wet, to pull her underwear up her arse, maybe even grab her hair and reef her head back, all that sort of shit.

The jab is still going on from the fighter in the red shorts. His thick jaw is set tight, his dark eyes intense and intimidating and all of a sudden, for no reason – we haven't even kissed – she moves her hand to the top of my jeans and slips her fingers under the button. I take a breath and suck in my stomach.

—*Down on the ground again and this time he's on top!* the commentator shouts.

The effort of the trip from Red Shorts pulls at his face, his lips stretching down and down. She is undoing my buttons, creating space. She has a hold of my dick. A full fisted grip. I'm worried now her hand's too big, or my dick is too small.

It's comfortably dark outside the spotlight of the TV. Despite the doubts, I'm loving it. But my jeans are too tight and she can't get any action going.

—Feel guh, yeah?

With her hot breath in my ear, I commit and shift the jeans out from under my arse.

Black Shorts with the chiselled six-pack counters.

—*And now we see him using those great grappling skills in reverse!*

She gets a hold of the tip of my dick like it's a game controller and starts to lash at the thing. It's amazing, but Jesus Christ, she has no mercy. She's in my ear again, licking it, breathing heavy, whispering:

—Yeah? Yeah?

Red Shorts' face is contorted out of recognition. His eyes disappear behind the strain and sweat while he tries to slip through the hold.

—He's just ragdolling him here in this position!

And she's squeezing my dick so hard I close my eyes. It's like a Chinese burn. I free my hand and spit on my fingers and lather the spit on my dick. That always seems to work in the shit I've seen.

The camera shakes close on Red Shorts' huffing face. Again the crowd volume booms. My eye then catches Tanya. She's oblivious to my stare, her profile perfectly outlined by the screen. Having her there while I'm getting cracked off is trippy. All the times I've imagined her close, boxing gloves raised before we throw ourselves together, onto each other. This is amazing.

But the rhythm is all wrong. She isn't pulling in small routine strokes like I'm used to. She's pulling and pushing like she's milking a cow. Pushing! Like forcing it back into my sack.

And then she stops and heaves herself off me and starts to kiss my shirt. And then my stomach. And then the top of my leg.

—He's mixing things up brilliantly, he's not just standing and striking …

I get nervous. A blow job is next level. Cian said if the girl doesn't gag it means your dick isn't big enough, so you have to make sure she gags. They always gag. And I just know, she's not gonna gag and then she'll laugh at me and not bother continuing on. I'll be disgraced – forever – regardless of a redner or not. But still I want it.

And Cian said you have to talk while she's doing it otherwise it shows you aren't able to stop yourself from blowing your load early. And that will be the end of your reputation as a serious lover. Another disaster. They don't seem to say much, the lads, other than, oh yeah, baby, oh yeah. I can muster that, surely. And your phone, Cian says, everyone always gets it on their phone. Otherwise how will anyone know it actually happened? And if you lie about something like this, you'll be thought of as a total loser, for the rest of your life!

The crowd oohh.

While she gives the top of my leg a soft, soft kiss I root out my phone from my jeans down around my knees. As each kiss moves closer to my dick my leg starts to tremble, as if electricity is going through it. I feel like I'm about to explode. I start thinking quickly about weird shit I've been sent before, like lads having sex with animals and all that.

It works, I'm still on, but not about to disgrace myself.

And suddenly, her lips leave my leg and her ear is on my lap. The weight of her head rests there like some sort of pillow. Dead. Limp. I'm on fire but she's stopped.

—*Much more difficult to finish from here, especially on a talented grappler ...*

Red Shorts has slipped and is sprawled on the canvas. I lean forward the best I can in my flitters state and try to see around to her face. She's passed out on my leg, inches from my dick! I throw my head back, whisper to the ceiling:

—Fuuuuuck ...

I'm a lover, not a fighter. Not the Jock. I am Dean. And I not going to settle for bronze. I'm going for a KO. An undisputed win. So I get my left hand and start to finish the job myself.

—*Again he's looking for the choke ...*

Tanya's silhouette is strong against the TV. The camera's close again on Red Shorts' pained face, his bloody nose. His eyes are innocent as he huffs and grimaces. Tanya's kind of smiling. There's a sadness around her, as if the vape smoke she's exhaling is softening her edges.

This is whopper.

—*Thirteen wins by rear naked choke coming in ...*

Almost there. And Tanya's face is so close. So close. So close.

—*He's got it deep, he's gonna finish this, he's gonna finish this …*

Want to fuck? You look like a freeeeaaaa …

—*Wow! It's all over, it's all over, he wins by submission!*

And my closed eyes see a flash of fleshy pink. The room's flooded with light. The overhead bulb is on. I am spent, my chest soaked, and Tanya turns back to see what's going on.

Our eyes meet. My kacks around my knees, dick in hand, staring at her. There's a sickening turn in her lips and a 'Fuck me.' Over my shoulder a small voice – Cian's little sister – is moaning:

—The bin's on fire in the garden.

She sees me and screams like she's about to be murdered. Runs out of the room. I have no tissue. I am deflated, stoned and kind of happy. A champion of sorts.

—*That's how strong his squeeze is …*

Red Shorts' arms are held aloft. Tanya is on her feet staring at me and Cian is up too, but looking to the door.

—Did you put water on it? he shrieks.

—No, the sister calls back from the hall. I didn't start it!

And then Cian – on his way out – sees me with my kacks down, and Sharon asleep on my legs.

—Fucking hell man, fucking hell! he says, his eyes near popping out've his head like a googly eyes filter.

He doesn't dwell on my dick, the mess, the girl, he just storms out into the hall.

They all leave the room tutting and grimacing at me like I've shit in their shoes or something and then she wakes up – Sharon. Her lip pulls down her face like she's got it snagged on a fishing hook and her eyes meet mine before she screams:

—What da fuck!

Because she's disorientated, she can't get up and I'm kind of stuck under her so I can't manoeuvre me kacks back and it's horrible. Real life. Reality. Horrible. Redners, shame, all those things you'd expect.

—That's the first time I've ever seen a guy tap out from standing ...

And in that moment, when I should want to dig the biggest hole I can throw myself into and never come out, I actually feel alright. Zen. Relaxed. Calm. Granted, the girl doesn't need to have woken up to the spoils of my wank, but in fairness, I made sure to keep her away from everything. And even while she screams and struggles to her feet, I'm not out for the count. I'm there, covered in jizz, but still alright.

I get my shit together and soak up my mess with the inside of my T-shirt. All the voices in the kitchen are a mix of girls shouting:

—Go in there and sort him out!

And Cian is roaring over them at his sister:

—Why didn't you put it out?

And the sister's shouting back:

—I didn't fucking start it!

I try to escape quietly. I might not be embarrassed, but I'm not thick. There'll be other Saturday nights to try and make things right. I hope.

Only, there, in the hall, at the bottom of the stairs, kind of waiting on me, is Tanya.

—You're a freak, you know that? she says.

I'm bamboozled by her words – the ones I've imagined her say for so long – and by her normal, not angry or aggressive face.

I shrug a, meh, and make for the front door. I don't want to get in a real row with her.

—Were you looking at me or the fight while you did that? she asks as I shuffle by.

There's no point denying it. I shrug again.

And then she says:

—Where you going?

The way she says it surprises me. There's a hint of something there. Something I can't put my finger on. Hope, maybe. At least I know from her tone she isn't going to hit me. I point vaguely at the door and look her dead in her gorgeous brown eyes and say:

—Home.

—Can I come?

I am stunned. I miss a step.

—Well? she says.

—What? I say.

—Can I come home with you.

It feels like she's hit me over the head. I'm concussed. Dazed.

—With me?

Where's the stars? Birds tweeting around, like in the cartoons?

—No, with your mate.

—Wait, I say, composing myself. I'm confused.

—That's a surprise.

—Wait, you want to come home, with me?

I can't read her face, her lips, her eyes. She shows me the palms of her hands, lifts her shoulders and says:

—Why not?

Like it's the most natural thing in the world to see a lad wank over you and then have him bring you home.

Without the burden and panic of a redner, I manage a moment of clarity.

—One thing, I say. Who got a Light-Heavyweight bronze medal for boxing at the Olympics in 2012?

—How the fuck should I know?

—And there's the knockout, I say, in the voice of a commentator, out loud like an awful eejit. I open the front door and sweep my hand before her like I'm some sort of Victorian gentleman. I'm giddy with the possibilities.

But she doesn't move.

—I've a question for you then, she says.

Fuck. Here we go.

I was so close.

—Go on, I say.

—Do I look lonely to you?

If this is a trick question, I'm doomed. She's testing me. Everything rests on getting this right. Honestly, she looked sad to me earlier on.

—Beautiful, I say, eventually. You look beautiful to me.

She smiles and nods.

—Cool.

I hold the door for her and she walks by. A unanimous decision. This is the greatest moment of my life.

Alright Our

Dean

I wake up with a jump and feel warmth beside me before remembering it's Tanya there. I must've spunked in my boxers while I slept. Even in dreams she has that effect on me.

—I just gotta run to the toilet, I whisper, and get out of the bed before she turns and faces me. My head is banging, and the night is a total blur.

Tanya is holding one of my boxing gloves in her lap when I get back, new boxers on. She's fully clothed and I'm both devastated but delighted this ordeal will be over soon. I've no idea what time it is, but it feels real early.

—I didn't know you boxed, she says, looking up at me with interest.

Her face is calm and open and I stand there for a second. It feels like a dream.

—Oh, you found them. Yeah, I haven't boxed since I was twelve.

—How come you stopped?

—My da.

I take the glove delicately from her and open the door behind me, stand aside to make space for her to go through.

—I stopped playing football cause of my da too, she says, still sitting on the edge of the bed.

—Cool, I whisper, covering the stains on the glove.

She looks at me like I've just farted.

—Thanks for letting me stay over last night, she says.

—Cool, yeah, I say.

—You enjoy it?

I'm freaked she might have smelt my jizz, seen I spunked in my sleep, so I'm all mumbles and looking away from her eyes. Her shoulders slump like I've disappointed her.

We get as far as the middle of the stairs before she spots – hard to miss – the two A3 framed prints of my da. In the first picture my da is every inch the Rocky he made me sit through as a young lad. In action at the London Olympics: his legs are glistening and set apart, his head hunched and his arm extended mid-punch. It was taken from just under the ropes and the shot has a heroic vibe. The second picture is of my da beaming on the podium, yellow flowers held close to his chest, bronze medal around his neck. His beloved medal.

My da keeps it nestled on green felt inside a wooden box the local town council presented him with. I lost it once, when I was nine. It fell behind the radiator in my bedroom. He got a hold of me by the shoulders and shook the absolute shit out of me wanting to know where I'd put it. He dislocated my neck. I was in a brace for two weeks and had to take half a Valium twice a day to relax the muscles. We told the hospital I was jumping on the bed. My ma told the school the same story and everyone got a good laugh out of that

—Wow, Tanya whispers.

She stalls it for longer than I'd like at the podium picture, inspecting it. I rub the back of my neck. Every day I pass these pictures. Every day.

I walk her to my front gate and say:

—I'd be happy to escort you home, if ye want.

—A gentleman too, she says.

We agree to follow each other on all our socials and she asks for my usernames. I giggle when I hear one of hers and she looks at me all surprised and she laughs then too.

Her laugh makes her look younger. Different to what I've seen before. She looks around as if she's just realized where she is and the smile fades. She coughs a little and fixes her hair.

After this weird pause, she says:

—I can walk home myself. It was nice meeting ye Dean. You're sound.

—Thanks Tanyeah, I say but she doesn't get the joke.

I watch her walk to the end of the estate and only turn for my gaff when she takes the corner.

I go back upstairs and stand and look at the messy bed. The boxing gloves are by my pillow. I lift them up and run my thumb along the leather. Then I creak onto the bed and sniff the pillow and slowly – eyes closed, concentrating hard – brush my face down onto the sheet, inhale, and go further.

Tanya

Nice morning for a walk

♫ I Just Had Sex (explicit version) – @The Lonely Island

Tanya squints into the camera as she walks through an empty housing estate. Her eyes are puffy and dark. Small shadows under them make her look older. A tall figure is in the background over her shoulder. He's standing outside a house, hands in his pockets, watching her depart. When she rounds a corner, she sticks her tongue out and raises her eyebrows before smiling and spinning

around in a mock dance. The sun is rising above houses in front of her.
>6852

When we kissed, me and Dean, even though I felt a bit woozy lying in his bed, I went for it and gave him a wank. He fell asleep straight after.

He's embarrassed about it in the morning. Maybe embarrassed about being with me.

Shes on the phone more than me!
♫ Motion Sickness – @Phoebe Bridgers
Tanya does a playful frown into the camera and flips the pov to a woman, jet black hair tied up in a ponytail, thin lips, drawn cheeks, at a kitchen table on her phone. She's in her pyjamas, a cup of coffee steaming in front of her, oblivious.
>116

Ma takes a deep breath to buy some time and then she places her phone on the kitchen table as if she's afraid the screen will break.

I was gonna tell ye, she says. I couldn't find the chance. It was a once-off thing while me and yer da were on a break. We were young. I was seventeen. It was a mistake. I loved your da.

A mistake? Like, I was a mistake?

Jesus Tanya. Course not. No. The one-night thing was a mistake. Me and your da, we loved you – still love you. Your da still loves you.

Can't believe you said I was a mistake.

I never said that, love. I never meant it like that.

Ye have the cheek to give me shit about a stupid ten-second yoke on WhatsApp.

That's different. Ye know that's different, love.

How? How is it any different?

She eases her chair out from the table. Her eyes stay closed for a second while she gets herself together. Her eyelashes have clumps of mascara on them.

It's totally different, she whispers, finally looking up to me. Everyone knows about you doing it. The whole world seen it. There's no hiding it.

And no one knows about your little mistake cause ye used me da to cover it up so ye did. When did he find out?

It's not like that, love.

When did me da find out?

Near two years ago.

That why he left?

Yeah.

No wonder he hates me.

We run these streets

♫ Hotline Bling – @Drake

Tanya is in her school uniform, smiling into a selfie, singing along to the song. A lad with a feeble moustache, thin face, black Canada Goose jacket and red cap, comes into the picture from her right, arms over her shoulder laughing and singing too. His eyes are clear and intense, his smile wide and one front tooth is broken in half leaving a small gap. The shot wobbles and goes black.
>1312

I get grabbed from behind. Paddy is there, big smile, hand down his grey Nike tracksuit bottoms, other hand pointing to the sky as if he's dancing. I'm in my uniform but wearing me black jacket with the fur collar and a pair of black leggings, so I look alright too.

What's the story, T? Haven't seen ye in ages, he says, as if nothing's happened.

Ye haven't messaged me in ages, I say, taking an earphone out.

Steady, yeah? I thought you were thick with me. Rihanna and Britney said you were still snapping over the video.

I never said that.

So you're not pissed? It was bad out, T. I'm not gonna lie. I feel bad for ye. I thought the cops were gonna come after me, smash down me door an all.

They called. I didn't tell them who it was in the video.

Sound out. I was gonna burst Sean.

Why didn't he take it down?

He did but some other lads copied it. Bad out, like.

Yeah.

A fat lad zips between us on an electric scooter. Paddy keeps one hand down his jocks and rubs his chin like he's thinking what to say next. He looks at me for a second.

Ye doing anything this Friday? Me and the lads are going to the Home with Rihanna and Britney. My ma is away in Limerick. Free gaff, yeah.

I wouldn't get in the Home.

He bites the inside of his mouth.

I'll get ye in, no bother. Ye up for it? The girls said you're not doing much since the video.

Yeah I have been. Sure I'm meeting someone.

Yeah? That you on the socials walking home from his gaff the other morning ye mad bitch?

Maybe. Anyway, he's mad into boxing and his da's an Olympic champion and all.

For real?

Swear to God.

Class, bring him down too then, yeah.

I'll think about it, I say, and go to put my earphone back in.

What ye listening to anyway? he goes.

Oldschool, I say.

Gissa listen, he laughs, and we share earphones and I hold my phone up and we have the craic in the middle of the street.

Dean

No one is talking – there isn't much point with how loud the music is. The techno shakes the room. Tanya announces my entrance with a flourish of her hand. Smoke swirls heavy and thick under the ceiling light. No one looks up. Two lads in caps are on the couch with a girl. She's on her phone. Another lad with a bong in an armchair has a cheap clone of Tanya on his lap. The TV is on, but the screen is just a blank blue.

Tanya shouts something into the noise and it's like she's given a small electric shock to the lad with the bong. His head jolts up and I see his eyes under the cap. Serious, deep blue things. His thumb flicks over his phone screen. The music suddenly drops. His smile brings out these cute dimples. I feel jealous. Tanya ushers me into the centre of the room.

The music remains low and there's this real awkward silence. I put out my hand to the lad with the bong and say:

—Alright, I'm Dean.

Everyone is watching.

—Your da was in the Olympics? he asks, sitting forward, clasping my hand and moving the Tanya clone off his lap.

She gets up with a tut and stretches and moans.

—When we going the Home?

—Whenever, the lad says, flapping her away, his eyes set on me.

—Yeah, I say. He got a bronze medal.

In the weird buzz and stoned silence of the room, despite my initial reservations, I'm actually alright now. Everyone leans forward expectantly.

The medal is wrapped in a thick purple ribbon. I unravel the fabric slowly to build anticipation and, when it drops from my hand, I hold it up for everyone to see.

The lad with the blue eyes reaches out to touch it.

—Paddy's cousin Trevor was Irish champion a few years ago, Tanya says over my shoulder, her breath warm on my ear.

Paddy nods along, his face set and serious now. He leaves the bong at his feet and gently takes hold of the medal.

—Here, when we going the Home, Paddy? a lad says from the couch.

In one pounce Paddy is on top of him, sparking a clatter off the side of his head. The sound of the smack makes me wince and think of my da.

—Would yis fuck up about the fucking Home, Paddy says, fixing his baseball cap and returning to me.

I retreat an inch or two discreetly, and feel Tanya's tits, small and firm, pressed against my back.

The vibe in the room is weird.

—Trevor was the best boxer you've ever seen, man, Paddy says, looking down at the medal in his hand. His dream was to box for Ireland in the Olympics.

The silence is so intense. Tanya nudges me. I clear my throat.

—Suppose it's a dream for every boxer, I say.

The peak of the cap lifts and his blue eyes squint as if the words I just spoke are written in tiny letters on my face. I don't know whether to smile or shrug, or run.

Paddy shakes his head, finally, and sucks his lips like he's tasted something sour. I steady myself, feel Tanya's presence tight behind me.

—Trevor wasn't like every other fighter. He got sick in his peak. Died a young lad, he says.

On the mantelpiece behind Paddy there's an old picture of a smiling boxer, drenched in sweat. He has one fist aloft and an arm draped over a young lad's shoulder. For a second I think it's me and my da. I look closely and see dimples in the small shadows around the young lad's mouth and the deep serious blue eyes of a young Paddy smiling back.

—Shit sorry, I say.

Paddy's brow darkens as if he's deciding something.

—Yeah? he says and looks down again at the medal in his hand.

He nods to himself and goes:

—It's grand like.

Tanya squeezes my arm.

The techno gets whipped up and Paddy shouts:

—Come on Deano!

I stand there unsure if he wants me to dance, or fight. Then he starts skipping on the spot, laughing and shouting out in a commentator's voice:

—Round one here at Madison Square Gardens …

I still stand there while he flinches and jerks his shoulders and starts to shadow box right in front of me.

Everyone is watching. Paddy is alone in the middle of the room, waiting. For the first time in five years, I plant my feet like my da used tell me to, like in the picture on the stairs. I become conscious of my stance and start to throw a few flashy shadow punches too. Everyone moves their legs to make space for our dance.

We duck and sway through the heavy smoke. The girls cheer. Our eyes stay set on each other's as we swivel around the rug. Paddy can't stop smiling. He pretends to catch me with a sweet right hook. I collapse onto the grubby rug, out for the count.

The room whoops. Everyone's smiling. Paddy holds out his hand to lift me up and puts his arm round my neck, breathing heavy in my ear.

—Get this into ye Deano, he says, and there's cheers again.

A bong is in my face. Tanya's nowhere to be seen. I've never done a bong in my life.

—Ah, it's grand, I say.

Paddy spins to anger so quick I can't tell if he's taking the piss or not.

—Don't leave me hanging Deano. You're in me gaff, don't be such a bitch. Take a whack of the bong with the boys!

—Yup Deano! someone shouts from the couch.

A funfair comes to Balbriggan every few years. Muck and straw and techno. My da brought me once. There was a punch machine all the punters hounded him to try. All the phones were out and he made me have a go. I was ten. Just about tall enough. I tried it and everyone laughed. So my da, three years basking in the bronze – before everything went to shit – stepped up and slammed the punchbag home. The numbers on the electronic board went up and up and the crowd went mad.

I think of my da's fist when I take a hit from the bong. The impact. It's like getting punched in the lungs. I cough so hard I think I'm about to be sick and the numbers keep on going up and up and up.

Princess

The last of mum's jollof rice is so dry and I'm like, wait, is there nothing else to eat? Becky looks at me across the kitchen counter with that fed up face of hers.

—You wanna make something instead?

Becky pulls a small bit of meat from her plate and puts it in front of Michael. The baby slaps his hands excitedly on the high-chair table and squeals with delight.

—It's been three days of this, I say, rummaging through the red peppers for meat.

Again Becky stares across the counter, her hand on the high chair like its supporting her weight.

—And? I don't see you going Dunnes to buy any food.

I'm being a bitch. I know this. Yeah, life's not fair. Yeah, we're eating three-day-old dinner mum made for us before she left for Nigeria, yeah, Becky's in the same situation as me – worse, since she's gotta work, and she has Michael to look after – yeah, yeah, yeah. Only I'm still moaning.

—That reminds me. I've been called in tomorrow evening. You're gonna haveta mind Michael, Becky says.

—It's Thursday. You know the library stays open late on a Thursday.

—You want to eat tomorrow?

I tongue a piece of beef lodged between my back teeth.

—Exactly. You let me work and you collect Michael from Claudine at five. No later. You know she gets vexed real easy.

—I need to work on my History topic. It's due soon.

—And I need to work on keeping us fed. Unless you want jollof rice tomorrow too.

—If we have to, I'd eat it instead of having to mind Michael.

—Do the fucking dishes when you're finished, Becky says and pushes back from the counter with a sharp squeak on the lino.

Becky startles Michael and his bottom lip wobbles. She stares at me as if she wants to say something more. Then she leaves the room.

Michael starts to cry after her. I pick him up and sit him on my lap. He needs a nappy change.

*

I do two hours after school in the pharmacy on Tuesday and Wednesday (so I can spend the evening in the library Thursday), and four hours on a Saturday.

I have a tag – silver Courier font – with my name stuck over someone else's. I have a uniform too which makes me feel good every time I put it on. It's the same as Rayo's only hers is black with a purple trim and mine is white with a purple trim. White. So every bit of two-day-old dirt, every little scuff or stain I don't wash out, is noticed.

The pharmacist is loud and opinionated, sure of himself and confident in everything he does. He lets the whole floor know what he thinks of a song or a bit of news. The weather is his favourite topic, not that he discusses anything with me. All said, he's nice – if a little distant. Rayo says I'm imagining things, but I don't know. It's a strange one. I have to remind myself how kind he was when I called in after he rang me. How he didn't have to give me this position.

He reassured me with grand flourishes when we first met: he'd show me the dispensary up the steps behind the counter and tell me about the formalities and protocols and procedures of being a pharmacist. He never has. He said he'd get me on the payroll for a small wage too. He never did that either. I haven't mentioned it to Rayo.

Rayo is his store manager, his aide-de-camp, Marie to his Pierre, so, yellow highlighter out, I behave around her as if I was around him. And I do whatever she asks, as if he was asking.

She likes to keep me busy. I think she wants to make sure my few weeks are a success – in the eyes of the pharmacist – which will make bringing her daughter in easier when summer arrives. She shows me how she processes prescriptions, how she deals with the customers, how she uses that soft, warm voice of hers in the face of ridiculous questions and statements.

—I'm sorry, do you speak English?

So many ignorant people I sometimes wonder if I'm back in primary school.

I'm beside Rayo after school on Wednesday, pricing the glucose lollipops. She is cleaning down the counter with an antibacterial wipe. We're chatting as we normally do.

—You get much homework today? she says, taking large sweeps of the counter.

—Not really. I gotta work on my History special topic.

—Yeah? My Damilola is finished hers a while now. What's yours on?

—The Black Power salute at the 1968 …

My phone rings under the counter and I answer in a cupped hand hush. It's Becky. Rayo watches me out the side of her eye, wiping stopped.

—I need you to collect Michael at five, Becky says, the hiss of people and cars in the background.

I keep the mouthpiece covered, move from behind the counter, onto the floor.

—I can't. I'm in til six, you know that.

—I'm not asking you, Princess. I'm stuck in town.

Rayo looks down her nose at me, her big, bright fuchsia eyeshadow fluttering lazily.

—Everything okay? she says.

I hang up.

—Eh, I might have to leave early today.

—Early?

She says the word like it disappoints her.

I go behind the cash register, leave the phone back, take the cloth and start working on the counter for her.

—It's not definite, but my mum isn't feeling well.

The bell chimes and a woman walks in. That's when I see Angel across the road from the pharmacy. There's always loads of traffic and he must think that camouflages him. He leans against the old bank wall, scrolling through his phone, or looking around as if he's waiting on someone. He's so cool there, his leg up against the flaking paint, like a North Face–clothed black flamingo. He's messaged and I haven't messaged back. This isn't the first time he has shown up.

I don't know what he wants.

The situation which unfolded when Pelumi and Isaac came into the bedroom was like the worst BZ reaction ever. All the bros got together and broke the symmetry of a beautiful moment. Things escalated way too quickly out of my control. What happened there can stay there because I've contained it now. I can't let it side-track me.

There's minimum entry requirements for Pharmacy studies in Trinity. Requirement one is 590 points. Then I need a minimum of a H6 in honours Maths and a H4 in Chemistry. That's why the HEAR scheme is so important, and if it comes to it, the interview. The points I'm heading for will leave me well short for direct entry into Pharmacy studies in Trinity. So, even though I see Angel, I try not to think about him.

I've decided to put Angel – thoughts of Angel, Angel's friends, Angel's influence on my life – as far away as I can. I need to concentrate on this work placement, my History special topic, my life, myself.

—I appreciate how important family is, Rayo says, bringing me back.

—So do I, thank you.

—But, you've also made commitments here, not just to me.

—I know but …

—Don't let me stop you, the small, middle-aged blonde lady says as she approaches the counter.

She has a floral scarf around her neck and a grey puffer jacket on, and flaps her hand as if she's asking us to continue.

—You seem to be having such a lovely chat. It's so nice to see a mother and daughter working together.

Now, maybe if this was the first time something like this was said, I'd laugh it off like Rayo is able to do.

I think of Pelumi standing over me, I think of having to do the interview for the HEAR scheme if it's oversubscribed. I think of Iwona and how she is still strutting around in her white lab coat in the pharmacy up the street. I think of how she robbed my idea and is now probably going to try and rob my spot in the HEAR scheme too.

Despite all this, I can't help myself.

—Do we actually look related? I say to the woman.

—Princess, Rayo says with a calm, wide smile.

—Well now, would you believe I'm not wearing my glasses and I forgot to put my contacts in this morning.

—Oh, but from where you're standing, we look the same? I continue.

The woman's smile flickers.

—Don't tease the poor lady, Rayo laughs. My daughter has her father's sense of humour! Now, how can I help you?

The woman chuckles uncertainly and taps her red nails on the counter. Before she can speak, Rayo excuses herself and turns to me.

—Princess, could you face off the shampoos? And try not to get any more stains on your uniform, dear.

Rayo and the woman chuckle as I leave, and I'm like, wait. I hold out the bottom of my uniform and look for the stains Rayo alluded to. To my disappointment, they're not hard to find.

Tanya

On de sesh with the crew

♫ God Save the Rave – @Scooter & Harris & Ford

Tanya is holding the phone at arm's length, at an angle, high above her head. Two girls, one with thick lashes and dark eyeshadow, the other with straight greasy hair, are beside her and dancing to the song. They're singing along to the song, bobbing up and down, cans of beer in their hands.

>837

Hey, you awake? I whisper in his ear.

Dean's eyes are closed and he has this content smile on his face.

I dunno, he slurs. I'm talking to … and I think I can smell her sexy smell. Tanya Guildea. So I must be dreaming.

Come on to the Home. I wanna dance with you. I wanna hang out, get a sneaky link going, what ye think?

His eyes stay closed, and his face is turning white, his lips real dry. He should never have taken a whack off the bong.

I'm not in your league. You look amazing, not just tonight. Like. Amazing, that dress, yeah man.

I get this lovely thrill, a small little high. No one else said anything about the new dress and I wasn't sure if Dean even thought I was good looking.

You're like, way out there and I'm just …

… talking shite and stoned, I say.

Yeah, I'm stoned. But you're still hot.

Hardly, I say and tut.

He finally licks his lips and I almost lean in and kiss him.

Everyone watches you, he says. Tonight, Paddy, his eyes, ye know. Those dimples. And the girls – your friends – they're so. You're funny and you take no shit. Jealous of you. I'm so stoned. I'm sorry. What am I even saying?

You don't need to talk, I say and lean in and kiss him. He doesn't react. He's passed out. Again!

Angel

Since everything's gone to shit between me and Princess, I wonder, yuno, just wonder if I shudda just been what Pelumi and Isaac thought I was. Cause now, no matter what I do, what I say, the boys see me different. Basically, whenever I can, I try and impress them. Especially now Pelumi's on the rise. I gotta stay tight. If yuno, yuno.

Stallin it on the wall, swinging my legs, knocking the heels of my dead Nikes off the pebble dash hoping Princess'll come by. It's been weeks. I send a message to Pelumi's cameraman Lorcan about my big plans for the future. I wanna know if he can give his brother a shout, who can then give his friend who owns the bando barber's down the town a shout. See if he's serious bout letting someone open it up. Find out what it'll take to get in the door. I hear footsteps and before I look up, swear down, I take a breath and close my eyes.

—Eeeyy, what a wasteman, bro, Isaac says when he arrives. Bro, you're getting a rep, innit. You hang out of this wall like some sort of pred trying to link up with them kiddies going the playground.

—Allow, I say. I just like it out here. My ma gives me shit bout studying if I stay inside.

Isaac clasps my hand, leans one shoulder in.

—That's my boy. Fuck that. Don't know why you did that TY shit. Bro, you're way too old now. School never did me any good, yuno. Your ma think you should be studying on a Saturday at …

He checks his phone's cracked screen.

—Two o'clock in the day? Eey, that's harsh Angel.

—I get a job like she wanted, she gives me shit about studying. I don't have a job she gives me shit about money. Swear down, all I want is that bit of paper to say I graduated, and that'll keep her happy, yuno.

And then Princess appears. Finally. This waiting around for her is long, but now I am popping.

Isaac sees what I see and sucks his teeth and mutters:

—This nitty.

But I shush him and ease off.

Her hair bounces with every step, a big afro like something from the history books, the Black Panther, Black Power stuff.

—Yo, Princess, I say.

Isaac shakes his head and walks away and calls back:

—I'm stalling it to Pelumi's.

—I'll follow ye.

—Wagwan, Princess, Isaac laughs and does a skip as he passes her.

She stares ahead, lips tight, arms folded and click-clacks towards me.

If ever there was a time to be fresh, this is the time. Swear down, I am stressed. Seeing her finally, having to say what I've been practising weeks to say, I am dying, and shook.

—Any suss?

She stops dead, arms still folded like she's still so vexed. Her eyes stare ahead at the entrance to the blocks.

—Did you really just ask me if there was any 'suss'? Are you for real?

I approach in a kind of a servant crouch, my back leaning in, shoulders down like I've been rocked.

—Sorry, allow, Princess.

—Allow? What am I, what do I look like to you? Am I one of them basic bitches in your music videos? Cause that's what it sounds like, and that's what it felt like the last time I saw you.

Obviously, yeah, I don't wanna go there.

—You know I'm sorry, Princess. Really, now that I can see you and say it, swear down, I am so sorry.

Her eyes move from the door and meet mine. Shitden, I feel so bad that I've caused this.

—I really liked you, Angel. I thought you were different.

I grit my teeth, look over my shoulder before replying.

—I am different. God knows I'm different from all them others. Swear down.

She snorts to herself.

—Yeah right. I've seen Pelumi's new track. And who's in the middle of it all, making like he's stabbing lads and spilling juice on the floor?

—That's just a thing. You know that.

—You deserve an Oscar if that's not the real you with your boys.

—It's a bit of banter, that's all. I'm working now. So I can save. I've got plans.

—Yeah right.

—Swear down. I'm in the deli in SuperValu.

—SuperValu plans?

—Yeah, plans. Not in SuperValu though. Allow. I can't be letting anyone know til they're ready, yeah.

—Whatever. I gotta go. I'm in work. I only came home to bring my sis some painkillers.

—In Bracken. That's fresh. You look too wavy in that uniform.

Princess brushes down her skirt.

—I've seen you, through the big window, shaping around like you run the show! I say.

—You spying on me?

—Hardly. Allow. I'm admiring you. From a distance, though, yeah.

She moves by and says:

—And that's not gonna change.

No lie, that's two footed man, but I don't blame her and I'm banged. She's different from all the rest. And I know she sees something in me too, yuno.

—I'm still me. I let you down. I know that Princess and I'm sorry.

She holds the door open, looking at the lift ahead, listening though.

—Maybe reply to a message now that you've seen I'm still me? I say.

—The only message I'll reply to is the one where you tell me how your plans for the future make you so different from all your boys.

She's gone before I can open my mouth.

*

Pelumi rings before I get to his gaff. Basically, I'm at his front gate.

—Wagwan, Angel, he says. Man, I need a trim hard, yeah? Stall it down with your clippers.

I stop dead and see Pelumi's silhouette in the front room.

—What's wrong with the Angolan?

—Never mind her bro. Don't even think of stallin it up here without your tools.

He must think I'm thinking bout it cause he goes:

—Chap, if you wanna be beside me in the next video, yeah, you'll get up these ends with your clippers and shit. I'm not even playing.

They salute me when I come in the room. They don't notice I'm panting. Pelumi has a slushy in his hand and he looks frassed. Isaac's flaked out on the couch, wasted too.

—Story boys, I say, shifting my barbering bag on my back.

Swear down, these boys are out of it.

—Bring yer clippers, yeah? Pelumi slurs.

I nod. Guy doesn't know I've got my clippers, trimmers, straight razor, foil shaver and shears in there.

—Get this into ye then man, Pelumi adds, holding out the purple slushy. It's lethal bro.

—What's that?

—Maggie, bro.

—Man get licked, Isaac sniggers.

I'm ready to go, do some business from the get-go, not get mad out of it on some cheap Jamaican Magnum wine. But as usual, mans gotta do what the boys do, yuno. Then Isaac goes:

—Yo, ye can't get him wasted if he's gonna give ye a trim!

—Shit yeah, Pelumi says. No maggie for you bro.

Pelumi sits up then, ready for action.

—Man, my trim is dead. I need a fresh cut for tomorrow.

—What's tomorrow?

Pelumi rolls his lips.

—Business bro, innit.

So basically, Isaac gets a kitchen chair for Pelumi and puts it in the middle of the front room. I can't lie, I'm a bit shook. Yeah, I've done Isaac, Mo and Harvey's, and it's low-key and all, but Pelumi never asked before, and I wanna impress. I gotta deliver. I gotta start making moves for myself too.

—Where's Delfina? I say, sizing up the back of Pelumi's head.

Pelumi sucks his teeth, slurps from the slushy.

—Bitch says she's busy. She's just vexed cause she thinks me and her daughter gonna twap.

—Eeey boy, Isaac laughs.

He's back on the couch, flat out, arms behind his head, delighted with life.

—And are yis gonna twap? I say.

—That depends on your trim tonight and that's my business tomorrow.

Isaac thinks this is too funny.

—So, see this trim, Angel. Don't fuck it up.

—It's calm, I say, snapping on my black latex gloves.

Pelumi turns, Isaac points and creases up.

—I'm not even gonna lie to ye bro, Isaac says, between breaths. Ye look like a fed!

—Hardly. They're my work gloves.

—They're your narc gloves, bro.

—Nah, man, I finessed them from the science lab in school.

Pelumi nods and salutes.

—Wagwan, Angel.

Anyway, it feels like the right time to say it, so I go:

—How much Delfina charge?

—Tenner, why?

I gotta play this sharp. Start high to get where I really wanna go.

—Cause I'm thinking of doing the barbering, innit. And a bit of bread be nice, yuno.

Pelumi just turns, holds that stare of his for ages.

—What ye saying, bro?

—Fiver for the trim, bro, yeah.

Isaac's giggling behind his hand like some wet yute. Pelumi's still turned to me.

—I will knock you out you try that shit on me man. Fiver! Pelumi says.

He kisses his teeth and faces forward again.

—Just gimme a trim. Man getting played out here by his mandem.

—What if then, like, ye let me take a Before and After shot for your socials? Then you give me a shout out?

Pelumi sucks real slow and loud on his slushy.

—Hey Isaac, he finally says, low, relaxed. Our man Angel is looking for clout, yeah?

Isaac nods, lips dipping, impressed.

—Angel lad looking to go clear of Delfina, Pelumi says, and they think this is too funny again.

—Allow, I say, trying to play it down, like it's not important.

—Angel been slept on too long, bro, Isaac says.

—Yeah man, I say, feeling positive vibes building in the room.

—Man wants recognition, Pelumi nods. That's all good. But swear down, if this trim is dead, me and you gonna have beef again and there'll be no Before and After for your barbering.

—I'm out here saving lives, innit, I say. Put some respect on these clippers.

It's all a bit of banter, but God knows I take a second to steady my hand when I turn the clippers on. I get ready to add the fade line with my half guard and Isaac goes:

—Ooohhh, and winces.

Everyone's creased up again cause they're wasted but I focus like I never focused on anything before.

*

The Polish mafia run the deli in SuperValu. I can't lie, I'm shy around them. Yeah, I'm a little bitch waiting to be told what to do, and I hate myself for it. If I could bring the vibes I have when stalling it down the street with the boys, I'd be on the rise, big man thing.

Instead, I'm quiet and weak. Though I'm not as bad as the other stranger on the deli staff: Khushdil, from Pakistan. He's like a slave to the customers.

—How are you, Sir? Thanks, Sir, enjoy very much, Sir.

If they think I'm saying Sir to the tapped elders they're gonna have to pay me more.

When I come in after school, they get me washing and brushing out the back. Never on the actual counter. Swear down,

I'm a glorified cleaner. That's alright, though, yeah, cause I don't
have to wear no hat, ruin my trim, nothing like that.

So I'm brushing up the breadcrumbs from the bakery when
next thing Lorcan the cameraman calls, old school, like, and I
know then it must be important.

—Yo, Angel. I was talking to my bro's friend. Told him a
mate was looking to use the barber's.

I leave the brush against the wall, lean on a table, freaked.

—What he say? I ask.

—All he wants is a month's rent upfront and a promise you'll
pay the electricity. He said he's already paid the insurance for the
year. He's a bit off his head lately, but he seems legit enough. Said
he'll probably be back soon, but if things go well, you can take
the spare chair.

—When can I open?

Lorcan laughs.

—You're eager. Once you got the month's rent, you can call
him and get the keys.

Before he hangs up Lorcan is all like:

—Yo, what's the suss man, haven't heard from Pelumi in a
while. What's going down? Any more tracks? When we doing
another video fam?

I play it sharp, I need Lorcan on side, but before I can even
say anything, Jerry the manager is tapping my shoulder saying
they're short and I gotta go help Khush.

The Polish mafia whisper about me as soon as I stall it behind
the counter with Khush. They're at their breads and the cakes, far
away from the steck elders in the queue, and the young ones looking
for sausages for their fat babies. I stick the dusty hat on, vexed my
trim's gonna be dead. My head's all over the shop, buzzing bout
that call and stressed now everything's so close. So close.

I've got my head under the glass, slopping out some Cajun chicken mix for this peng thing when I spy Pelumi's opps coming up past the pastries and rolls and coffee machine and shit. Swear down, the last thing I need is these paigons.

It's Paddy Mac's plugs Mart O and that lad Callum that gave me hands a few weeks ago. They go round starting on anyone who strolls down Mainstreet on their ones, throwing digs, pressuring lads all the time.

No lie, I hand over the plastic container to the peng ting and fix my stupid white hat and I'm pressured already. Verbals are coming, I just know it. Man needs gwop, I say to myself and then they see me. There's three of them. Shitden.

—Alright our, Mart O calls, big madman smile.

His other boys clock me too and one of them, the tall lad, has his phone out, pointing the thing at me.

Khush steps in and says to them:

—What can I get you Sirs?

This gives them all a laugh.

—Here boy, Mart O says to me, ignoring Khush. Boy get me some chicken, yeah?

Khush hasn't got a breeze what's going down. I'm thinking the Polish mafia gotta be at the breads ready to step in. They gotta have my back, yeah?

The phone is over the counter, up in my face. Them boys are laughing. I am pressured. Basically, yeah, I'm stressed.

—Ourlad, chicken! Get me some chicken boy!

They are so gassed seeing me behind the counter. Elders with their trolleys and baskets are stopped and watching now. Khush goes to grab some chicken but one of them goes:

—Nah, man. I want to be served by this lad.

The camera is still in my face.

I need the cash.

Man got plans, innit?

I lean down and scoop up a handful of chicken pieces in my gloved hand. I'm thinking of the black PVC gloves I wear for my barbering. How I wish I was barbering now.

I put the chicken into the small clear plastic container and weigh it.

This tall guy filming with his phone smiles, smirks like he's so chuffed to see me pressured. He turns the camera to his face and sticks his tongue out and goes:

—Lil Pel's crew serving up fresh fried chicken like the bitches they are! Yo Pel, who's Blazing Boy? Who's Blazing Boy?

I hand the chicken over the counter and one of the lads takes it and turns to the camera and goes:

—Lil Pel's chicken is shit!

From the get-go, I was ready for it to get activ, so when one of the boys fires the chicken at me, I dodge it easy. It hits Khush on the chest. But I'm shook. I'm not gonna lie. I wanna throw hands but Khush is all:

—Hey, hey, hey, arms out trying to calm everything.

The three of them walk off whooping and yeeowing.

I say thanks to Khush for having my back and as I do I see the Polish mafia, Konrad and Pawel, behind the bread counter, watching. I feel bad for Khush having to get involved, he's old like forty or something and has kids and shit.

I get down on my knees and pick up the bits of chicken and the container. I don't mind being on the floor, on the cold tiles, on bits of lettuce and cheese. It's calm. Not exposed. I feel like staying down here, outta the way for the rest of the day. God knows this shit is long and I'm not meant for it, but mans gotta keep grinding and believing. Some day soon, yeah.

I'm chuffed Princess agreed to meet me. It's a start. If yuno, yuno. I'm stalling it in FLC, at the window inside the door, so I can dash if need be. But Princess is late and I'm not gonna lie, I'm getting a bit vexed cause being left on your ones at a table and none of my boys with me is bad out. I flick through my phone and message Lorcan since I've got time. Ask him some questions because I wanna get shit locked in before I tell Princess. Reassurances, yuno, that it's all good, and the barbershop is ready to go.

The table beside me is filled with a disgusting elder, slabbering his chicken all over his scabby cheeks, his eyes nearly closed he's so out of it. Another table has a family, a ma and a da and two yutes, but the yutes are too shook being seen having a family dinner in FLC to even attempt look at me and chat shit about being on my ones.

Anyone that goes by, yeah, looks in at me and thinks, That guy's lacking. If Paddy and his boys see me they'll come in and cause beef. There was no other seats and this waiting is long but I'm not standing on the street on my ones like some tapped yute either.

Even Bossman Franco comes out from the back with all the scraping and frying and looks down at me like I'm a weirdo. I take out my curl sponge and get working on my head. I smile and tap my nails on the salty table, then flick through my phone with my greasy fingers smudging the screen.

The door whooshes open, the old hip-hop vinyl hiss and scrape of Mainstreet flies in. It's five past nine, on a Thursday night, and she's still wearing her school uniform, and she's still got her clapped school bag on her back. She looks peng though.

That smile. I'm so gassed. The uniform skirt goes to above her knee and them socks are pulled up and her legs are fire. I'm popping. Her hair is in a short afro. Normally, yeah, I'd say it's lacking if mandem has an afro. Man is broke that got a fro, yeah. Only Princess, swear down, she has a pink scarf in it, and she is on point. She is a peng ting, and I put away my sponge and get up cause it feels right. I wait til she has her bag off her back and sits before I ease back down too.

—Hey, I say, all calm, but really I wanna tell Franco to blast out Tupac's 'California Love' and hop up on the table and dance!

—Hey, she smiles.

She slides in across from me. The neon lights in the window wash over the side of her face. She looks as if she's glowing, her edges are bright and sharp like something from Naruto.

—You coming from work, that why you couldn't link up at the blocks?

She blows out a breath, shakes her head.

—Nah, the library.

—Eeey, I go. Study is rinsed.

—That why you're never in the library now? she says.

—Mans been busy, innit.

She looks at me like I'm jarring. I can't stop smiling.

—I've been busy, I say, correcting myself, putting a bit of respect on it. I'm getting things done, yuno. Getting my life ready, like you.

—Like me?

—Yeah. Look at you. Living your dream. Job in a high-end pharmacy, gonna ace the Leaving, yeah? College girl. You're going clear.

She smiles.

—What you order? she says.

—Mango juice.

—That it?

—I was being a gentleman, yuno. Waiting for you.

—A gentleman?

—That's me, innit.

—So you're a gentleman now, okay.

—God knows I'm gonna try.

—You weren't much of a gentleman in Pelumi's house the last time we linked up.

I try push back from the table only everything's bolted to the tiles.

—Allow, Princess, please. You know I'm sorry. Don't be extra. Swear down, I said sorry, yeah.

—I just need you to know that you let me down, Angel. It's not something we can just laugh off.

—Allow. Is this why you agreed to meet? Make me feel like shit? Cause I do already. Every day, every day I feel like shit cause I didn't help you. Stand up to him.

—And if it happened again, would you stand up to him?

—God knows.

—Yeah, she says in a whisper, confused, looking over my shoulder, like my words were spoken by someone behind me.

She catches Bossman's eye.

—You wanna order? he calls.

It's hard to hear him over the sizzling and the metal scraping.

—Kid's snack box please, Princess says.

—Kid's?

—Yeah, kid's, she reaffirms, serious face.

—You want anything drink?

—No thanks, she says. I'll share his mango juice.

Bossman smiles and she turns back to me.

—You'll give me a sup of your drink, right?

—It's calm, I say and then put my hand up. Yo, Franco. Junior box and two mango juices, yeah.

He gives a thumbs up.

—No problem, no problem.

Our attention returns to the dark blue table, the grease, the salt.

—Obviously, yeah, I made a mistake bringing you there. It's on me. But I'm changed. I'm like you, just like you.

She tries not to snigger. Shitden that's harsh.

—How exactly are you like me?

—No need for the verbals.

—I'm sorry. I'm intrigued.

—Ambition, innit. Vision for the future, yeah.

—What, in your music videos miming stabbing someone with your 'Rambo blade'? Ambitious, well done.

—Allow. That track, 'Blazed Boy', is gonna get a million views in the next few weeks. A million views.

—A million euro?

—Views.

—Oh. Wow, I thought you said euro – as in money.

I tut, edge back.

—You're dropping bars on my crew again. That's bad out.

—I'm not dropping bars. I'm interested in where you're going with this.

—Yeah, well, he's got management interest. English tour getting lined up. He's going over there in a few weeks for this major YouTube channel. Labels interested. Big things happening.

She nods along, looks me straight in the eye, her face still soft and lit pink on one side like she's stepped out of an *Attack on Titan* skyscape.

—That's cool. I'm happy for Pelumi, Ireland's number one thug-for-life driller.

Bossman calls from the counter. Princess roots in her bag for a handful of coins. No joke, twenty cents, fifty cents, ten cents. Man needs a bag to carry them to the counter.

—You finesse your piggy bank?

She shrugs, no smile.

—Something like that.

—Oh, shitden.

—It's okay.

—Ye don't need to pay now anyways.

I jump up and grab the tray. I feel bad out for chatting wass about her coins so I offer her a chip. This makes her laugh. I'm chuffed I can still do that.

She lifts her mango juice.

—To ambition and getting out of here.

—Amen, I say, and we sip from our straws.

—But you know he'll drop you quicker than he drops bars on his opps.

—He won't drop us. We're his boys. His crew.

—All you are is boys to fill up his videos so he can look cool.

—Hardly, I say.

But then I think about the other week when he was chatting about too many light skins in the shots.

—I mean, she goes on between sups of her juice. There's nothing to be gained by getting seen by one million people on YouTube talking about fighting and stabbing lads.

—Well, I say, hyped I have an answer to this. I'm actually on the up because of it.

She holds a chip at her mouth.

—How?

—That's why I messaged you. To tell you about my barbering.

—How is being a clichéd thug helping you with barbering?

—Pelumi, swear down. I gave him a trim the other day. I've steck DMs. All wanting me to give them a trim. I've been saving from my dead job in SuperValu and I'm close, this close to getting a barber's sorted.

—You serious?

—I can't say yet, it's not one hundred percent. But how do you think I'm able to pay for your dinner tonight?

—You didn't pay for it.

—Really?

And I take out some of the very fivers I got from yesterday's trims after school and I place them between us on the salty table. Obviously, yeah, I feel like a star in the hood.

Princess tries not to smile, but she is chuffed.

—You're grand, she says, lightly flicking the paper back to me.

—I'm grinding away, two jobs, allow. Like I said, I'm changed. Mans a gentleman now, innit?

She shakes her head, tries to lose the smile, but I know, yuno. I know she's gassed.

—A gentleman?

—A gentleman. Soon to be a bossman, gentleman.

Princess

He's across the road from the pharmacy again, pretending he's busy on his phone. Then Pelumi and Isaac arrive and they give each other the big man high fives and fist pumps. They don't look in my direction, not that they'd see me kneeling on the floor. Pelumi points down the street and they move off. I take an unsteady breath, and I'm like, why'm I shaking? I've highlighted that moment in pink: Pelumi is never gonna get a chance to threaten my life advancement again.

My gaze drifts back to the pharmacy floor, the empty carpet. Rayo is looking down at me from the counter and she offers me a warm, encouraging smile. I smile back and get to work.

I'm out the front to the left of the counter, polish in hand, cloth in the other, when the lady comes in. All the sachets of shampoo, the cough sweets, the condoms, are lined up in a tight little legion of products across the carpet. The smell of the polish is strong and I'm wiping away deep in the back of the shelf, just like Rayo asked.

Rayo greets the lady and I glance up, only I can't really see past the middle-aged swell of her stomach. She's wearing that light puffer jacket and flower scarf combo all the middle-aged white women in the town wear.

I don't pay any attention to the opening exchange between Rayo and the lady. It's only when Mr Brogan's voice enters, do I tilt my head up.

—It'll be a shame to lose your custom, Mr Brogan says.

—I wouldn't normally, only the other chemist is closer.

—But don't you live in Oakwood? Rayo says, a rustle of paper following her words.

I see Rayo hold up a small prescription.

—In fairness, now, my reasons for leaving are really none of your business, the lady answers.

—Oh, okay, Rayo whispers.

—I support all this type of stuff, the lady says, nodding down to me. But if I don't feel comfortable no more getting me prescriptions, ye know.

—I'm sorry you feel that way, Mr Brogan says.

I return to the back of the shelf. The bell rings above the door and suddenly Rayo is standing over me.

—You'll have to get this mess cleared away, she says, pointing impatiently at my lined-up products.

—And here, she says, leaning down and spraying me with a sample perfume. Air your work clothes properly before coming in here. Your top stinks of damp.

—I could only wash it last night, I say, still on my knees, embarrassed under the misty flower bomb.

I don't tell her I had to steal washing powder from the Home Ec room yesterday.

—Then you dried it too quickly. Stinking up the entire counter. We have standards here. You need to have standards. We can't be losing any more customers.

I hate myself for simply nodding. I'm like, wait, my smell? For real? Is she deaf? I know she can smell, but is she actually deaf too?

I don't say anything. Instead, I get back to work. And then I'm like, wait, more customers? How many have they lost because of us already?

*

Thursday afternoon into Thursday evening into Thursday night is my favourite time of the week. The library stays open until nine. All the fake, wannabe studiers shuffle away between five and six and, for the next three hours, I can pretend the large open spaces of the library are mine. I can enjoy the silent atmosphere without having to battle for space. Enjoy being able to work without distraction.

Whatever seat I want, it's mine to take – at the window on the recliner; up the steps in the corner on the spherical chair;

in the middle of the floor at the huge circular table on a simple wooden upright seat; or at the MDF alcove unit on the second floor on a stiff steel frame chair with a slim cushion. I usually opt for a large round table and spread out my books to give me a sense of what I need to cover.

Today I got lucky when I came in. An old man wearing one of those tweed farmer caps was folding away the local rag of a paper – the *Fingal Independent* – at his window seat, so I loitered in the non-fiction section and waited for him to vacate the space.

Yellow highlighter: Nothing in this world comes easy, without a fight. Even a good seat in the library has to be secured with dedication and commitment.

*

From nowhere a TY student is in the pharmacy on Work Experience on Tuesdays and Wednesdays. And she gets a black uniform top. All the scuffs and stains she wants and not a bit of washing needed.

Not that she has to worry about getting her uniform dirty. She stands with Rayo now, like a good little puppy. All dark chestnut hair, thick fake eyelashes, lovely rouge cheeks and fake-tanned hands. Erin is her name and she's so enthusiastic and personable it turns my stomach.

Thankfully we only work together for one hour each day. She leaves at five and I come in at four.

Things I normally do on my own, I'm asked to do with Erin. Things get done quicker, great, like, then what? I'm left standing round like a loser while she scurries back behind the counter to smile and secretly scroll through her phone.

Today it's the sanitary towels that need moving to a new display to make space for a full rack of sun-tan lotion. Rayo gives me a big thick cardboard box of Always and lists our instructions.

—God, this is so embarrassing, Erin whispers, as we're on our knees emptying the shelf.

—How?

—What if, like, someone I know comes in, and like, sees me up to my tits in pads?

She takes a look at the sun-tan lotion bottle.

—God, I need factor 50 no matter what. I wish I had leather skin like yours. I'd save so much on my fake tan.

She snorts to herself, so innocently. I smile back, politely.

After we're done, Erin tries to take the big cardboard box. Only I stop her with a sharp tug on the flap. A small pack rattles around alone in the carboard. Erin says there's space for it on the shelf, but I tell her there isn't, grab it from her and make my way down to the back of the shop.

Erin follows me. Our eyes meet across the storeroom floor, empty boxes and plastic wrapping between us. I keep my hand in the opening of my bag, the purple Always pack bright between the zipper.

I'm so embarrassed and I hate myself for being embarrassed. For getting caught.

We watch each other in silence. Erin shakes her head in disgust and leaves. I take the pack out of my bag and hide it. I leave the school bag open and place it beside Erin's so she'll see it's empty when she leaves. I hate myself for having to perform like this. For having to pretend like this, convince this girl I'm not what she thinks I am.

I walk back out onto the shop floor. Rayo and Erin are behind the counter, talking low while Mr Brogan is busy up the steps behind them. The classical music swells through the shop, a slow and mournful sound.

*

I'm in my runners that Becky ruined, so I have to walk slow anyway.

—Eey, you'd be quicker getting home doing the Moonwalk, Angel says, spinning round and displaying how fast he can move while doing it.

I laugh, pretend to slap out at him. All of my unspent loose coins jangle, so I pull back.

—I'm tired, is all I say.

—Yeah? Bossman's chicken not give you energy?

—I need more than chicken for all my study, the pharmacy, my special topic.

—Let me take your bag for you.

—No, it's falling apart.

—Allow, mans a gentleman, innit. I'll be gentle, yeah. Let me carry some of your weight.

We walk through town, the warm neon lights from the takeaways, the traffic lights, the car lights, the drone lights. The chaos of the night doesn't infiltrate the calming bubble Angel surrounds me in. I'm content, happy.

—Yo, look at me, Princess, mans on the rise with all my study, yeah?

He does this exaggerated walk, both hands holding the straps of my bag on his shoulders. His energy is so positive. His smile so playful and infectious. He makes me laugh. His whole vibe is like electromagnetic waves, like alpha radiation. I can feel it absorb into my very being, my tissue.

—Do I look like a nerd now? he says.

—Oh, so that bag makes you a nerd. So I'm a nerd too?

—Nah, nah, nah. You're too leng to be a nerd.

—Wow, okay.

—No lie. You're like, beautiful, but with low-key study vibes going on.

On we walk, Angel continuously dancing round me like a giddy electron. We can't stop smiling at each other and I'm like, who is this guy? Why is he interested in me? I want to be with someone who wants to be with me. For the right reasons. Not just to lips. To jeet. A sneaky link. I'm not some girlo he can find down the canal. I want more. I thought he wanted more. He had me convinced he wanted more.

—Do you ever rest?

—Do I ever rest? It's calm. I'm just juiced.

—Juiced, why?

—Cause I'm walking home with you, innit!

To have someone tell me something good about myself – other than old men sending me random DMs telling me how sexy my ass is – is cool. I need something positive in my life. Because the pharmacy, if I'm honest, the customers, the day-to-day working and dynamic of the place, it's not everything – anything – I'd hoped it would be.

—I'm sorry to ruin your buzz, but I gotta go do some more study.

His face darkens.

—Study's rinsed. You've done enough.

We cross at traffic lights, car lights blind us as we go.

—I can't stop. I gotta get this pharmacy course. Get my pharmacy.

—That's done. Swear down, relax.

—Okay, well then I still gotta work on my History special topic. That's not done.

He kisses his teeth.

—Hardly. What you doing it on anyway?

—You know that Black Power salute Tommie Smith and John Carlos did in the Olympics in 1968?

He shakes his head. I stop walking, nestle my chin into my chest, hold up my right hand in a fist. He explodes in recognition, pulling his hand over his mouth to contain the excitement.

—No way! That's cold.

—I thought it was. My teacher's too eager to be seen as a woke cheerleader to actually revise it properly.

—That shit's on point though, yeah?

We walk by the police station, the high tower pulses red.

—You'd think I'd be inspired, but I'm like, wait, this shit happened over half a century ago. Half a century and the same issues are rampant in America, here in Ireland too.

He nods along, his hands still holding the straps of my bag on his shoulders.

—I know they deserve to be written about, only now I'm thinking, wait, what I've lived through these past years is history too, you know?

—God knows.

—These years, my life, your life, these are historic times too.

He chuckles.

—I dunno bout my life.

—I'm serious, Angel. Grand gestures from like a century ago are cool and all, but I should be writing about people achieving things now, small simple things like this guy Tunde who owned a pharmacy on Mainstreet a few years ago. I should be researching him, finding out how the fuck he did it.

—True dat.

—These times are unprecedented. This is history now and learning about guys who wore a glove and held up their hands during a national anthem is great, only I'm like, wait, surely the struggle now to live and become something positive is just as important to acknowledge? And if I don't do it, then who will?

—Shitden, Princess, I'm not gonna be able to help you carry all that shit weighing on your shoulders. This bag is heavy enough.

He stops dancing round me and stands and looks me straight in the eye.

—I'm not gonna lie, what you're saying is like, out there, wavy shit, yuno. But swear down, all this shit has got you shook. You need to chill, yeah?

—That's easy for you to say. You've got your life on track.

He shakes his head, all shy.

—Hardly. The only bit of my life that's going good is when I'm linking up with you.

I look over his shoulder at the apartment block. Try compose myself.

—I gotta go.

He takes my hand.

—Allow. The only way you're going home is if you Moonwalk there.

—I can't Moonwalk.

—Not with them dead runners you can't. Let me show you.

We both turn our backs on the apartments and Angel starts to beatbox and shuffle, my change jangling in my bag pocket as he does.

*

Becky's eyes are dark and they make her look old. Her cheeks that were chubby and always smiley, are drawn. Her braids are in bits, all loose and clumpy with a whole lot of dirt underneath. She doesn't know it, but the light from her phone doesn't do her any favours when it's held so close, especially when she sits in the dark like now. And it's always about an inch from her nose after Michael snapped her glasses.

This isn't the time to talk about money. No time is these days. Becky is always on edge, and I can't blame her. My mum is staying in Nigeria longer than we anticipated. My gran is refusing to give up. If I was her, I'd do the same. I'd fight. Always fight. Mum doesn't want to leave her. I understand, totally. Only her absence is having a serious strain on me and Becky. It's hard to maintain a relationship when life – electricity, gas, dinner, exam papers, nappies, baby food, pens, chores – continues to make demands, to ask questions of us and pull us apart.

—How's work? I say, to lead into my request, forking up my pasta like it's a casual question.

—Shit.

—Okay.

—I'm serious. Get a good Leaving, Princess, so you don't have to listen to absolute melts complain about their husbands not giving them enough money while you polish their fucking nails.

—No pressure, I say.

—I'm not even joking, Princess.

She never looks up, just scrolls through her phone while talking. She even puts food in her mouth without looking at her fork. Her tonsils are lit up, the saliva stringy and thick. Her lips blindly search for the food like a horse taking an apple from your hand.

—Well, eh, since you think my Leaving is so important, I don't suppose mum left any money to pay my exam fees?

—How much?

Still she scrolls.

—Hundred and sixteen.

Her fork hangs in mid-air, a drip of bolognaise falling in her bowl. Her left thumb moves off the screen. Her nails are a bright, shellacked white. She finally looks up.

—You're talking cap, right?

I shrug.

—You have to get a job, she says.

—I have a job.

—A job that pays.

—I will.

—When?

—When I'm in college.

—You won't get to college if you don't pay for your exams.

—I thought you could pay.

Her neck gives way and her head drops, the top of her scalp spotlighted by her phone, the dry scalp grainy and dense.

—Me? I'm barely able to pay for Michael's milk. And you want me to somehow get one-sixteen?

She kisses her teeth.

—I'm not being mean, Princess, I can't. We can't afford it. You need to get paid or get a new job quick.

—Please, Becky, I say.

She shrugs, like it's no big thing and returns to the phone, the shadows thick and gruesome on her face.

Tanya

Young ballers

♫ Mask Off – @Future

The camera settles on young kids, no more than ten, in Nigeria jerseys, kicking a worn leather football on an estate. Tanya flips the pov to selfie and smiles before the picture wobbles. Her head blurs and comes in and out of shot. Front pov again and the kids salute Tanya and pass to her. She passes back and gives the peace sign.

>116

I can tell Barry's had a few drinks by the way he opens the door and calls out onto the road with his voice all slurred. I turn and make my way over. He leans against the porch wall.

What ye doing with them? he says, a bit too loud for my liking.

What's it look like? What took ye so long to answer the door? Me da there? You drunk?

Don't encourage them.

What's that meant to mean?

He shrugs and puts this mush on and nods to the house next door.

Last thing ye want is them feeling like they belong.

The kids?

Don't be thick. Immigrants.

Cop on, Barry. You're drunk.

Easy for you to say. Ye don't have to live beside them.

Is me da here?

He'll be back. Come in anyway. I'm having a drink.

It's five o'clock Barry. I'm not drinking with ye again.

So ye take the dress I got ye, wear it down Home and now don't want to know me? Ye didn't mind having a drink with me a few weeks ago, did ye?

You got me drunk, Barry.

You weren't drunk.

You felt me up.

You didn't stop me.

When's me da back?

The ball bounces off the wall under the front window. One of the young lads apologizes and scurries away.

Your da'll be back in a while, he says. Come on in. Come on. Just hang out. And if your da doesn't come back, I'll put a good word in for ye anyway. Help him ignore all that Balbriggan Connected chat. You know there's other pictures going round of you.

You're talking shite, Barry.

I'm telling ye. Yer da hasn't seen them. No one really did. They were taken down real quick.

Then how'd you get them?

He smiles a lazy, drunk smile and leans against the wall to let me by.

*

I come in from school. Another shit day hanging out in the toilets vaping and dancing to stupid songs for some of the girls' videos. All I wanna do is have a green tea or something and go up to bed. Then I open the kitchen door and me ma and 'Chris' are sitting there all quiet like they've been waiting on me. It all makes sense now. I take a hold of the door handle to keep myself from collapsing. It's a shock seeing him there. Right there in me kitchen.

Hiya love. Sit down there, me ma says with this weird, respectful voice on her.

I'm grand here, I say, giving Chris's weird haircut a glance, nothing more.

Tanya, this is an old friend of mine, Chris …

I know who it is.

Wait love! Me ma says.

Alright Tanya, Chris goes.

Come in, take a seat love, please. I'd like yis to meet, my ma says, and scrapes a chair off the tiles.

I tut and look at him like I don't care.

We've met before. On the street and in Millfield, I say.

Chris was telling me, love. But, that's not the proper way to meet.

I just wanted to meet ye. Introduce myself.

Why?

Come on, Tanya. Ye know why, Ma says.

I wanted to see ye. Talk with ye, Chris says, smiling to my ma as if he's doing an audition and she's the judge.

Grand. Fine. You've talked with me. You've seen me. Now fuck off.

Tanya. He's trying to …

My sigh stops my ma in her tracks.

I know this is weird, Chris says. It's been mental for me too. Since I found out. But, like, I'm here in the town, like. I'm yer da and I wanna do what I can to get to know ye …

You're not me da, I snap. You'll never be me da. Me da's Derek.

That's coola boola. But I'd like to get to know ye too, if that's alright.

Coola boola. I'm not five, freak.

Tanya! My ma gasps.

Look at the state of him, Ma. He's a creep so he is. On me social media all the time and all.

My life is boring asf
♫ Ain't Shit – @Doja Cat
Tanya is lying on her bed, hair spread out on the pillow. She looks into the camera, wide eyed, her head moving from side to side trying to find the best angle. She shrugs before exhaling a cloud of smoke.
>88

Dean

First thing Cian says when I answer the front door is:
    —You get your da's medal back from them yet?
    I shush him in a hurry. My da passes by the kitchen and stares up the hall.
    —How the fuck you know about that? I say.
    —They were all wearing it in the Home on their socials. And I didn't see you in any pictures.
    —Yeah, well…
    —What your da say?
    —Nothing. It's grand.
    The medal box is always open – in the corner of the big dusty cabinet the landlord refuses to get rid of – in the back room. To get to the medal you have to stretch over the clothes horse beside the radiator. My ma asked my da to paint over the black mould in that corner ages ago, but he never did. He doesn't really go over to that side of the room because of that, so I reckon I'll be alright, for a few days at least.

Cian blows a short laugh:

—That lad Paddy rob it on ye?

—Course not, I say.

All I can remember is looking up from the rug and seeing Paddy's clenched fists raised in celebration – the medal around his neck – and everyone laughing.

—That must be the fee to hang around with them then. You know it's sold, Cian says.

—I'm actually getting it back tonight.

—I thought we were goin down Deli Burger?

—Another time.

—Ye know that lad Paddy is the lad in the video with Tanya.

—I never watched it.

—Maybe ye should. They're losers.

—Everyone's a loser to you, I say. Maybe take a look at yourself first.

Cian takes a deep breath as if he's ready to argue, but instead he turns. His grey tracksuit bottoms are stained at the arse from always being worn and never being washed.

*

Paddy's voice echoes through the tunnel. A train passes overhead, the pale windows lighting up the darkness for a few seconds. I stand and watch it thunder by. Once the track has stopped rattling and I'm in the dark again, I move.

On the embankment over the beach, I inhale through my nose, exhale through my mouth, slowly, as if I'm about to slide between the ropes and enter the ring.

Trawlers are waiting on the tide to come in. Their lights shiver on the calm sea. In front of the white reflections, I make out Tanya and Paddy and the rest of them on the roof of the lifeguard's shack. I think of Tanya's video. Wonder should I watch it.

Normally, if I'm out on my own and hear laughter and shouting like theirs, I'll do everything I can to avoid it. Instead, I whisper, Fuck it, and take the steps down the embankment.

Paddy and Tanya's legs are dangling heavily off the edge of the roof.

—Deano, ye mad bastard, what's the story, our? Paddy says.

He stands and puts out his hand to help lift me up.

The top of the shack is like a cement boxing ring. A big HI covers the whole floor in faded white paint. Marto and Callum are crouched over a two-litre plastic bottle of coke in the far corner. The other two girls are dancing for their phones.

Tanya gets up when she sees Paddy isn't going to sit back down again. She gives me a smile, just a little press of her lips.

—He forgot your medal, she whispers, like an apology.

Paddy holds up his hands.

—Nah, T. I didn't forget it. Deano has to earn it.

—But it's not mine. It's me da's.

—Bit of banter. Do something for it, like, earn it. Knock a lad out.

I look to Tanya to see if he's serious. She shrugs. Gives a grimace.

—I'll fight ye for it, a voice says, and suddenly Marto is beside me, his big leery head only up to my shoulder.

—Leave it out Marto. I didn't mean one of us, Paddy complains.

—Give it to me, Marto says.

The girls' faces go dark when they put their phones away.

—It was great craic in the Home with it. Moths loved it. I'll fight him for it. Sure his da didn't even win it proper.

Paddy frowns like Marto is becoming a distraction, a pain. Marto sways in and out of my shadow, his stupid pale face appearing too close. And then he says:

—I googled his da. Did you? He's a faggo …

My hips turn, my shoulders swivel into it and I extend fully. Left hand, left step coming down at the same time, pressure on my lead foot. Pop.

I don't over-commit. A simple snap. A jab. Something I practised and practised under my da's critical stare for years. The jaw jolts and the legs give way. I even surprise myself.

Marto is sprawled under the crossbar of the faded H.

—Deano lad! Paddy whoops.

I bend down to check Marto's okay and that's when I smell the petrol. It's dripping out of the coke bottle in his hand. A small puddle glistens beside him.

—Get up to fuck, Marto, Paddy says, and I take a breath of relief.

I'm pumped, absolutely buzzing. I didn't know I still had it in me. My fist is sore, and I hope it won't be a problem later if I want to crack one off in the new Cian style.

A small flare sparks in the corner of my eye and Paddy says:

—Get up ye fucking wimp.

Before Marto can even move, Paddy flicks a match.

The petrol rises into a small blue bloom and a thin layer of it licks over Marto's runner. He gasps and jumps to his feet, launches himself off the roof and legs it to the sea.

Our laughter follows him over the rippled sand. Paddy especially finds it hilarious. Tanya and her mates have their phones out. Behind us a small flicker of fire remains over the dark patch.

—That was some jab, Deano, Paddy says, watching Marto run.

—That was mental with the match, I say.

—Bit of craic. Not like the dig you threw though. Serious boy. You could do damage.

—Ah, it was just a tap. Did I win my medal back?

—I thought it was yer da's?

I look closely at Paddy. The eyes, the stubble start of a moustache over his top lip, the cap high on his head, as if he's afraid it'll ruin his hair. I'm as tall, maybe even taller than him.

—I'll show ye the stance, I say.

He comes close and we turn to the fire.

—Right, I say. Ye don't wanna stand too tall, or square on.

He nods and I talk him through it.

*

—Ye made sure not to wear your Adidas tonight, Cian says.

Even in the dark, he notices my shoes straight away. Other than the shoes, we have nothing to talk about. I expect him to say something when we walk under the weak boxing club lights. Nothing.

So instead, I do.

—I'm thinking of going back in there next week.

—Where? Cian says, looking ahead, stiff in his new pressed shirt, the oversized collar.

His nervousness annoys me. I rattle the big spray-painted door.

—In there. The boxing club ye dope.

—Yeah right.

—Serious. Me and Paddy. He's always wanted to, so I said it's grand. Just walk in, chat to Ryan, pay your subs and put the gloves on.

—Ye never asked me to go?

I laugh him off and get moving again.

Paddy, Marto, Tanya and Rihanna are waiting for us under the viaduct at the harbour.

—Come on, Deano, they call.

—Deano? Cian mutters with a chuckle.

—Yeah, Deano, I snap back.

The pink neon HO E sizzles brightly above the three dark figures standing at the top of the steps of doom. They're watching us.

Cian nods a quiet, embarrassed hello as an introduction to Paddy. I just do a random:

—This is Cian.

To try and distance myself from him.

The small bouncer surveys the growing queue, his chin raised, looking down his nose from his platform. We all wait for a sign from him to progress.

—Don't say anything, I warn Cian through gritted teeth.

Tanya and Rihanna go ahead of us. They're wearing these tight dresses with no real fabric on the side, just strings, and if you kind of close your eyes you can imagine they're naked. I'm two steps behind Tanya as she climbs. I nearly trip.

The three bouncers stand to the side and let everyone pass, until me and Cian make the top.

—Not tonight lads, one of them says.

I take a moment to compose myself before saying anything. But Cian whines:

—We're with Paddy.

—Here, Paddy, the small bouncer calls.

Paddy has opened the door into the club. The beat is massive and the heat hits you like a Libero's pizza oven.

—Paddy, you know these lads?

Paddy points at me.

—Yeah, Deano's sound.

Then points at Cian.

—Don't know him.

And just like that, the big bouncer steps aside and opens his arms wide for me to go on through.

Paddy and the girls are waiting at the opened door. The sound is already swallowing me, swamping me like the Russian crowd on Rocky after the Drago fight.

—Dean? Cian says, like how dare I do this to him.

There's no time to feel bad about what I'm doing. It isn't like I'm the one not letting him in. It isn't like he needs a hand getting home. Sure we didn't even talk on the way down, we would barely have talked on the way back.

—Another time, Cian, yeah? I say, and turn.

The smell of sweat, the heat, the music, the sex. My destiny. My friends.

No dry ice this time. The place feels smaller now. Paddy and Marto don't smile. They don't even dance. Tanya and Rihanna go straight for the dance floor and I want to go with them. Paddy takes a hold of my arm, shouts in my ear:

—Where ye going man?

—With the girls, I say.

His eyes crease up and he looks disgusted.

—Get some fucking drinks into ye man. Fuck the dance floor.

We go up to a balcony and drink, standing there watching everyone laughing and grinding below us. Paddy and Marto spend the night smirking and shaking their heads. I can't tell how much is too much. Paddy is buying me vodkas and coke or whiskeys and coke, doing shots with me and I'm in absolute ribbons. Delighted but.

Angel

Pelumi's gotta free gaff. There's bare heads there, smoking and drinking. It's vibes though.

Isaac and Benni are playing FIFA and the beats are massive on Isaac's big Bluetooth speaker. In one hand Pelumi's got a bottle of Jack Daniels and in the other his maggie.

—Wagwan, Angel, he shouts, flaked on the couch beside me. What's that SuperValu shit up on the socials?

Isaac shakes his head, laughs:

—Man, them boys owned you, Angel. That tall guy was chatting bare wass bro.

—They never owned me. Those lads are a pack of fools.

—They pressured you bro, Isaac says.

Pelumi swigs from the whiskey.

—Hardly bro, I tut.

—They had you shook, Angel. They called you out too, Pelumi, Isaac goes.

—Hardly, Pelumi says.

—I wasn't stressed.

—You pussied out bro, Isaac shouts.

And Pelumi's watching someone's phone now, holding his chin, nodding as a clip plays.

—Swear down, it looks bad on the crew this clip does, Pelumi says. They posted that shit.

—Man needs a job, innit, I go, trying to be heard over the music, the phone and FIFA.

—Not if you're getting pressured on all the socials.

—Say nothing.

—I'm serious bro. That shit gets Paddy clout. Calling me out. Makes us look like bitches. Mandem don't work behind a fucking deli counter serving wet yutes like a slave.

—Allow.

—I'm serious, bro. Mandem can't wear that SuperValu uniform, get pressured behind a counter on all the social and be in my videos. Pattern up. Ye get me?

—What about Jordan in Burger King? Eniola in McDonald's? And Dalton in that Chinese in the garage?

Pelumi turns to me, dead serious.

—See any of them in the videos these last months? See them here tonight? Man, I'm going clear. I am ready for the top, and I'm not having no clout-chasing white boys call me out on socials, making me look like a bitch, knocking me off track. I'm going London in three weeks bro. I'm doing Next Up. They've got over a million subscribers. The bars I spit will be seen by a million, two million heads. Swear down, I am not having my cred ruined by these wastemen, and my crew been seen serving yutes like some sorta slave. You only get so many chances, innit. Gotta make them count. My flow is my way outta here, bro. You aint gonna ruin it. And God knows, I need a trim for London and you're slave boy deli-counter hands aint going near my head again.

Pelumi leans forward and grabs the phone from Isaac. He shouts for FIFA to be turned off and the music to be changed to just a backing track beat. Pelumi goes Live, there and then, spitting bars about Paddy and the tall guy that disrespected me – and him. Everyone oohhs, and shouts approval with every bar dropped. Pelumi, no lie, is on fire and this tall boy Dean is getting owned.

*

Basically, Pelumi's gaff is popping all week long. His ma's still away – as usual – and it's activ. No FIFA tonight, just flaking out on the couch with Pelumi and Isaac. The three of us packed tight, sharing a spliff and supping. There's bare heads here too.

The maggie is a weird buzz. And into that the grass has my head frassed. One of the boys takes a picture of the three of us and Pelumi holds up his Jack Daniels bottle and goes:

—Yup the boys! Here's to Next Up, yeah.

All I can barely manage is a smile cause I am licked.

Obviously, Next Up is next level for Pelumi. Seeing him drop his bars at that spot on the river in London at night, with the city and all the skyscrapers in the background, is gonna be a mad thing. Isaac and Benni are buzzing bout it too, since them boys gonna be by Pelumi's side. The producer for that has got hard beats and he'll make Pelumi straight bang!

Isaac's Bluetooth speaker is shaking the room. My eyes are so heavy, and next thing, no lie, I start tripping – or at least I think I'm tripping cause a white elder – probably about thirty or forty, strolls into the room like he owns the gaff.

Swear down, my mind says dash cause this guy's a fed for sure. Or if he's not a fed, he's the landlord. And if he's the landlord he's gonna be pressured by how activ his gaff is.

Next thing the elder strolls straight over to Pelumi in his dead green bomber jacket and this dusty ass baseball cap.

God knows he's a narc gonna bust us, only instead of taking out handcuffs and grabbing Pelumi, he smiles and waves to him. Obviously yeah, I'm too wasted to dash, but I'm sure Pelumi's gonna throw hands.

No lie, Pelumi gets up from beside me and grabs the white guy's hand and shakes it! Then he turns to me and goes:

—Here Angel, get up, yeah, make some space for Neil.

Like I said, I'm wasted, man can't even lift his head, so I'm not budging. Instead Pelumi says:

—Here Isaac, get up there, make some space for Neil and give him a pull on that, yeah.

—Thanks guys, but I'm good.

—Have a swig on the whiskey then yeah?

—All good. Seriously.

—Get licked on the maggie.

—Ah, no. Grand thanks.

—Isaac, go out the kitchen yeah, and get the man some water. What a dry shite.

The couch shuffles and shakes and Isaac leans on my leg to get up and then I can smell Neil sit down and press up against me. Pelumi shouts:

—Thanks for coming down, Neil.

—It's all good. Glad to be here. Great to see what your scene is like.

—Yeah, it's popping bro, Pelumi shouts over the music.

—Popping?

—Activ like.

—Activ?

—Busy.

—Oh, course, cool. Energetic. Yeah.

Nothing, this guy, swear down, Pelumi normally wouldn't have a bar of lads like this.

I start to drift off but then:

—I've sorted your flights and hotel for London.

—Nice one, Pelumi says, his voice high, like a kid after being surprised.

I think my cheeks lift.

—Didn't I tell you I'd sort it, dude? If I'm gonna manage you, I'm gonna manage you right, White Guy Neil says.

—Safe bro.

Pelumi is so eager and thankful I nearly snigger into the arm of the couch.

—I've sourced another producer too for when you get back. This guy is so hot right now. Bit more mainstream. Like I said, you need to be making the move to more conventional rap. Transitioning. Respectfully.

—Bless man, bless.

—And I've got another production company to do your next video.

—Yeah? I like Lorcan though man. He's on point.

—Yeah, your past videos are good, but amateur hour is over, dude.

—Allow.

—I'm just here to tell you the truth. You've outgrown him.

—Oh, alright, it's calm, calm.

I can't believe what I'm hearing. Pelumi is just acting like this white guy's plug.

—What you up to now for the 'Blazed Boy' views?

—Seventy K off one million, yeah.

—Wow, White Boy shouts, like he's just won the lotto. I mean, wow! Do you have any idea? Like, that is incredible. It's out, what six, seven weeks? No mainstream artists in Ireland, not one, could dream of numbers like that in that space of time. What you have right now, dude, it's off the scale. When you hit one million you gotta throw a party. Go Live and make a big deal of it.

—Cool, Pelumi says. Yeah. I like that idea. Nice one, bro.

—Cool. And no whiskey anymore, dude. You gotta stay clear-headed, focused on being who you need to be to make it.

—What? Chap, you're jarring.

—You wanna drink whiskey and make a fool of yourself, get arrested, stabbed, injured before London? Fine. We won't work together then. Otherwise, no more hard drink. That's for amateurs. I don't work with amatuers. You gotta be a pro now. My pro.

Pelumi calls:

—Yo Isaac, come here, bro, listen to this. Tell him Neil. Listen Isaac. Flights and hotels and shit are booked for London, bro.

—Deadly, Isaac answers, his voice now coming from above me. Where we staying?

—About that, Neil shouts.

Pelumi's 'Blazed Boy' is starting up. The elder goes on:

—Listen, as much as I'd love all you guys, this whole room to be there and all, I could only get flights for two. Me and Pelumi. I gotta be over there and work on a few things. And the hotel room is only for two. Me and Pelumi. Like I said, I have to be on site to make some connections. And Pelumi, well, Pelumi is Pelumi, right?

Pelumi's voice is so deep and full of bass on the speakers. The floor is shaking. Ridiculous flows. The beats make it straight bang!

—What about Pelumi's crew for the video? Isaac goes.

—I get your concerns. Respectfully, one hundred percent, White Boy Neil says. I've spoken to the promoter for Next Up. He's got four or five Black guys who can stand behind Pelumi and be his crew for the night. It's all good.

The beat shakes the room and Pelumi's slick chorus cuts through loud and swear down, the whole house hears the line and shouts with him:

—*Man don't show, where he go? Man done run, I fucking know. Blazed boy! He's blazed boy!*

Tanya

The girls that get it get it

♫ Yoncé (Homecoming Live) – @Beyoncé

A montage of short selfie clips of Tanya in a nightclub: dancing, vaping, posing in the mirror of the girl's toilets. Her arms are around a short girl with a ponytail. Another girl, large with big hoop earrings, is doing shots with her. Tanya's tongue is out and she is smiling, looking down on the dance floor from the balcony. Dry ice clouds the shot and green laser lights blind the picture. The last clip is of two lads; one with a cap high on his head, small moustache, the other is tall and thin, unsure of himself. They do shots and then scream into the screen.

>1588

In fairness to Barry, he got me a deadly dress from Bohoo that has all the girls raging and all the lads staring.

What's the story with your man Deano? You linking up with him? Rihanna shouts over the beat.

Yeah, kind of, I shout back in her ear.

He's more interested in Paddy than you, Britney roars, leaning over Rihanna to be heard.

Stuck together, Rihanna laughs.

Bromance, Britney adds.

They just talk shite about boxing, I say.

Defo not you anyway, Rihanna replies and her and Britney laugh into their straws and take a sip.

We all look back out over the dance floor and point out the state of some of them.

Paddy say anything to you about the video? Rihanna shouts.

He apologized.

He not say anything about his story afterwards?

What story?

It was up there too.

No it wasn't.

Britney nods and leans in again. It was, she smiles. He put it up about a week after when you deleted your account.

Whatever. At this stage, I don't give a shit. Ye see Sarah O'Neill's story last night?

My name gets called from behind us and Paddy is there waving for me to come over. He's all smiles with his arm over Dean's shoulder. I look back at the girls as I go. Britney and Rihanna aren't smiling anymore. Dean and Paddy watch me approach like they're imagining what's under the dress. I squeeze in between them, patting their legs. They're both drunk.

Here T. Pick. Me or Deano, Paddy says.

Pick what?

Me or Deano. I'll allow ye. No bad buzz.

What am I picking?

It's cool, Dean slurs, stretching across me to Paddy. Leave it. Me and Tanya are cool, yeah Tanya?

The girls are watching us with their straws in their mouths.

Nah, nah, nah. It's okay Deano, Paddy says. She can have one of us only. Which one?

None, I say.

Nah, ye can't cop out like that, Paddy laughs.

Leave it, Paddy, Dean goes.

Deano here or me?

Okay, okay. Dean.

Paddy lifts Dean's arm and shouts, We have a winner!

Paddy gets up and staggers over to the others and then they all turn to lean over the balcony and look into the smoky mess of bodies.

Don't mind him, Dean says. I'm just lucky enough to be here, beside you. That's enough for me.

Why are you ignoring me all night? Did you see those pictures too? Did Paddy show them to you? I say in his ear, so close I can smell his aftershave.

Pictures? I've never seen nothing. I don't need to. I think you're beautiful. We're talking now aren't we?

Any time we do anything, you're always ignoring me the next time I see you. Like you're embarrassed by me.

How could anyone be embarrassed by you?

He hiccups and lets his head rest against the back of the couch.

You mean that? I say.

His eyes close, and he sways his head with the music.

Course.

I sit on his lap to wake him. Straddle him to get him going. Put my chest in his face and lean down and kiss him.

Whenever you're drunk you always say the nicest things, I scream over the music.

His eyes stay closed but finally there's some movement. He sits up suddenly, brushes me off him, his hand rising to his mouth, heaving. Then he pukes over the edge of the couch.

A hangover will last a day
♫ Drunk Memories with nightli – @nightli
A selfie of Tanya on her bed, holding her head. The screen flips to photos from the night before. Tanya dancing, eyes closed, hair in mid-flight, smiling. Tanya posing with two girls and two lads in different stages of drunkenness. Tongues out, peace signs, middle finger salutes, gang signs.
>76

He's the weirdest guy, Dean. It's like, he says these lovely things and then the next time I see him you'd swear the words never passed his lips and he's all about Paddy and getting his stupid medal back. I feel guilty about that. I'm the one asked him to bring it that time.

Of course, this only delights Britney and Rihanna cause the last thing they want to see is me linking up with someone like Dean, someone Paddy obviously respects.

Why am I even hanging out with people that make me feel shit about myself? It's impossible to ignore them when they message, ignore them when they call, ignore them in school. So I just go with it and hope someday Dean remembers the cool things he says to me. Maybe when we're all on the lifeguard's shack he'll say something to prove everyone wrong, and convince me that I'm worth knowing. Worth being with.

Creepy ass man wont stop staring
♫About Damn Time – @Lizzo
Selfie shot of Tanya standing against a shop window shrugging her shoulders. The pov flips to an old man across the road watching her. The street is busy. It's late and yellow taxi signs parked along the path shine like glow sticks. The green pharmacy sign spins and the FLC neon meal deal signs darken the picture exposure. The shot zooms in on the man. He is obscured by passing traffic. The pov goes back to Tanya. She gives the finger and mouths the words to the song.
>23

Da? Da! It's me da, open the window, I say.

He rolls the window halfway down.

Hiya Tanya.

His eyes are bloodshot and have massive bags under them. He hasn't shaved in a while. I can smell his car freshener through the small gap.

Hiya da. You working?

Yeah, look, I've gotta do a pick up. Chat to ye again.

Da! Wait. When?

When what?

Will ye chat to me again?

What? I dunno. Whenever. In a while. I'm working.

I miss ye da.

Thanks, love. I'm tryina sort me head out. These've been a few mental weeks. Your ma told me about Chris calling.

But I told him to fuck off. You're my da. And I miss ye.

Look, I gotta go.

The car moves away a few feet, the red brake lights come on and I think he's changed his mind. Then the yellow taxi light shuts off, the red tail lights disappear. He's in darkness as the car revs down the hill.

Princess

I can't bring myself to ask Rayo for pay. Instead, I have to put up with Becky doing extra shifts late on a Wednesday and Thursday. This means no study for me because I have to collect Michael at five from Claudine and keep him occupied until he sleeps. Only then can I study, and by that time I'm normally too tired to really take anything in.

I'm on my way home from the library to collect Michael when I see Angel at the monument across from Deli Burger.

Michael's minder said if I was late once more, we'd have to find someone else. I'm already late.

Obviously, I can't stop and talk with Angel. When I see him these days it's like my heart is a Gummy Bear being dropped into potassium chlorate. I'm a rush of emotion, expectation, excitement. I'm a gush of purple heat in a reaction to his positivity. Only this evening, I'm under so much pressure I can't even think about basking in this feeling.

—Wagwan Princess, he says, a cheeky smile.

—Not today, Angel, please. I can't stop.

He skips in line as I dash by. The river flows heavily under the monument and this noise mixed with the traffic adds to the chaos of my head, my heart.

—Where we stallin it?

—I've a headache. My eyes are sore. I'm late to collect Michael.

—Allow Princess. I thought you said we'd buzz up to FLC today?

—Plans change. My sister's plans changed, so my plans changed.

He's struggling to keep up. And then my runner comes off. My foot just slips out of the heel, and I stagger and catch a glimpse of my big toe.

—Let me carry your bag, he says and reaches out for it.

I shrug him away, bending over to block his view of my sock, and shove my foot back in, start moving again. I take a hold of both straps on my shoulders, feel the heavy bounce of the books.

—Eeey, he says. I was looking forward to some of Bossman's mango juice and fries, yeah?

—Well, I can't. That's life.

—Allow, I was only saying.

We stop at the traffic lights. I'm not angry with him, I'm angry with Becky and my life. I slap the silver circle to make the green man appear quicker.

—I'm only buzzin with ye, Princess. I don't really care about the mango juice.

I don't turn to look at him. If I did, I reckon I could cry. Fall into his arms and sob.

—I was just hoping to talk to you about my barbering, yuno?

And to stop the tears, to push the thought of Angel saving me, supporting me, I turn to him and sneer:

—Why?

—I dunno. Cause I wanna bounce ideas off you, yeah? My options, yuno?

—Options?

I laugh. The little man finally glares green. Cars ease to a stop.

—Yeah, yuno, options.

—Get real, Angel. Grow up. The barber's is never gonna happen. You're in the deli for life.

—Eeey, harsh, he goes.

I take off across the road, my words, those cruel words, hanging like nitrogen dioxide in the air.

There's no time to explain how I'm feeling. Only once across the road do I glance back. Angel is stood at the traffic lights, hand on the pole, watching after me, stunned. I hope my words haven't poisoned him. Toxic and destructive, corrosive and heavy.

I'm like, wait, just because my dreams are collapsing doesn't mean I have to take it out on Angel. Seeing him progress, hearing him talk about progressing underlines how I've stalled – maybe even gone backwards. I can't stand this, so instead of taking control of my own life, and concentrating on what I can do to improve my situation, I'm trying to knock his. Even us up. What a lousy thing to do. What a lousy person to be.

*

Me and Erin are outside on the street, newspaper scrunched up in one hand, window cleaner spray in the other. We're meant to be doing it together, only it's me who is literally getting my hands dirty. I'm physically scrubbing the newspaper over the window, mixing the window spray with the seagull shit, creating a greyish black paste as I circle it around.

Erin, her lilac nails too long to grip balled up paper, holds the bottle at arm's length. She screams when a breeze blows the spray back in her direction.

—Jesus, I'm nearly blinded. My mascara will be running down me face.

—Go on Erin, ye ride ye! comes from across the road.

Erin turns around in mock shock, her lips shrinking into a proud pout. I keep wiping the gritty shit with the newspaper, the white suds dripping down too quickly to catch.

—I'm scarlet. Thank God they're paying us to do this shite.

—You're on work experience though, I say.

—Yeah, and?

—He paying you?

She tuts and does a random spray on the window.

—Course. Think I'd be doing this for free?

When I stand back and analyze my current situation in the pharmacy as if it's some sort of sociological experiment, I come to the conclusion that the experiment – as well as being ridiculous to begin with – was only ever going to fail. There were too many negative external factors preventing the trial from being conducted with any sort of integrity.

Erin gets put on the till too. I'm like, wait, maybe she smiles better or something. And then, she gets brought up the steps to the back, Mr Brogan's hand on her shoulder, leading her around. I mean, that's it. All I can do is look on, polish and cloth in hand as he escorts her round the room, opening presses, pulling out trays, laughing as he does.

No one should be doing what I'm doing for free. What I'm witnessing in the pharmacy isn't work experience or life experience. It's the wrong experience. Micro-aggressions and low-key trauma are not services I should be paying for with my free time. Luminous yellow highlighter, general observation: Cynicism doesn't come without a cost. Pink highlighter, specific life-advancement threats: Other people will let you down.

*

I walk by Iwona's pharmacy every time I'm on my way to work. I go by as quick as I can so she doesn't see me. She's always there though, still wearing the impeccable white lab coat, always chatting or laughing. The pharmacist is there with her a lot, arms on her hips, a relaxed pose, as if they're equals. I think of the HEAR interviews. My competition. I think of what I need to do, and keep doing.

Maybe I'm asking for too much. Maybe I'm being hypersensitive, seeing things that aren't there. Looking for excuses, reasons why I'm not succeeding, why I'm not happy, why I should be paid. Maybe it's the pressure of the past weeks, the stress. Maybe I'm giving off negative energy and it's beginning to show, impact on how people perceive me.

Whatever is causing these situations, it can't go on. Especially with mum still being away. Either I get paid, so Becky doesn't have to work longer hours, so I can then study more, or I don't get paid, Becky still works longer hours and I don't study more, or I don't work, study more and Becky works longer hours. Something has to change.

—Rayo, I whisper while the store is briefly empty and Mr Brogan and Erin giggle away up the steps.

She closes the large diary and puts her pen down beside the cash register.

—Yes, dear?

She smiles and the thick hair in front of her ears catches in the light.

—Em, remember Mr Brogan said he'd pay me?

She glances over her shoulder.

—Did he?

—Yeah, he did. Like, I'm grateful, really, for this opportunity. I am. Only, things at home are difficult, and I need to either study or help my sis with money …

Rayo steals another quick glance before she fixes her collar and escorts me towards the front window.

—Child, she says, a hushed impatience in her voice.

We stop at the window.

—You're looking for money, after all I've done for you?

—You've done for me?

—Yes, I've done for you.

She lowers her voice, those bright eyelids flickering furiously.

—You think he wanted you here? You really think Mr Brogan came up to me and said, Well, Rayo, what we need to become is a charity for Black girls in the town who have dreams to be like me.

Rayo kisses her teeth with disdain, dismisses me with a wave of her hand.

—You saw me put your CV in the bin. I know you did. And I saw your face. I saw how disappointed you looked. I have a daughter, and a conscience, you know?

She lets out a long breath.

—I see you look at me like I'm a fool when all them white ladies talk to me like I'm a foreigner, like I'm not educated. I have a degree, in International Business Management, but that doesn't matter to you. Well, remember, it was me who gave you the chance. Me! I was the one who took your CV out of the bin, I was the one who convinced him to let you come. See that top you're wearing? That's mine. See that white work-experience girl up there? His niece. Who he organized to take on last year. You come along two months ago and shuffle in here like we owe you something and now you demand money for our trouble? I know about the sanitary pads too.

She stares at me, deep into me and shakes her head. I feel so, so stupid. So naïve. So embarrassed. This is not what I thought it would be. This is not what I'd hoped for.

—Thank you, Rayo, I say quietly, with respect. Thank you for looking out for me. I appreciate it. I do. Only, I can't …

There's too many things I want to say. Need to say. I turn and go to the storeroom and grab my bag. The work shirt unbuttons easy. Rayo is still at the window. I hand her the shirt.

—Please, thank Mr Brogan for the opportunity. It wasn't for me. And thank you for helping me Rayo. Now I need to help myself.

There are no tears on leaving the store. Angel's across the street – the North Face, one legged flamingo pose.

—Yo Princess, you good?

—Just walk me home, please, I manage.

He puts his arm over my shoulder and leads me up the street, whispering as we go:

—It's okay, yeah, it's okay.

Dean

In our usual spot, Paddy, Marto and me are watching all the saps swaying and moving like weirdos on the dance floor. Tanya and Rihanna keep looking up to us and waving. Tanya especially, keeps gesturing for me to come down.

—Not a hope, I call back.

She puts on this little girl pout and shakes her ass.

—Get this into ye, Paddy shouts in my ear and we do shots.

Marto peers over Paddy's shoulder. Dry ice gushes onto the dance floor like it's at the bottom of a space rocket. The beat drowns out the hiss. Paddy leans in and points down at Tanya.

—See that fucker there.

—Tanya? I say.

—No, ye mad bastard. The lad beside her. Look at him.

Reds and oranges start to pulse through the cloud like fire. I try to focus on the shapes, the lights throwing everything out of whack. Paddy's in my ear again:

—There. Right there, ye muppet. There's a lad recording T on the sly.

—What?

—I swear to ye. He's taking the piss out've T.

—Ye sure?

Paddy's stare is like a warning.

A few whiskey and cokes later and me and Paddy are in the

smoking area, standing under the door. Paddy keeps on looking up to the corner of the canvas roof.

—There used to be CCTV there, he says.

I'm too drunk to reply.

Tanya arrives, all smiles and sweaty from the dance floor. She hugs me real tight and I almost pass out in her smell. Paddy points to someone trying to get by Tanya in the doorframe.

—There's that lad now, Deano. Knock him out.

I can barely see straight.

—Knock him out, man, Paddy insists, his bottom lip cracked and stretched.

Before I have time to even make a fist, Paddy launches past me and smashes an empty pint glass over the lad's head. Paddy's elbow thumps off the back of my neck and Tanya screams and ducks. The lad falls to the ground in a heap, roaring. Blood oozes down between the fingers clasped over his face. Paddy tugs my shoulder and reefs me and Tanya over the crackling mess and back into the dry ice, and into the noise of the club.

—The next time I say to give a lad a straightener, you give him a fucking straightener, Paddy spits in my ear.

—Why?

—Don't fucking question me, man. If ye want yer medal back, don't be questioning me. These drinks don't come for free.

—Leave him Paddy. That was bad out, Tanya shouts.

—I don't know what's goin on Paddy. Where'd you even get the glass?

—That's what we do. That's what it takes. Ye need to be prepared man, ye gotta be prepared.

Tanya

NittyBoppin to Blaze Boy
♫ Blazed Boy – @Lil Pel

Tanya has the phone held out on selfie pov. Two other girls, one with thick lashes and dark eyeshadow, the other with straight greasy hair, are beside her and dancing to the song. They look serious as they concentrate on the moves. It's dark and their phones light them unevenly. A cement floor shakes into view, and a flash from a lighthouse can be seen in the background. They finish in a charge of laughter towards the screen.
>1554

Rihanna's all out've breath after dancing and laughing and she goes, That tune is banging, isn't it?

Yeah, he's going big in London I heard, Britney adds.

What'll Paddy do? I ask, and we all laugh.

We're having the buzz.

You send in your sex CV to be part of his girl crew for the next video? Britney says.

We all look ahead at Paddy, Callum and Marto sitting down the other end of the roof, facing out to sea.

I can shake my ass better than any of those bitches posting shit, Britney says.

And I can give head better than that slut from Oak Wood, says Rihanna.

Who?

Sarah O'Neill.

Paddy'd go mad though, Rihanna whispers, like the thought disappoints her.

Sure he wouldn't be watching that, would he? I say, and we all burst our shite laughing.

The lads look over their shoulders but can't hear us. They turn back to the horizon.

He's gonna cause a row with Pelumi anyways, Rihanna says.

Or he'll get Deano to, Britney says, and the two of them laugh.

Deano's a bit of an innocent boy, isn't he though? Rihanna's eyes are creased up.

He's cool. Paddy thinks he's sound, I reply.

Paddy just wanted his medal, Britney whispers.

He's giving it back, I say.

Rihanna scoffs at me:

You mad? I've seen it hanging in his room.

When were you up there?

Yup Rihanna! Britney says and shines her light on her before dancing over to the lads.

Rihanna takes out her vape, the purple tip brightens her face as she inhales.

Deano's harmless, she exhales. But ye think Paddy'd have him around if he didn't box? I'm telling ye, there's gonna be a row with Pelumi soon and Paddy needs a crew. He's freaked after the last time down the train station and everyone showing Pelumi all the love now he's getting famous.

He didn't say that about Dean did he? I say.

What do you think? D'ye really think someone like Deano should be hanging round with Paddy and the lads?

I think he's sound.

That's cause he's the only lad in the Brig who says he hasn't perved over your video. Paddy needs him for the boxing is all.

Nah, Paddy's not like that.

Paddy's rep got done after the scrap down the bandstand.

Why else ye think your video with him got shared?

That was a mistake. Paddy said his cousin put it up taking the piss.

Rihanna laughs and shakes her head.

Mistake? Paddy got loads of street cred again after that. You made him a legend cause it got in the papers and all.

Paddy said he was freaked about it.

Paddy talks shit to everyone.

Nah, he said he was sorry about it.

He said he'd give Deano's medal back too and there it is, hanging over his bed.

That's different.

Look Tanya, me and Paddy are linking up now. If ye wanna keep hanging with us forget about the video and keep Deano sweet, yeah? Paddy needs him round. His cousins are coming up for a few weeks so that's when it'll kick off.

Dean

The screen is so bright I have to squint. Paddy's holding the phone too close to my face. Everyone's breath smokes around me like we're back in the Home. It's so dark all I can see is the blur of YouTube's red and white and then Pelumi appears. He's sitting on a random couch, game controller in hand, and he goes:

—Yo, yo, yo, this your boy Lil Pel going Live.

Maybe he's doing a reaction video on GTA or something. A thin beat starts from behind the camera, a small snare and a round bass drum and then a piano note plays and he lets fly:

My boy Angel got got by surprise,
Man tyrna grind nine to five—

I ain't into the talking ting,
Samurai sword in the yard
It gonna swing—
Bare wet keyboard warrior Dean he's new,
Paddy's gonna get mouth fucked like Tanya
If that's man's crew—
Dean's da goes down bare times
Like Neymar—
This man's VIP in every Dub
Gaybar—
I warned my cats that blood gonna spill,
Dean chat that wass bro
Your da's too fat like Uncle Phil—
If mandem sees you, Tall Boy's dead,
Gonna get my Rambo and shank man in the
Head—

A slow, sad piano break loops over the beat for a second and then he goes:

Slenderman Dean
Yer da's a queen.

Laughter from Pelumi's audience, so much laughter, fills the final second before the phone gets whipped away.

Everything is darker than before. My eyes sparkle, tingle in the black vacuum on top of the lifeguard's shack. My ears are ringing, my stomach hollow, my chest tight. Everything is off balance. My head is melted.

—Five K views already, Paddy says. He's made an absolute show of ye.

—Us, Marto adds.

I don't respond. Can't. I am discombobulated. Paddy's voice sounds like it's underwater.

The push and pull of the tide returns. Tanya and Rihanna and Britney and Marto and Callum start to come back into focus. Their phones light their faces and everyone, bar Paddy, moves away from me.

—You'll need this now, ourlad, Paddy says, holding out something at his waist.

I don't look down, but it's got to be the medal.

—Ye gotta be ready for the shots that are gonna come your way now that you're one of the boys. Every man needs to be ready to protect himself and his friends, you know what I'm saying? We gotta be strong and show people we're strong otherwise they'll try and take the piss out've us again.

I clench my jaw, look into his eyes and say:

—Okay.

He sounds just like my da.

I hold out my hand for the medal. Instead Paddy places a stubby Dealz penknife in my palm. It would do well to break the skin of an apple, never mind an enemy on the mean streets of the Brig. I accept it with a serious nod of gratitude.

I want to throw it in the sea.

Tanya is with Rihanna and Britney across the floor. She's the only face not lit up by the glow from her phone. Her eyes reflect the other screens.

—Dean doesn't want that, she announces.

All faces go dark.

—She's right. Deano'll never use it, Marto says. Look at him, he's shitting himself even holding it.

—You don't know shit, I say, getting sick of this little prick trying to cause more grief.

I clench my fist round the knife.

Paddy watches me closely, almost like he's making up his own mind.

The little metal corkscrew grooves are smooth and warm in my fingers.

—I know Pelumi musta read that Reddit on your da, Marto says. I know that shit.

He has a glint in his eye. He's been waiting to say that since I put him on his back.

I snap forward and rock him again.

Tanya

2 much testosterone on these streets

♫Money Calling – Da Beatfreakz (feat. Russ Millions, RAYE, wewantwraiths)

The camera shakes in front pov. Six lads, hoods up, all in grey or black tracksuits, some in Canada Goose and North Face jackets, are ahead, walking down the street. Brief flashes of street lights flare the screen. The silhouette of another group appears in the distance. At the top of Tanya's gang, a lad with a light moustache, cap high on his head, turns back to search for someone. The screen turns to a tall guy. He's nervous looking, holding something small, hidden in his fist.

>186

Come on, Dean, I whisper close to him so the others can't hear.

He shakes his head without turning to me.

Don't be stupid, I hiss, trying not to raise my voice.

This is it Deano, Callum goes.

You ready man? Marto says.

Pelumi and Paddy face off. Everyone else hangs back, watching them.

Got your knife ready? Marto mutters to Dean.

Come on, Dean – I repeat – I'm not hanging round for this shit.

Again he just shakes his head.

Fuck ye then. I'm off.

And I back away from the madness. There's cheering voices from Pelumi's crew, tension in Paddy's crew. A crowd is watching from inside the windows of FLC. Bossman Franco is shaking his head like he's not having this. I don't blame him.

Angel

We're all buzzing to get into Bossman Franco and get warm inside. It's dark and there's steck puddles and I haveta watch how man walks. The heel of my right crep is wasted so I'm up on my toes, like I'm wearing high heels or something. I keep bumping into the boys, having the banter, shaking shoulders and shit so no one notices me on my toes.

And then, who comes strutting up the street? I spy them under the pharmacy sign, the cap, the dead grey tracksuit, big white socks, Nike Air Max, hands down their jocks on their balls. Paddy Mac and bout five of his crew. The same boys we gave hands to down the train station only a few weeks ago.

All my boys go quiet, but keep on walking. We shape towards each other. The splash of car tyres is all man can hear. I do the sums quick. Think, shitden, there's more of them than us. If I was to dip, the boys would notice. This is gonna be a scrap, and we're outnumbered. Only then I realize I forgot to add myself. So we're even. But yuno.

Pelumi moves out front, like the driller he is. Swear down, if it wasn't for Pelumi, I'd run. Pelumi though, yeah, he'll sort it – or get into a scrap just so he can use the footage for clout, or get action for some new bars – sort it that way.

—Play it sharp, boys, yeah, Pelumi says back to us, barely turning his face from the action ahead.

And then I see a light, like a small torch from Benni's hand. He's gone Live already for Pelumi's socials.

Shitden, it's gonna get activ.

From the light off Benni's screen, I catch a flash of a blade in Isaac's gloved hand. Isaac's getting ready to drench man down.

We're outside Spar now, two baked beans for two euro. Paddy and his boys stop dead, just clear of Pelumi's swinging distance.

—Alright our, Pelumi says.

I'm not gonna lie, Pelumi is wavy as fuck. Mans a legend. His voice is strong and loud and he's straight up, shoulder back, on fire.

—What you say to me? Paddy goes, chest out, chin raised, like he's the big man and he didn't get hands from Pelumi a few weeks ago.

He looks like he wants a knock.

—Alright our.

—You can't say that to me, Paddy says, thick now.

—Whatever bro.

Pelumi's not backing down, his legs spread wide, his shoulders back. Then I see one of Paddy's boys got a blade too. Big fuck-off kitchen Rambo and from what I'm hearing these boys are mad to shank. Mart O and Callum meant to be mad into scrapping too.

There it is, one of our boys and one of his boys with a blade and it's getting hot.

—You lads can't say it. Alright our. It's a Balbriggan thing.

—Hardly chap. Allow.

—I can say it. My lads here can say it. Aul lads from the Brig can say it. But you can't say it, ye get me.

—You're jarring bro. I'm from the Briggz. My boys here from the Briggz. These wet ends are dead, yeah, but they're mine.

—They're not yours, ourlad. They'll never be yours.

—What ye saying bro?

—I'm saying, no I'm telling ye, ye can't say Alright our. You lads don't even know what it means.

—Shut yer mouth, pal, yeah.

—Ye see. Ye haven't even a breeze what yer saying. Alright our is you asking me how I'm doing – and then yer telling me to shut me mouth? How can I tell ye if I'm shutting me mouth?

Paddy's boys smile at this bit of smartness.

—Nah bro, Pelumi goes on. That's not what I'm saying. I wasn't asking how ye were. I'm saying wagwan, fam. I'm seeing you and saying you're alright, our. Mandems giving you a salute, innit. Mans seeing you and yer alright. I'm telling you, bro, that I think you're alright. So you're alright!

Shitden, Pelumi has crisp bars, yeah. Everyone knows that. God knows his flow is unreal yeah, in the studio and on the street. But, swear down, hearing him spitting out the truth here on this shitty block, while cars creep past and heads peer out the windows all shook at the crowds, is lethal.

Paddy is all like, duh, duh, duh. Man doesn't know what to say.

Silence. Still the cars roll by, making that slick wet sound. Still that blade shines in the background and still Benni's got his phone out. The pharmacy sign spins a green puddle on the path and my socks are sapped and I swear down, it feels like ages, but Pelumi is only taking a break.

—And you, Pelumi goes on. If ye weren't such a fucking savage gripping yer balls like they're gonna drop off, you'd say back to me, Alright our, and we'd both dip then, chuffed, yeah, cause we saw each other and said we're alright. Mandem gave good vibes, yeah, by telling each other we're alright. But no, man stops there and cries You can't say that.

All our boys go:

—Eeeyyyy, and wince like Paddy just got rocked.

The knife behind Paddy's waist flashes. Isaac shuffles close behind Pelumi. I'm a bit stressed. Not gonna lie.

Paddy licks those cracked ugger lips of his. His eyes stare. You can tell he's stuck for what to say.

—Don't blame me man. That's the way things are round here. You lads say fam, we say our. If ye don't like it, ye know what yis can do ...

—We can say whatever the fuck we want. That right boys?

All of us cheer and shout:

—Yeah bro.

We sniffle and spit.

—We make our own rules. If I wanna say our, I'll say it, right boys?

And again, we all go:

—Dassit, Pelumi!

And cheer like a mad thing.

—We run these streets, we run this block. No son of an Olympian bitch boy goofy fucker, or some fake roadman with a blade gonna change nothing. That right boys?

—Dassit Pelumi, yup Pelumi.

Paddy is pressured and he steps up, goes head-to-head with Pelumi.

—Let's settle this out then, yeah.

—Allow, Pelumi says, holding his hands out, shrugging his shoulders like this is all calm. Settle what? Me saying our?

Swear down, for the first time ever, Pelumi sounds a bit shook. Don't think none of the other boys cop it. But I do. Normally, Pelumi would throw hands first, chat shit later. He wouldn't have a bar of Paddy going head-to-head like that. The way Pelumi says his line, yeah, there's a definite drop in it. Dunno, but there's definitely something lacking.

And no lie, from nowhere, like a mad thing, Bossman Franco dashes in between them, his eyes massive and black, a hurley over his head and he's shouting:

—Fuck off the streets!

Some other tapped elders with aprons round their necks appear behind him, all red faces and wheezing. And these boys start swinging hurleys like mad things too!

Next thing, more elders with dirty aprons flapping like fucking superhero capes come out've Deli Burger! Basically, everyone scatters and we're all laughing and blazing back to our ends, 100-metre sprint Bori Akinola style.

So much for FLC, Bossman and his mango juice. So much for tryin to keep my socks dry, my heels high. So much for Pelumi the driller. Mans backed down for the first time ever – and only Bossman Franco – of all people, saved him from looking like a bitch.

Dean

The face of the hurl slaps me on the upper arm and it stings like a mother fucker. I collapse to my knee in the shock. It comes from absolutely nowhere. I'm at the back so I get it first and turn and see the hurleys and hear the scuffle and the shouts. I leg it like I've never legged it before. Full on shoulders back, hands raised, karate-chopping the air.

Once I'm off Mainstreet I slow to a jog past the Pool Hall and Casino, through the low-hanging willow tree branches, down the canal and under the viaduct. I near go on my ear and break my ankle on the greasy cobblestones. My chest is burning when I make it onto the beach. The chaos left far behind. A hurling team of cooks running riot on the street, Franco in the thick of things, roaring and swinging like a mad man. I can't stop smiling. I put my hands on my waist and walk, head high, taking deep gulps of fresh, lung-stinging air, smoke streaming out like dry ice down the Home.

Callum and Paddy, and one of Paddy's cousins, are already at the lifeguard's shack, hands behind their heads, panting.

—Why didn't ye do anything? Callum gasps, bent over, holding his knees. That lad was laughing at ye.

—Pelumi? Paddy says.

—No, the other lad. The SuperValu lad. He deserved an awful slap, Callum adds.

—I was going to, but then everything went mental, I say.

—Ye can't let lads like him take the piss, Deano, Paddy goes. Ye have to sort that shit, or you'll be seen as a bitch. You're not a bitch, are ye?

The red lighthouse light flashes across his face. His eyebrows are high, like he's on the verge of being surprised.

—I was going to knock that guy out, swear.

—You have your knife with ye?

—Course.

—Next time fucking use it then.

—Next time I see him, swear to God, he's a dead man.

The words are ridiculous coming out of my mouth. It feels like someone else is saying them.

Tanya

Best way to get where I wanna go

♫ Ooh Ahh (My Life Be Like) – @Grits

Tanya sings into the screen in selfie pov. She's in the back of a car, the rear window lit up by shopfronts and street lights. Her head rests against a window. First a gang of lads at Spar, then shops and fast-food signs. They all go by in a blur behind the glass. They disappear in the distance out the back window of the car.
>102

Barry comes out of Bracken Cabs and sits into the passenger seat of a taxi. I get there in time and knock on the boot just as the car starts to move. The driver says, Who the fuck are you? as I hop in the back.

Ah Tanya, Barry slurs, ye coming back to the gaff?

His eyes are near closed and his heads bobs like it's too heavy for his neck.

You know this one?

That's Derek's daughter so it is.

Aahh, right, I see, the driver says, his eyes staying on me for longer than they should in the rear-view mirror.

Had a few pints so I have, Barry says through a small hiccup.

We tear off, flying down Mainstreet until the lights go red outside the hotel, across from Barry's barber's.

When ye opening your place up again ye mad thing? The driver pokes him with a finger, two little jabs to get an answer.

Barry belches, Sure I've got plenty of cash still doing nixers in me kitchen. Couldn't be arsed with the shop. Got too used to the good life after lockdowns.

Would ye not rent it out at least? Make some sorta cash, the driver says.

I've thought about it. Some kid wants to open it for himself and his gang.

Well that's something, I suppose.

The driver sniffs and taps his fingers on the steering wheel, waiting on the lights. Barry snorts.

Nah, amn't I after finding out he's Black. I'm not having an African barber's under my name.

I can't help myself so I go, Your name's not even on the sign. It just says Barber's.

What's it to you? Makes no difference.

Just give them the keys, Barry.

Jesus, this one, wha? the driver giggles, his eyes back in the mirror, watching me.

She's only a kid, sure. I'm not giving them lot the keys. I'm not that desperate, Barry mutters.

Now, now, Barry, the driver says.

The lights go green, the car starts to move.

Ye just gonna leave it closed instead? I say.

Course I am. I can do what I want with it.

True, the driver nods.

That's bad out, Barry, I say.

Jaysus, the driver laughs, this one your business manager?

Barry shakes his head, holds up his finger, It's my shop. I've signed the lease. I can do what I want with it.

Ye don't have to be such an arsehole, I say.

That's you told, the driver laughs, nudging Barry again.

Barry turns round with a grunt, blinks slowly before fixing me with a stare and saying, It's my shop, Tanya. I decide what happens with it. I'm in charge. Don't go forgetting that now.

Dean

Maybe it's because he's standing over me, but my da looks larger, fatter than I've noticed before. Like his face is being submerged into his neck and all his chins. His nostrils flare. He still has the huge chest, only now it heaves in man boob wheezes. It isn't the person I pass every day on the stairs. It's hard to believe this mess was once him.

—Where's my fucking medal, Dean? he shouts, not even giving me a chance to sit up on the bed.

It isn't a question. It's a demand. His fists are balled pink, the knuckles white.

—What? I say, putting my phone away.

Getting ready.

—Don't *what* me. It's gone.

—What's gone?

—My medal. Where the fuck is it?

—What would I want with a *bronze* medal? I say, in the most disgusted objection I can muster.

After all these years, you'd think I could see one of his backhanders coming. I'm barely sitting up. Can't even defend myself. It's quick, and efficient and stings like a motherfucker on my ear. I'm glad the wedding ring's gone.

—Find it. I swear to God, Dean. Find my fucking medal or it won't be a backhander next time.

He slams my door behind him, the gust of wind from it whipping the Queen poster off the wall.

Cian calls to the house literally five minutes later. No one answers of course, so I have to go down to him.

—Noodle Box? is all he says.

My ear's throbbing, my head ringing.

—Nah, can't go on my own, I say.

—I'll be with you, he says, his foot resting on the edge of my porch.

—I meant without the lads.

He looks confused and after a second he goes:

—This about that SuperValu thing you did?

I shrug, my hand still over my ear.

Cian grimaces.

—That was a bit childish, Dean.

—Says you.

—Come on, you're hardly gang material.

—What would you know?

—I'd know you.

We look everywhere but at each other. My ma creaks on the bottom step of the stairs. She gives Cian a weary Hiya over my shoulder before flip-flopping down the hall in her slippers with a sigh. Her perfume lingers for longer than it should do.

—Another time, Cian, yeah? I say.

—They're all wasters, those lads.

—Don't be a thick.

—Get your medal back?

I shush him aggressively, stepping off the porch to cover the question.

—Your da find out yet?

—No.

—He will, I'm tellin ye. Those lads are snakes. Everyone knows yer man Paddy's cousin was the one who put up Tanya's video. Where'd he get it? Paddy'll use you the same.

—Nah, he won't. He's sound out.

—Fair enough, he says and turns.

—We're mates, I call after him.

He stops, looks back as if I've said something hopeful.

—Me and Paddy. We're mates. We've got each other's backs. Cian gives an exaggerated double thumbs up before morphing it into the fingers and walking off.

Angel

Pelumi sits into the chair and goes:

—I swear Angel. This better be on point for London, bro. I aint lying. You get man vexed and I'll get Isaac's blade and drench man down.

—Chill bro. You're gonna go from 'Yo baby, you got any spare change?' to 'Yo baby, let me change your life!'

The boys are creased up and I fix my gloves and wait for the hype to die down.

—Seriously, though, Pelumi. Go Live for me, yeah?

—Live?

—Yeah. Man don't need a fiver.

—Good, cause you aint getting any, innit.

—Nah bro. Just go Live.

—Yeah?

—Yeah.

—You've quit the deli, yeah? Say mums.

—Mums, I say.

Cause it's true, man got all the cash together.

Pelumi holds out his phone and Isaac takes control of it.

—I'll talk through the trim and answer any questions and shit, I say.

Pelumi shrugs.

—Man, no one is gonna watch that shit.

Isaac waits for the go-ahead and once Pelumi nods, Isaac holds up the phone and starts the Live.

Obviously yeah, I'm under pressure with Pelumi's trim for London gonna be all over YouTube, Pelumi getting vexed if I fuck it up, and now going Live on his socials. But yuno, mans gotta do what mans gotta do.

So basically, I look at the phone, clear my throat and give it high energy vibes.

—What's happening people, it's Angel here, barber boy from the Briggz and I'm about to give your boy Lil Pel the greatest trim mans ever had. Shout out to Next Up crew in London cause that's when you're gonna see the mandem going hard with his slick bars and with fire in his fade, innit!

Pelumi holds up his hands, fingers in our gang sign K beside his face. Swear down it feels mad. But I gotta keep talking, gotta start barbering. Next thing Isaac whispers:

—Two tonne already watching bro. Don't fuck it up.

So I turn on the clippers and raise my voice over the buzz.

—Alright, you know the suss, if you wanna ask me a few questions on the Live, stick it on the chat. No verbals, yeah? Barbering is all about the good vibes, yeah. If you're tryna hop on for a chat, let me know. Otherwise, I'm gonna get busy with this nappy head here.

Isaac laughs and Pelumi looks up at me with a tut, thick, but I can tell he's dying too.

—Two-fifty, Isaac whispers, and Pelumi says:

—Shout out to my boy Angel, trim master, barber for the K3P crew, bringing fresh trims to these ends!

I'm not gonna lie, I am chuffed.

Obviously, yeah, I get it together and look at the camera and go:

—Alright, so, today Lil Pel is getting a low skin fade.

I talk over the clippers and just get going. It feels lethal.

—We begin with a one and a half guard to start the blending. Just an initial guideline, yeah?

Isaac turns the camera to me so I can see all the Likes, the pale blue hearts dashing up the screen in a big hurry. It's amazing.

—Join the lines at the back, point to point. Then man needs to add the shape and make it more defined.

—We got bare comments bro, Isaac calls over the buzz.

—Yeah, what's been said?

—Bare mandem wanna know if you'll give their dead heads a trim.

We all laugh.

—Nah, nah, nah, Pelumi says, his head ducked down still in position for my blade. This boy is our crew. No transfers! No transfers!

I get back to the trim and the love is coming in fast and I am so chuffed with life. I am in the zone, God knows, high like nothing ever before.

—I'm leaving more hair around the front, yeah, cause this is a low fade, and man wants to see the shape-up going round. You'll know what I mean at the end, yeah?

—Yo, we got some yutes wanna hop on, Isaac says. We let them?

—Yeah, all good, all good, I say and turn off the clippers and wait.

—Wagwan bro, the yute says before the top of his head appears on the screen, mad nappy roots.

—Wagwan, I say. Who's this?

—Yinka, the voice says.

—Story Yinka. Where you at?

—Blanch, yeah.

—Cool. Cool. You a fan of Lil Pel, yeah?

—Yeah, but that's not why I'm on.

—Calm.

—Where can I get a trim from you bro?

Isaac thinks this is too funny behind the phone.

—In the Briggz, bro, I say, playing it low-key.

—Safe, the yute says, and then you can see his eyes.

—How old are you bro?

—Fourteen, yeah, but my trim's dead. I need a new barber, yeah?

—I'm your boy then.

I can see all the hearts in blue go wild now, flying up the side of the screen like a water fountain. There are three hundred yutes on this Live.

—Alright Yinka. Mans gotta dash. Mans gotta get back to the grind. Bless, safe.

But before he dips the yute says:

—Hey, hey, hey, where in the Briggz can I get the trim?

Shitden, Isaac is watching over the top of the phone. Pelumi is right under me, and that little yute has his younger eyes on me. Lorcan said all I had to do was call the guy and he'd drop the keys down to the barber's. I've been afraid to. But mans gotta do what mans gotta do, so I just go:

—Mainstreet Balbriggan, yeah. This Saturday is my opening day. And after that, four to eight Monday to Thursday, two to six Friday and all-day Saturday. My barbershop is the red building beside the blue bookies with the smashed-up window. Stall it in. Tell your boys to stall it in too. And that goes for all the bare heads watching now, yeah.

Isaac looks at me kinda confused and Pelumi turns his head up, all deep eyebrows.

—The Live is activ, bro, Isaac says.

He turns the camera round to his face and he sticks his tongue out and goes:

—Wagwan. Send them requests in. Angel's barbering is going off!

—I'm out here saving lives! I shout, pumped, buzzing.

No backing out. No looking back.

I'm not gonna lie, the rest of Pelumi's trim is a blur cause my head is gone, already thinking about making that call to the guy. Paying the month's rent. Getting the keys.

Obviously, yeah, when it's done, the fade is fire. After I sponge Pelumi's head and he gets up and sees the trim in the mirror, he is gassed too.

There's steck comments and DMs to Pelumi asking about my barber's, and all the boys are creased up and wanna know how I got myself a barbershop on the QT.

—No face, no case, I say, low-key. If yuno, yuno.

*

I get the number from Lorcan – who seems a little weird with me on the phone. He's all tuts and sighing and leaving mad big empty silences. Basically, yeah, I reckon he's heard about Pelumi and the new production company.

—I saw the Live you did with Pelumi. You said the barber's would be open on Saturday, Lorcan says.

Swear down, I can't tell if it's a question or he's thick with me.

—Yeah, you said once I had the cash I could get the keys. I've got the cash, now all I need is them keys.

—Just, ye know. Ye didn't need to go advertising the fact it was you opening the barber's.

—What ye tryna say bro?

—Nothing. Nothing. Here, ye got a pen? Take down this number.

I'm hyped, so basically, as soon as I get the number I hang up quick and call the lad who owns the barber's.

—Yo, this is the lad looking to use your barbershop, yeah, I announce, respectful and all.

—Who's this? the voice says.

—Angel. Lorcan's mate. Barry, yeah? He said to ring you when I got the cash together for the barber's.

—Angel?

—That's me bro.

—Where ye from lad?

—Briggz, innit.

—How'd you say you got my number?

—Lorcan gave it to me.

—Okay.

—Yeah, I got the month's rent for the barber's. We all good to go? Lorcan said I could get the keys from you Saturday morning? At ten? Outside the barbershop, yeah?

—That what Lorcan said?

—No lie. We all good?

—You one of Lil Pel's crew?

—Nah, man. I'm out on my own. We good to go?

—No bother, lad. No bother.

And he hangs up.

*

My mam's in the kitchen when I come in from school. Normally she's in work at this time. All man wants is a glass of boba tea, but my mam's in her work uniform, holding a T-shirt of mine in her hands. No lie, straight away I can tell she's vexed. So what do I do? I dash. Pretend I don't see her.

She's all:

—Angel! Angel!

But I don't respond and then she goes:

—*Eza yo, yaka awa!*

And then I know I'm getting grabbed over something.

I jog to her, all innocent, like I only just realized she was home.

—*Yaka awa. Nazo benga yo*, she says, arms folded, my T-shirt wrapped between her fingers.

God knows, when my mam speaks Lingala, there's trouble, so I always try and bring her back to English. It slows her down, calms her.

—Sorry mam. Had to go the toilet.

—*Ozo yoka ngai sikoyo?* she says.

—Course. How come you're skipping work?

—*Ko salela ngai mutu makasi te*, she frowns, and I lower my eyes and see her big toe tapping impatiently in her sandals.

—I didn't mean to be cheeky. Sorry mam.

She takes a breath, and I look up and she smiles at me.

—Okay, she says. Answer me this, why do you have other people's hair on all of your T-shirts?

—Oh. I'm barbering mam. For cash.

—Barbering? For money? How much?

—Serious bags. I'm really good at it, swear down.

—Excuse me?

—Sorry mam. I'm doing really well. Everyone wants a cut. And I've got a shop sorted and all.

—No, no, no.

—Allow, mam.

—Excuse me?

—Sorry. Please mam. Listen to me. I'm really good at it and everyone wants me to be their barber. You gotta understand.

—What about your study? What about the job I got you in SuperValu?

I shrug, smile my smile for her and say:

—You know the way you love *bébé na yo*?

She tries not to be gassed, but if yuno, yuno.

Tanya

Still in the ends hanging with my bff

♫ Do We Have a Problem – @Nicki Minaj & Lil Baby

Tanya vapes into the screen. She is sitting on a couch in a darkened room. A laptop lights her from below while she sings along to the words. She flips the view: a lad in the kitchen, dressed in shorts and a white vest. He has a big chest and thick arms. He opens the fridge and takes out a drink.

>186

You said he'd be back by now.

I thought he'd be back. And then he rang after I messaged ye.
So what am I gonna do for an hour?

Barry leans against the kitchen doorframe, arm up over his head like he's posing. His armpit hair is rank.

You like hanging with me, don't ye? Bit of adult conversation instead of all your shite talk about computer games and homework and all that. Wanna drink?

I'm not having vodka, I say.

242

Red Bull do ye?

It gives me bad vibes now.

I unlock my screen, press record and then lock it again. I position the phone on the coffee table near Barry's end of the couch.

That's from all yer clubbing, the bad vibes with the Red Bull, he calls from the kitchen.

No, it's after that night you got me drunk. How'd you know I was clubbing again?

Ye know I follow a few of yis on your socials.

There's so many weirdos following me.

I saw ye with the Jock's medal. He know yis have that? He'd kill yis.

He'll kill Dean.

He flip-flops back over in his Adidas sliders. He puts a can of Red Bull on the coffee table, and sits down with a sigh beside me.

Who's this Dean lad? he says.

A friend.

Like me?

You're twenty-six. Dean's seventeen. He can't be like you.

Exactly. No one you know is like me. And that's why you're here now, isn't it.

I came to see me da.

Don't be such a tease, he laughs.

He leans in and tries to tickle me.

Stop it, I say and brush him away.

He puts his hand on my leg.

Come on Tanya, he whispers.

I thought you wanted to chat and you're putting your hand on me leg, feeling me up.

Do ye not like that? You've nowhere else to be going. You've no other friends to be hanging out with. I'd thought you'd like a bit of attention.

I shift away from him into the corner of the couch, not feeling it at all.

Course I like attention. And I have got other friends, I say.

I've seen your friends. The lad from the video that always wears the cap. He really your friend? Those girls really your friends? The girl kissing him in all the pictures? Why wasn't she the one in the viral video?

Stop it …

Admit it. You've no real friends. I'm here, now. Yer da's not here. You're friends aren't here. Dean's not here. I'm here. It's not for nothing we keep meeting alone on this couch.

You're the one organising it.

And why wouldn't I? You're gorgeous. You know well we have something.

Didn't seem like that in the taxi. Acting the hard man in front of the driver.

I wasn't acting the hard man.

Talking shit about your barber's.

I wasn't talking shit. Amn't I after taking the piss out've some young lad. Thinks he can just stroll into me shop Saturday morning like I'm a fucking charity. Not a hope. He'll turn up, but I'm telling ye one thing, I won't be there. And besides, you were annoying me. I'd had a few. We're all good now.

He goes to tickle me again. I slap his hand away.

Okay, okay, he says. We'll wait for yer da. And see what he thinks of ye coming in unannounced.

I'll say ye invited me.

Fair enough. And I'll just happen to have the screen-shots of you and your mate Paddy that yer girlfriends put up a few weeks ago.

Barry takes out his phone, flicks across the screen and holds it up.

See. Yer a little tease so ye are, he says. Down on yer knees making a show of yer da. Think he wants to see that going round again?

If he doesn't think I'm his daughter anymore, why would he care? You said you'd have a word with him anyway.

I have. I'm working on it.

I should go, I say, and shift my legs.

Stay. Come on, Barry moans and pats the couch. Stay. Last thing I want is to be sitting here on me tod listening to those savages next door stomping round.

Then go the gym or something.

I'd rather stay here with you.

Then have a word with my da, please, to get in touch with me. Me ma can't get him anymore either.

I will, I will. Just sit down and we can have our chats.

I'm not drinking vodka. And I'm not watching any of yer videos.

Barry gets a text from my da that says he won't be home til much later. I don't get up. I sit and watch Barry scroll through Facebook and Instagram. He taps on videos and gives out about immigration and the lack of housing and jobs for Irish people. I wait, frozen, watching his hands, those nails, his index finger flicking. My leg stays tensed, waiting for his touch, unsure how I'll feel if it comes again.

Cant sleep need green tea

♫Remember (Acoustic / Sped Up version) – @Becky Hill (feat. David Guetta)

Tanya is in a selfie at a kitchen table. 2:10 am is across the screen. Envelopes are stacked behind a wooden bowl containing a blackening banana and a bruised apple. Underwear and T-shirts are on a clothes horse over Tanya's shoulder. She sings along to the song while flattening her hair on her shoulders.
>24

Has he messaged you?

Not for ages, my ma says, ripping open her chip bag and flattening down the inside white flaps. She gets the red sauce and squirts it all over the place.

When was the last time he messaged then?

I dunno. A few weeks ago.

Did he say anything?

I dunno. Does it matter?

I want to know what he said to you.

He asked about Chris, okay.

Chris?

Yeah, Chris.

Oh.

She sucks her thumb and finger.

He wanted to know if he'd been around. If he'd met you yet.

And what did you say?

She picks at a little burnt crispy thing and starts to chew on it for longer than it should take to chew a normal chip.

I said Chris wanted to meet you. And I was going to organize it soon. Then all that mad WhatsApp stuff happened and everything went crazy and I never heard from him.

I miss him, I say scraping a chip off the bag, trying to clear away the mess.

My ma does a few messy red sauce lines over the chips again.

I know love, she says. But ye can't be living like this. If he doesn't want to talk to ye, leave him for now. Ye can't be pining after men all your life. You've got to take control. Take hold of your life. Live on your own terms – not anyone else's. Don't be waiting on other people to make you feel good about yourself. Or make you feel like your life is good. Be your own woman, d'ye hear me?

Mmhh, I say, and keep on eating.

Look at me, Tanya. Do ye hear me?

I miss talking to him. Playing football with him.

My ma shrugs and clicks her tongue on the top of her mouth.

You're not eight, love. He can't be playing ball with ye out on the pitch anymore. People grow up. You have to grow up. Ye need to realize that. Decide what ye want in life and take action. That video thing was horrible, but you got on with things. So do the same with yer da, or whatever else is out there stopping you from being happy.

Me next chip has so much vinegar on it I wince. My ma laughs at me and I smile back.

Need a taxi

♫ Wish You Were Mine (Radio Edit) – @Philip George
Selfie pov as Tanya walks down the street, fixing her hair and vaping. Young lads outside Mr Wu watch as she passes, bopping their head to the song and calling after her. Tanya turns and laughs before swaying her head back into the screen, eyes wide and embarrassed. The pov flips and a taxi is seen up ahead.
>76

Tanya, out. Come on. I've a fare coming, he says.

I need to talk to ye da. Please.

Another time.

Please da.

He sighs.

I'm working. I'm not in the mood.

Ye can't ignore me forever. You're my da.

Finally he turns round.

I'm not though. Am I? Not anymore.

Two dopes with shopping bags appear outside the car.

My da brings his window down and goes, Just a second folks.

Then he meets my eyes in the rear-view mirror and says, Sorry Tanya, I've a fare. Another time.

Of course you're my da, I say. You'll always be my da. That lad Chris is a nobody. He'll never be anything to me. You're my da. And I miss you. I love you, da.

Ah Tanya, he whispers, and takes a breath.

I can't do any more. Say any more. Give any more. He just presses his lips and stares at his fucking handbrake. A small alarm goes off when I open the door.

Wait, love, he says, and looks to the dopes with the shopping bags and goes, Apologies folks. You can get the next one.

Princess

Angel messages, asks if I'm feeling better. Of course, I say, nothing's wrong. Only everything's wrong and I feel hopeless. Totally hopeless. My dream of making something of myself, going to college, getting that train out've town every day, seems more distant than ever. And I'm like, wait, how is that even possible? How has my CAO points capacity decreased, the ability to impress in an interview lessened? It's like the more I've done, the farther away my goals have become. Maybe Tunde's Pharmacy on the Mainstreet was an anomaly. For all I know, he has left Ireland. Gone somewhere that encourages diversity, entrepreneurship. Maybe these streets aren't for me. Aren't for people like me. Maybe I've been aiming too high, asking for too much, expecting too much.

It's two minutes to nine on a Thursday and I'm packing up my books in the library. There's three weeks left until the exams. I've done a solid five and a half hours. No food, no liquids, no break. Just pure reading and underlining.

I whisper goodbye to the old librarian as I shuffle across the carpet. He is slow to respond, his chin nestled into this chest, his glasses at the end of his nose as he frowns with strained eyes to see me. He beckons me over.

I stagger down the steps afterwards. Lost. Dejected. Ready to shuffle home and just cry. Only when I look up, Angel is waiting to surprise me outside on the street, wide smile, big eyes. I wave to him without energy or enthusiasm.

—Hungry for some FLC? My treat, he says.

I reach the bottom of the steps and I can feel he's delighted to see me. And I am, really, the same: delighted to see him too. Only I'm now feeling so sorry for myself after what the librarian told me I don't want to ruin Angel's buzz, be a downer on the evening. It's not as if I'm like his favourite Hange Zoë at the best of times.

—Yo, you good?

I literally bite my tongue. He doesn't need any more of my negativity.

—Shiden, Princess. I do something?

I take Angel's hand and lead him across the road to look back at the whole library.

The top of the building seems normal, the roof, the tower in the corner, right above the big stone sign with 'Carnegie' chiselled into it.

—What we looking at? Angel says.

I nod to the tower, the cone roof with the weather vane on top.

—We doing some low-key Briggz history project?

—See that turret?

—Allow. This is long, yeah.

—Okay. Forget about it. Let's just go to FLC.

—Hardly. We're here, looking at that …

—Round turret, there. Like something from a castle?

—Yeah, yeah, he says, his voice lifting when he spots it.

—This is a Carnegie library. The red-brick part there on the corner. It's really old.

—That's calm.

He giggles, thinks I'm playing a game.

—One hundred and seventeen years it's been there. No problem. Only today, of all days, they found a crack in the roof. A structural defect the old man says.

—Oh.

—Yep. I won't see that old librarian for a while now.

—What, the elder retiring?

We continue to watch the turret.

—Nope. He says the library has to close for emergency repair works. Like, tomorrow. Insurance risk. Public safety risk, in case it blows down, or falls backwards and crashes through the new glass ceiling.

—Shitden.

—Yep, shitden. I've given up work to study, and now, I've nowhere to study.

—Shit Princess, he says, and turns to me. That's harsh. I didn't know you'd finished in the pharmacy. I know how much that meant to you.

—It makes sense, doesn't it? The library, the one place I relied on, the one place in this town that felt like home, is kicking me out when I need it most.

He leans in and hugs me, tight, his arms around my shoulders. He smells so fresh.

—Mango juice? he says in my ear.

We giggle into each other's necks and it feels good. It feels safe in his arms, feeling his heat, his breath on my skin.

—You're paying, I whisper.

—Oh really? Well then you'll definitely be carrying your own bag.

We laugh again. Even in my darkest moments – everything with my mum, my gran, my job, the library – he still manages to make me smile. He makes me feel good: if not about myself, at least about the moment I find myself in.

*

We're late and Angel sits with an uncomfortable cough onto the stiff grey seat nearest the aisle on the last row. I smile, smooth the skirt along the back of my thighs and take a seat beside him.

—Yo, I dunno bout this, Angel says.

I laugh and lean into him.

—Relax, it's just a service. Take off your cap and people will stop staring.

He whips his basketball cap off and starts to brush his hair down with the palm of his hand. You'd swear his head was on fire the way he does it over and over.

—Seriously, though, why we here?

His head is tilted to try and look inconspicuous, his eyes darting round the hall.

My kitten heels sink into the thick blue carpet, feel the welcoming give I remember from my old church. Only in this place, a red strip of carpet goes up the middle aisle and covers the tiered circular design of the altar, making it look like the lava-covered remains of an ancient Roman amphitheatre. The hall is only half full, empty seats dampen the colour scheme. Flat screen TVs shine purple from the corners behind the altar. Then a beat starts up from a golden drumkit in the corner, beside the bottom step. It's loud and echoes around the empty spaces. A small kid is all smiles as he whacks away with loose confidence. About seven people – women in skirts, suit jackets, hats, headwraps – stand in a blaze of greens, whites, oranges, reds and yellows and make their way to an idle forest of microphone stands beside the kit.

—I'm not gonna lie Princess, I think I prefer the library.

—Yeah, well, so did I.

He kisses his teeth.

—Shitden, this place is dead.

—It's not. I used to love going to church.

—This one?

—Course not. I've never gone to one in Balbriggan before.

—So you brought me for protection?

I tug his arm, bring him close.

—Support.

—Hardly, he says, and shakes his head.

THE LORD REIGNS PARISH is on a massive banner adorning the back wall. Thin green laser lights spin weakly across the white letters. A strip of lights strobe along the cornice, warping shadows as they go.

Unannounced, and all of a sudden, this tall guy in jeans and a white T-shirt starts to pound on conga drums. Piano notes pierce through the PA, way too loud for the room. A light synth accompanies them. Still the little kid flails gloriously on the drumkit, cymbals catching the lights, smashing down. The bass drum is solid and establishes a reliable beat. Something I can hold onto.

—FLC is like, one minute away.

—That's your place.

—It's not my only place.

—Yeah, well, this is mine.

My foot starts to tap.

—For real? I didn't think you went to church.

—I did. When I was like, fifteen. Give it a minute. You'll love it.

The women stand behind the mics and start to hum. The people in the hall stand up. Eyes turn to us and I'm like, wait, so you don't get a choice here? I tug at Angel and we stand too.

—I know this song. You'll love it.

—Hardly. You gonna sing along?

—When I feel the power of the Lord, yeah, for sure.

—Eeeyy.

Hips start to sway. The sound is loud and the room so colourful. My eyelids flash the primary colours when I close them. The aroma compounds swirl in the air, esters, cyclic terpenes stir in my olfactory bulb. Cosmetic fragrances of perfume and hairspray stimulate my papillae. My arms start to loosen. I can get lost here, close my eyes and be at peace. Only people continue to look over their shoulders at me and Angel, and I lift my eyebrows as if to say, hi. No one returns the gesture. The women bend their elbows at the hips like in my old church and bop and lean over as if they're going to lose balance, but the Lord will keep them upright. The ladies start to sing at the top of the hall:

You are the mighty God, you are the glorious God. What manner of man is Jes—us!

I start to hum along, work my way into the song. I close my eyes, give myself up to the power of the moment, the music, the love in the room. Feel the joy and the freedom I felt when I was between mum and Becky – when I was fifteen and the whole world was open to me. Then a deep, coarse saxophone, disastrously out of tune, imposes itself unapologetically over the song and the little boy on the drums misses a beat. But still the ladies sing:

You are mighty God!

And I close my eyes tighter until a loud male voice freestyles to what sounds like a different song entirely, in a completely different key, over the choir. Gideon! The pastor no less. He is in a grey suit, and his bald head looks so shiny. A tall man puffs his cheeks out behind the ladies and blows the sax for all his worth too.

Angel sniggers into his chest. He tries to hold it in, but his shoulders betray him. The kids sitting down in their best tracksuits, legs spread wide, bored, stare at him, embarrassed, angry. Angel's laughing highlights how powerless they are to object to their parents about being stuck here.

—Stop laughing!

—Allow Princess, seriously, what we doing here?

The saxophone floats over the piano like oil on water. The women hold on to the microphone stands, eyes closed, as if the song will collapse if they let go. The drum fills are too long and baggy, and Gideon continues to stray liberally with the melody, his brown microphone shaking before his face. I close my eyes again.

—I swear, I'm not giving verbals today, but this is long, Angel whispers.

—Please Angel, I insist, still trying to connect.

—What? No shade Princess, but this place is clapped.

—I loved church before I came to Balbriggan.

—Respect, but you were fifteen the last time you went to church. You're not fifteen no more.

He looks at me with his disarming eyes, sad and understanding all at once. I scan the room, the lasers snaking over the back wall, the man blowing out his big cheeks, eyes closed, giving everything he can to his saxophone, the women swaying uncertainly to a beat they can't find, a tune they can't hear.

—I've nothing else.

He puts his arm around my back, squeezes me softly.

—That's a bar. You've got me, yeah?

Tanya

When he gets you a new dress
♫ Mary on a Cross – @Ghost
Tanya is on a couch in a dark room. She brings her fist to her mouth and tongues the inside of her cheek a few times while moving her fist back and forward before covering the screen with her hair as she laughs.
>42396

Spending time with Barry is a weird thing. He makes me feel good about myself but in a strange way. It's like he knows there's something wrong with me and he's the only one who can fix it. Cause he's older he knows about things. About me. And what I can do to be more mature and stuff.

I got ye a new dress, he announces.

Ah, Barry, I'm grand.

He flips open the laptop and it lights the room.

You deserve it. I told ye I'd look after ye, didn't I?

He turns the laptop round so I can see the screen, the dress.

Seriously Barry. I'm grand, I say. How can ye even afford it when you've given up your barber's?

I told ye, it's grand.

It's not grand. You're being an arsehole, I say.

How?

Telling some poor lad you're gonna give him your barber's and then not.

Relax will ye. I don't need to open it anyway.

Yeah, but …

Give over. I've got ye the dress so ye may quit giving me grief and saying ye don't want it, cause it'll be delivered in a few days. Green will suit ye. You'll try it on for me, won't ye?

Would ye stop? State of me.

He looks up from the screen when I say this. Stares at me with this smile that freaks me out, like he's excited about something behind my head I don't know about.

Don't be so hard on yourself, he says. You're gorgeous. Bet I'm the only one who tells ye that.

No actually. Dean does.

Who's Dean?

This lad that's real nice to me.

Tall lad in some of the photos? He's a kid. You're too mature for lads like him. Bet ye he doesn't buy ye nice gear for the Home, does he?

No. But …

Exactly. You deserve it. Helping ye improve how ye look, I am. Make ye look like a superstar. And you'll model it for me, won't ye? Go on. A little favour. One little favour, and that's us settled.

What'd me da say if he heard ye saying this to me?

How would he hear it? You'd never tell him.

Why wouldn't I?

Cause we're friends. And ye don't want him seeing those pictures I have now that yous have made up again.

How are we friends if ye keep on talking about those pictures?

I'm not. I'm just telling ye how badly your da would react if that kinda shit was all over the gaff again. And I'm the lad making sure it's not. I'm just telling ye what I'm doing for ye. One thing is all I'm asking. Ye try on the dress for me, when no one's around, and we have some time together.

I know I have choices. There's choices out there. I'm just not sure what they are.

I'm not that size Barry, I say.

What?

That's an eight you've ordered. I'm not an eight, especially in Zara sizes.

I'll order another one then. It's no bother.

You do that so.

Who gives you butterflies

♫ All the Stars – @Kendrick Lamar & SZA

A speeded-up montage: a heart emoji over an X-ray of a chest, then butterfly emojis circle the screen before resting on the heart. The word Him appears and the image freezes.

>109

Angel

Basically, I say:

—I wanna show you something. Walk with me, yeah?

And I link her arm.

She knows nothing about going Live with Pelumi's trim. About me talking with the lad who owns the barber's. She's had her head in her books. At this stage, study is rinsed though, yeah.

As ever, man has to keep sketch for Paddy and his boys if I'm not with my crew on Mainstreet. The odd car passes. The neon lights from FLC glow bright and Deli Burger on the corner is all fresh white windows since there's no heads in there. Everything's quiet and calm and feels different.

We pass by FLC and she's confused. I know she walks slow, but shitden, swear down, when we pass FLC it's like her runners got chewing gum stuck to their soles. I nod for her to keep walking and on we go in silence til I stop. I turn to our reflection in the barbershop window. A tall orange street light is over our heads and we stare back at ourselves in the dusty glass.

—What we looking at? she says, and I think she might be hangry.

I'm not gonna lie, mans a bit stressed, yeah, seeing the barbershop waiting and all, so I take out my curl sponge and start to rub my head, right there where we're standing.

The shop is small. The wooden window frame is a real sharp red, but the paint is old and starting to peel. The door is just a frame with two big windows. The opening times are in small white letters stuck inside the glass. There's black bin liners stuck up behind the letters.

The main window is massive. There's steck bin bags stuck up inside that window too. 'Barbershop' is in plain black across the top of the window. On each side of the word there's these poles painted red and blue and white. They look like the marshmallows I used to finesse in Dealz, all swirls, with a little white ball on top. That's the window me and Princess stand in, our reflections dimmed in the dirt, but framed together, yeah, like some old-school album cover faded in the sun.

Swear down, if mandem were strolling by, they'd think the place was some bando. But standing there with Princess, I am on fire and this place feels like the centre of the world. I feel calm now, and I put the sponge away.

—Saturday, this is gonna be my barbershop.

She giggles and looks at me.

—What?

—No cap. I just gotta meet this guy Lorcan's brother knows.

—Who's Lorcan?

—Pelumi's cameraman. Never mind. But like, I gotta get the keys from the chap. Barry's his name. I saved up the deposit grinding in the deli. Swear down, I've got bookings already for the whole of next week.

—You can't drop out of school.

—School's rinsed.

—Seriously, you can't drop out.

—Hardly. My mam would bate me. I'm opening after school every day until after the exams.

She looks back to the window like something new has just happened there.

—What about your Leaving?

—I'm doing it. It's calm. But swear down, barbering is what I wanna stick to. I get a buzz giving trims. I got bookings, bare bookings already. Ten euro each. Six a day after school, ten, twenty a day Saturday. But it's not just the bread, yuno. It's an art though, yeah, barbering. And I'm in. I am on the rise.

She turns to me with this mad look in her eyes, real intense like.

—I've never heard you talk like that.

I hold out my hands, take the shop in.

—For real. This is more than just about me though. Barbering is more than cutting hair. Like Delfina, yeah, up in Oakwood, queues out her door, giving trims in her hallway, yeah. That's dead, yuno? Not proper. Hiding away like that. This is about being on the Briggz Mainstreet. Opening our doors and having youngers stroll in and being all, yo, this guy's Black like me. This place is gonna belong to me, yuno, but basically, them too. That's fresh.

Princess sniffles, looks back to me with these glassy eyes and I'm like, shitden, what have I said now?

—I know exactly what you mean. You're right, she whispers, wipes away a tear and comes right close to me.

She says it like I've surprised her. Like she can't believe it. I dunno if that's wavy or if she's jarring without even knowing it. I don't want to ruin the buzz so I just smile back.

She leans in and we lips. Real slow but really into it, with some mad meaning.

Someone shouts from out've a passing car:

—Get a room!

And we laugh into each other's necks, the way we do, yuno, like we're stuck in this mad tight bubble of just us and good vibes. Mainstreet is quiet again but God knows, it's popping.

—So when do you get the keys? she whispers.

—Saturday morning. I got the cash together and he's meeting me right here.

—Cool, she says. Do you want someone with you?

I nod.

—Yeah. I'd love that. But I'd love you with me tomorrow night too.

She worries her lips.

—I dunno. I gotta study.

—Hardly. Come on. Sesh down the beach. One night. Live your life Princess. This is our chance to celebrate.

Dean

A car alarm sounds somewhere across the estate. The Doberman from two doors down barks against the side gate. A Manna drone pulses across the sky, its electronic hum slicing through the night.

—You okay? I say.

Tanya squirms, gives a weak smile.

—Course, why wouldn't I be?

—Dunno. Just, you calling up here, instead of that gaff you're always posting from.

She seems tired, distant, lost in her vape smoke.

—Whatever. Haven't been here since …

—Since the morning I offered to walk you home, I say, trying to forget the dry spunk in my boxers.

She looks at me like I've hurt her.

—My head's just wrecked with some stuff. I thought we could hang out. Go for a walk or something.

Tanya looks like she's fresh out of a PrettyLittleThing model shoot or a Boohoo ad. I'm in my socks – holes on the big toe and the heel – dirty Penny's tracksuit bottoms and a jizz-stained T-shirt. She's wearing a pristine pink Adidas tracksuit. The top is high, like a belly top – I can see her smooth pale torso, her belly button, an inch below – and her bottoms are so sexy, skin-tight. She has thick white socks on, pulled just above her ankles, and these shiny white sneakers. Don't even think my hair has been brushed today and hers is up in a shiny bun. Her eyelashes are dark and long, and she looks straight at me like she's waiting on an answer. Everything says go for a walk, but there's no way I'm good enough for her.

—I dunno. I'm not feeling it. I've to think about Lil Pel's crew too.

—Come on. That's all bullshit. Those lads don't give a fuck bout Paddy. And they don't even know who you are.

—You not see Pelumi on YouTube? Paddy said ...

—*Paddy said*. Get a grip Dean. What did Paddy say? Paddy say there's a gang war?

She laughs to herself. Her eyelashes start to flutter impatiently.

—There's no gang war. Pelumi's going to London. You think he cares about Paddy? Paddy needs Pelumi to seem tough in this town. If Pelumi isn't rapping about Paddy, Paddy's just another waster on these streets. That's why he shared the ...

She stops, tightens her hair.

—That's why he took your da's medal and won't give it back. Cause it gives him something no one else has. And it gives him control over you.

—Course he'll give it back, I whisper, stepping down from the porch, discreetly moving her from the door.

She arches an eyebrow, claps her hands.

—Come on, let's go for a walk.

I laugh.

—A walk? We're not eight-year-olds.

She groans, thick now, so I say:

—I would, but I can't.

—Stop saying you can't. Jesus Christ. Paddy's using you to make new trouble with Pelumi. How can you not see that? It's because you box. You're useful.

—Like the way you were useful.

She steps back, takes a breath like I've caught her under the belt. Her vape comes out and it glows purple before she's lost in the smoke again.

—I'm sorry, I say. That was bad out.

—It's okay, she says with a wave of a hand. I'm not thick. I know it was Paddy who shared it. He needed to get his rep back. Only I'm the one who got the reputation.

—Reputations don't mean anything, I offer. It's what you are now, or will be, that counts.

She exhales a forest-fruit-scented, shallow laugh.

—Says the lad living off his da's reputation, Deano?

—It's just til I get the medal back. It's a bit of craic.

—What if ye don't get it back? You gonna be a fighter for life?

I shrug, like whatever. My neck spasms from muscle memory and I can almost taste the Valium.

—I'm serious, she says. Reputations stick. I should know. And you're doing a good job of living up to yer da's – throwing digs and getting into fights. I thought you were different.

—You told me to bring the medal.

—Yeah, I wanted to show you off. Show them I wasn't a waster. I could do better than them. I didn't want you to be another Marto or Callum. Paddy's little bitch.

I try not to smile at this hint of a compliment. I think of the club. Paddy's elbow on my neck, the crack of the pint glass, the blood coming out between yer man's fingers.

—I'm nothing like Paddy. You know that. I'm just messing til I get my medal back.

—I'll believe it when I see it.

—If you're so against Paddy, why you still hanging round with them then? I say, not to argue, more to understand.

—Why do you?

I think about saying because I'm a loser, and being near Paddy and being seen with someone beautiful like you makes me feel confident and better about myself. Instead I say nothing.

The drone hovers outside the house across the road. It sounds like a kite in a strong wind. We watch its red lights flashing, see the McDonald's package shiver down on the white string. The noise is thick and intense, a threat.

Princess

We walk home together hand in hand, looking up at the stars behind the orange street lights. Angel can't stop smiling and sighing contently as we go. I glimpse a falling meteor and gasp, but before I can think of a wish I see it's just a drone delivering McDonald's to one of the estates.

—This is just the start, Princess. My place first, then yours, he says.

—I know.

He squeezes my hand.

—You don't seem like ye know. For real. If I can do it, you can, yeah.

I'm ashamed to say, I'm devastated. I am feeling sorry for myself. How have I ended up behind Angel in the standings? How am I on the lower podium for our Black Power salute in defiance of all that's holding us back? How am I playing catch-up?

But then I'm like, wait. This is a first.

Angel is a first. Of my generation. Of locals. In this town.

Yeah, I should be a first. And it's killing me that I'm not. Like Angel I need to be making a mark in my community. Only then I realize, wait, if Angel can do it, if Angel can get the keys to Mainstreet, can get a piece of this town for himself, what's to stop me from doing the same?

He can be my inspiration. These times are unprecedented. Angel's gonna make them precedented. And I can follow. I'm gonna be right beside him when he opens that door – and then I'll be doing the same someday, only my keys will be for my pharmacy.

—Saturday morning Princess, yeah. Me and you. No Bossman coughing in our chicken.

—Nope.

—No library closing cause some wasteman spotted a crack in some bando roof.

—Nope.

—No dusty church playing no clapped tunes.

—Nope.

—That's it, Princess! Come on!

And he holds up my hand as if we're sharing the podium on this deserted Mainstreet. He whoops down the empty road and I whoop too, our delayed lonely echo the only recognition we need.

Tanya

Life of having a lad bsf
♫ True Love – @P!nk (feat. Lily Allen)

The shot zooms in on a lad with a thin moustache who is lying on his bed, fully clothed – socks on his feet, crisps on his chest. He has his hands behind his head and he is smiling at the camera. His dimples create small shadows on his cheeks. The pov flips to selfie and Tanya sticks her tongue out.

>215

I close his bedroom door and stand there.

First time I've ever been up here, I say.

Yeah? You're too busy up in Deano's anyway, Paddy says.

Maybe I am.

Knew it. He's all about you.

He's all about you.

Nah, he pissed me off there the other day, gave me shit when I showed him something on me phone.

What was it? I say, interested now.

Pictures.

Of what?

You.

Yeah right.

Seriously. The ones from ages ago.

What ones?

Down the lane. The video me cousin put up.

Oh.

Swear to God, on me ma's life, Deano says he's never seen them. The video, the pictures, nothing. Not even a sneaky peek. So I gives him the phone, and what does the cheeky bastard do?

What?

He goes and deletes them all on the sly. And then when I catch him he has the cheek to tell me to grow the fuck up.

I've heard Dean never saw the video and thought it was

just the girls taking the piss out've me. To hear it from Paddy is different. Means it's true. And since it's true it hits me different. Like when you're winded on the pitch, caught off guard, gasping for air. Only in a good way. A positive way. It's weird.

Why'd you keep the video anyway? And ye never told me there was pictures.

Relax. It's no big deal, Paddy says picking his teeth.

Ye cudda told me.

What's the point, like? They're gone anyway after Deano deleted them on me.

I'm glad he did.

Lad thinks he's a roadman. He's never getting that medal back now.

Because he deleted pictures of me?

It's not about the pictures. It's him thinking he can act the hardshaw in front of the boys and mess with my shit. They were my photos.

Thought you said your cousin posted them.

Why you here anyway?

I wanted to find out if you were gonna give the medal back.

What's it to you?

Just wanna know.

Well, ye know now.

That it?

The medal is hanging off a knob on his press at the end of the bed. I reach out and take it. Paddy springs off the bed.

Leave it, he says.

I never gave ye any hassle after that video went up, I say.

Give us the medal, T. I'm not even joking.

Paddy takes two steps and breathes through his nose on me face. His jaw is tight, I can see him work his teeth.

What ye gonna do? I say.

Just give us the medal back.

Touch me and I'll go the cops, tell them it was you in the video. You're nineteen Paddy. I'm sixteen. Know what that means?

Paddy leans forward and puts his forehead against mine.

Ye looking for a knock? he says.

It's up to you.

Paddy licks his lips and exhales. The cheese and onion off his breath is rank.

Dean

The full moon is like a spotlight over the sea. Its white reflection swells forward quietly on the high tide. The slow, red flash from the lighthouse mixes with the spinning disco lights from the Home. Added into all the lights, the sounds of the Friday night smoking area makes the beach seem real busy.

As usual we're sat on top of the lifeguard's hut.

—Do ye have my medal Paddy? I say, because it's time I said it.

Paddy looks away to the lights of the club.

—Thought you were gonna earn it by knocking the SuperValu lad out. He's the reason you got owned by Pelumi.

—He shat himself, Marto giggles, his lips sealing around the coke bottle.

—I told yis I'd do it the next time I see him. You'd swear yous were knocking lads out every day.

—We don't need to prove ourselves. You do, Callum slurs.

—We've done our bit, Paddy goes on. I've showed the town what we're like. So has Marto, and Callum. You've done nothing.

—Only talk about your da's medal, Callum adds.

—I thought with a boxer in our crew we'd be running the streets, Paddy says. Maybe that's the difference between bronze and gold.

He says it with a smile, like it's just a bit of craic. He means it though. Callum and Marto snigger into their bottle.

Paddy cops I'm thick.

—Chill, he says. We can't all be legends.

I don't know if he's talking about me, or himself, his dead cousin or my da.

A heavy beat suddenly echoes through the tunnel above the beach. Voices, laughter, deep booming shouts follow. The rattle of a shopping trolley, spikes and sparks.

We all turn and look up to the constant crash of the trolley taking the steps. There's a blur of figures under the orange lights. My heart drops into my stomach.

The music becomes clear once the trolley is on the beach. Just what I thought. Drill. Although it's hard to make out exactly who they are, I reckon we all know.

—There's your SuperValu lad now, Deano, Callum says, with this real satisfied smile.

They don't bother looking in our direction, the crew – maybe they don't care who we are. They keep to the hard sand at the water's edge, walking towards the harbour end of the beach.

There is laughing, so much laughing it highlights how dead it is where we are. A small bonfire gets lit and shapes start to dance around it. They chant, football chants with Pelumi's name, over and over. It looks like great craic.

Someone tugs my arm. Paddy's in close:

—Here, take mine.

The glimmer from his blade is at my hip.

—Nah, I somehow manage. It's grand.

—Take it, he whispers forcefully, at my ear. Don't leave me hanging here, Deano.

—I've got the one you gave me, I say.

Paddy nods solemnly and edges me forward. We drop off the roof. Marto and Callum follow.

—Do this and you'll be a legend forever, Marto says. Seriously man. No one will ever think about dissing you on YouTube again.

—He's right, Callum adds. We'll own the streets after this.

I stand all tense and serious, staring over into the flames and the shapes near the sea.

—Get in, do it, and sprint back, Paddy says. Once ye make the steps you'll be grand.

—We'll wait for ye there. Or if ye get in a scrap, we've got yer back.

I continue to stare ahead, not trying to see anything, but to look serious to the lads.

—Do it Deano, do it, Paddy says, his warm breath on my face. You'll get yer bronze medal back and I'll get ye a gold as well.

I'm shaking, trembling secretly in my big hoody. Everything, my whole life, is burning through my mind, and a question, one question keeps repeating: How the fuck have you ended up here?

The lights from the Home flash pink across the water. I can almost taste the dry ice, smell the sex, the perfume, the sweat. Tanya. That's how I've ended up here. And here, now, is a place Tanya isn't. I have no choice but to act. Do what I need to do.

So I move. The knife is in my hand. I start jogging, jogging as best I can over the deep, dry sand.

The waves wash softly, the bonfire orange on the white froth. Faces flicker. Shadows warp features and then I see him at the water's edge. The drill gets louder, the tight beat so strong and definite.

Silhouettes duck and weave in the sand, doing dance moves I could never muster. Flames light up faces, all happy and laughing. The SuperValu lad is leaning into a girl, smiling. She's enjoying whatever he's saying. Some others have hands in the air, shouting out lyrics over the flames. And still, for some reason, I'm jogging towards this madness.

Why?

What am I doing?

Why am I doing it?

I speed up like a skateboarder would to clear a ramp. I commit.

SuperValu lad. On the edge of the fire, beside a girl. Both with their backs to the sea, their heels almost licked by the tide. And he glances at me. And smiles a simple, pleasant smile as if to say:

—Alright our.

As if I'm just some randomer.

I slow down. I'm no threat. The jog eases. My breath streams out in fast bursts. I'm just some lad walking the beach. We're not enemies. We've never been enemies. I don't want to fight anyone.

I lift my head, start to salute him when I'm grabbed from behind. Hands have a hold of me and there's laughter as I'm forced towards the bonfire. I try to dig my feet into the loose sand, jolt free. I don't even have time to shout. They're going to burn me alive. Like a witch.

I'm picked up, off my feet, two, three lads maybe. I struggle but I'm moving, being moved. And they fire me into the sea.

Laughter follows me down. The water is only a foot deep, but I fall flat into the surf. I'm soaked and breathless, even if it's too shallow to cover me whole. The cold sucks the air out've my chest.

There's mocking cheers from the shore. Phone lights are on me like I'm being rescued at sea. They're recording of course.

One hand offers to help me up.

Angel

We all stall it down the beach with Isaac's big Bluetooth speaker and a shopping trolley full of booze and bits of broken pallets for a bonfire. Princess stays real close, and Pelumi is the main man, his bottle of whiskey held up in the air like the World Cup trophy, rapping over all the songs. She smiles and all, but I can tell Princess is feeling a bit pressured.

—I'm tired, she says after about ten minutes.

—Hang out just a bit longer, I say.

I dunno, I'm feeling sentimental or something bout all this.

—You've got tomorrow morning, remember.

—It's calm, it's calm, I reply and turn and put my arm around Pelumi's shoulder and start rapping with him.

Him and Princess haven't chatted at all. Not gonna lie, Princess is keeping it low-key, and that's cool.

Pelumi leaves his bottle on the sand and turns to the water to piss. This guy is so wasted he can barely stand up. I grab his bottle of whiskey and turn to Princess and go:

—Yo, Princess, to the future, our future!

And take a gulp from the nearly empty bottle. I don't even know why I took up the thing. In a way I wish I didn't. I don't like headache, and Pelumi's bottle of whiskey gives me one. Not cause it's whiskey. Cause it's not whiskey. It's iced tea. Swear down. I am shook.

Princess sees my face and goes:

—You alright?

I respect Pelumi too much to chat about him being a fake. I just place his bottle back down on the sand and say nothing. Then I see that tall boy from SuperValu. He's stalling over with these big scared eyes and he nods, Alright our, and I'm like, fair enough, that's calm, and I nod Alright our too.

Next thing Isaac and Benni grab the guy and Pelumi shouts:

—That's a paigon boys, in the sea, in the sea!

And the lads dash the chap in the water.

I dunno, the iced tea aftertaste is still on my lips and seeing Pelumi pretend to be licked and chatting wass about paigons doesn't sit right with me. So I go:

—Leave it out boys. He's harmless, that's bad out.

I help the lad up out of the waves not even caring if I get my creps wet. It just seems like the right thing to do.

Obviously, Pelumi and the lads are not having a bar of it and their verbals are so long, but Princess just squeezes my hand and I feel wavy. I've caught feelings for Princess, yeah, but that's not it. I'm all about the positive vibes, and I don't feel them no more chatting shit about opps. If yuno, yuno.

Princess

It's fun for a while at the bonfire. Angel keeps his arm around my back, makes sure I feel comfortable. Pelumi hasn't said anything to me, not that it matters. He's too hyped about England and performing for his adoring crowd to bother with me. He has this bottle of whiskey he swigs out of and keeps on saluting everyone with, as if tonight is his last appearance in Balbriggan.

When he leaves the bottle down, Angel snatches it up on the sly and drinks to our future. Pelumi watches him from the shadows. I catch his lazy, serious eyes staring through the flames. Just as Angel's returning the bottle to the sand, some white dude comes out've nowhere, looking all scared and nervous only Angel just nods to him as if they're friends. Pelumi and some others tackle the guy and throw him in the sea and everyone starts cheering and stuff. Angel is the only one to help the white dude out of the water. I can't help but smile and hold his hand that bit tighter when he returns to me. He's the only one who stood up for that guy. The only one who was ready to go against his crowd. Do the right thing.

Pelumi appears beside us and I expect him to give Angel grief about the bottle. But instead Angel turns to him and they do their handshake and pat each other on the back like they're old men who haven't met in years.

Pelumi stands there, and for the first time ever he seems unsure of himself. Maybe I'm standing on a slope, but he doesn't seem as big, or as intimidating as before. Those big eyelids are nearly closed, and his lazy eyes try look down his nose at me and he nods his head and rubs his top lip a few times with his finger. I don't break the stare.

—Look, eh, bout that day in my gaff, yeah, Pelumi says. I'm not gonna lie, Princess, that was a mad thing. I was only jarring, though, yeah? I didn't show you the respect a woman of Angel's deserves. He rates you, yeah? And I respect Angel. Mans changed, innit.

Angel nods, serious and we squeeze each other's hand.

—It wasn't funny. And you need to show respect to all woman, regardless of who they're friends with, I say.

—Safe, Pelumi says, with an agreeable shrug.

—You say it was only a joke, but what would you have done if your sister didn't come in giving out about us all being in her room?

—Allow. Nothing, yeah? Mum's life, nothing. I shouldn't of pushed you on the floor, though. I get that, yeah. My bad. But that's it.

—It's enough.

—No disrespect. No shade. I'm a new man.

—New man? Angel says, looking at the bottle of whiskey between them.

Pelumi holds it up.

—Mans going clear, yeah? Mans gotta do what mans gotta do.

They nod to each other with some ridiculously intense mandem meaning and Pelumi spins back to his crew and shouts:

—Boys, boys, big up Princess boys, yeah!

And everyone cheers. Pelumi hails me with his lifted whiskey bottle and swaggers off. I'm embarrassed when I catch myself smiling. It feels good to have everyone recognize my name. Pink highlighter: Beware the insidious thrill of a cheap ego boost.

—It's getting late. I gotta study tomorrow, I say.

—You're still meeting me to collect the keys at the barber's, yeah? Angel says.

—I wouldn't miss it for the world.

We kiss beside the bonfire, the warm lick of the flames making the beach feel like home. As much as it's a big deal for him, getting the keys, walking in the door, it's a big deal for me too. I need to witness Angel's first steps. See it can be done.

Dean

Cian answers the door, his eyebrows raised, lips in a pout, unimpressed.

—Rough night down the beach?

I'm absolutely freezing, shaking in my heavy, soaking tracksuit. An embarrassment and disgrace. Even the guy from the SuperValu deli took pity on me.

—How'd you know? I say.

—It's on all the socials.

I hold up my busted phone, water still dripping from it. Cian squints.

—You not even seen what Paddy put on his story?

I shake my head.

—Don't suppose you've still got a spare phone?

—Yeah course, he says, a smile trembling on his lips.

Then he turns his screen to me and says:

—I told ye they were wasters.

There's the flashing pink lights of Home, and the loud beat from the dance floor. I'm on the couch near the smoking area, head back, mouth open. Going on the shirt I'm wearing, it's the first time I went to the Home with them.

Tanya straddles Dean and starts kissing him. Dean's eyes are closed, he doesn't react. She holds his face in her hands and the flashing lights make the shot go blurry for a second. The shot comes back into focus as Dean suddenly heaves to life and Tanya falls off him onto the couch. A projectile stream of liquid gushes from Dean's mouth, clearing the arm of the couch. The beat distorts the sound until laughter, close to the screen, breaks through. Dean the queen! covers the bottom of the shot in a large font.

And a little yellow face Queen emoji pops up.

Cian takes his phone away from my face and winces. There's no hint of smugness.

—Fuck.

I put my hands behind my neck to stop my head from falling off.

—Fuck, I whisper again, and hope Cian doesn't hear the wobble in my breath.

—He's an arsehole. Fuck them, Cian says.

He comes away from his front door and sits on the doorstep.

His hall light reflects a dark puddle where I'm standing. A seagull squawks its short call from someone's roof. A drone buzzes in the darkness overhead.

—My da's medal, I say. He's gonna fucking kill me.

I sniffle casually as if it's the cold and wet.

—Dean the queen. That's gonna stick. If not that, then I'm Slenderman Dean. I mean, for fuck's sake.

—You can always go back to being the Jock's son, Cian says.

We share a small, pathetic giggle.

—Nah, I'm a lover not a fighter, remember? I say, trying to sound upbeat.

—You are in yer bollox, Cian says, standing up. The only loving you got was a solo wank on me ma's favourite fucking armchair!

Cian's sister powers down the stairs and stops.

—No dick out tonight Dean, no?

She disappears down the hall.

—Ye looking for a taste of it? I call after her and Cian's face is a mixture of disapproval and amusement.

—I prefer when you're a fighter, he grins and pats me on the shoulder.

—I don't, I whisper.

We both look away quickly.

—Well, ye wanna come in? Cian says after a second, unsure of himself. My ma's out.

—Friday nights now too?

—Fuck off. Come on, I still got a bit of that hash.

My runners squelch when I move. I take a handful of my freezing jumper and squeeze it out.

—Ah, I gotta go home. Get changed. Tell my da about the medal and get a bating.

—Ye can get changed into one of my tracksuits, Cian says. Come on. I'll get my old phone for ye.

His potato house smell reminds me of something I haven't felt in a while.

Tanya

Nah Im rich

♫ Forever – @Labrinth

The camera zooms in on a coffee table and a couch. Noodles hang out of a toppled silver tray on the table, beside that is an opened laptop with Facebook's blue dimming the screen. An ashtray with half-smoked cigarettes is on the other side of the laptop. Next to that cans of Red Bull are crushed and bent. A bright green dress is draped over the arm of the couch in the background.

>225

Look what arrived today. Ye gonna try it on for me now? he says, all smiles.

The dress is hanging from his arm like a large glob of green slime.

Not tonight, Barry. You're drunk, I'm not in the mood.

Come on, don't be such a tease. I'm sober now. Ye said you'd do it, so do it.

I'm not in the mood.

You're being such a child. I thought you'd be more grown up about it. Do it, come on.

His phone rings upstairs, the echo of the bathroom tiles making it louder than it would normally be. Barry throws the dress on the couch and says, You'll be in it when I get back. Right?

I left a voicemail on Dean's phone, and I messaged him telling him where I was and to call up. So when the doorbell rings, I hope it's him.

I open the front door. Dean's there, in the darkness, standing back from the porch. When he sees it's me, he approaches and I laugh cause I thought he'd be sapped. Instead he's in tracksuit bottoms that are too short for him, a pair of Nike sliders and a jumper with sleeves near his elbow. He's scarlet and waves from his hip, as if his hand is tied up.

I'm so glad this is the right house, he smiles.

I don't know what to say, I'm just so happy to see him. I lean forward and before I know it, I'm hugging him. He puts his arms round my back and it feels so nice to be close to someone.

I'm glad you're here, I say. I've got something for you.

His face when I take out the medal is class.

No way! I thought it was defo gone after tonight, he says.

That was bad out what happened ye on the beach.

Is it up everywhere? he says.

Yeah.

See Paddy's story as well?

Yeah.

I'm sorry you were in it too.

Don't be thick, I say, reaching out to grip his hand. There's nothing to be sorry about.

I don't know why, but I hug him again. I don't know what to say. I just hug him because I don't know how to thank him. How to say what it means to me that he deleted Paddy's pictures. To have someone look out for me without wanting anything in return. I take his hand and lead him into the front room.

This the Jock's son? Barry sniffles, sprawled back on the couch, looking up lazily from the laptop on his stomach.

Barry, this is my friend, Dean. Dean, this is my da's housemate.

Da's housemate? Barry repeats.

Alright, Dean says.

We move over to the chair in the corner. Dean sits on the arm of it.

They throw you in the sea there tonight? Barry says, picking up his phone.

Eh, yeah. How you know that? Dean says.

Barry's phone volume is loud and you can hear Lil Pel's voice and the sound of waves and a splash and people laughing.

Barry creeps on everyone's socials, I say.

Dean the queen? That you, yeah?

Leave it out, Barry. You're drunk, I say.

Do that with all the ladies? Puke on them when they sit on ye?

Maybe all the women do that to you, Barry? That why your girlfriend cheated on you? I say.

Fuck off, he snaps back. I'm only having a laugh with the lad, aren't I our? You shudda given those lads down the beach a straightener.

Ah, it's grand. I probably deserved it. Being an eejit I was.

Yer da wudda knocked a few lads out, telling ye, Barry says.

Well, I'm not me da, Dean shrugs, and him and Barry watch each other across the room.

Dean leans down from the arm of the chair and goes, Pelumi's mate from the SuperValu deli was sound. He helped me out've the water. There was no need for a scrap.

Yer just making excuses now, Barry says. Didn't seem like there was no need for a scrap what I saw.

I look up to Dean and say, That deli guy is the barber lad. Angel's his name.

Barry grins and laughs to himself.

Angel? That's the little shit thinks he's getting my shop.

What you're doing's bad out, Barry, I say.

Relax, our. The lad lied to me. Tried tell me he was a local. Not a hope. Little shit gave me lip a while back on the street with his gang too. What comes around, goes around.

I tut. I couldn't be arsed arguing with Barry but he's annoying me now.

What he do that was so bad? I say.

They wouldn't move outta me way when I was coming out've Spar with a few bottles.

That it?

It's enough.

He seemed sound to me, Dean says.

Barry makes this face, like he's confused all of a sudden and he goes, In fairness to ye, Brian, why don't ye fuck off home. No one gives a shit what you think.

It's Dean. And I care what he thinks, I say.

Dean, fair enough, but yis can stop all this woke talk. It's my barber's and I'll do what I want with it.

Barry nods to the dress beside him, and then meets my eyes.

And I always get what I want, he says.

Dean's hand is warm on my shoulder and I think, what

about what I want? I feel brave with Dean by my side. Braver. I feel like I've still got choices, control. Fuck him.

So I open my phone, find the clip and press play. My volume is down at the start, but I turn it up quick.

A bare switched-off lightbulb hangs from a ceiling directly over the phone screen. Tanya leans across and glances into the screen and disappears from shot. A shadow passes, a male voice gets louder.

Come on Tanya.

I thought you wanted to chat and you're putting your hand on me leg, feeling me up.

Do ye not like that? You've nowhere else to be going. You've no other friends to be hanging out with. I'd thought you'd like a bit of attention.

Course I like attention. And I have got other friends ...

The laptop clacks on the coffee table.

Where'd ye get that? Barry says, sitting up.

I recorded ye a few weeks back, I say.

Gimme the phone, Tanya. Swear to God, gimme the phone.

He storms around the coffee table, knocking off it with a slight stumble. Dean gets to his feet. The chair rocks a second. Dean then stands in front of me. I can't see past his arse in the too-tight tracksuit bottoms.

Sit down or I'll put ye down, Dean says.

Gimme the phone Tanya, Barry goes.

He's face to face with Dean now, but obviously talking to me.

I can't stand up because Dean's against my legs. But still I say, Sit down Barry and stop being such a racist prick.

Barry leans his head into Dean.

I'll knock this lad out, I'm telling ye.

Try it. Go on, and I'll put ye on yer back, Dean says.

Barry is on his tippy toes going eye to eye with Dean. Dean's fists are closed, his elbows bent, standing the way he did that night in Paddy's. The front door sounds and da can be heard coming in. Barry steps back and shakes his head.

Sit down Barry like a good lad, Dean says.

Barry just sways there, looking from me to Dean.

My da walks in smiling. He has a battered leather football in his hands.

What's going on here? he says.

Dean steps to the side of the chair.

We were talking about Barry's barbershop, I say. He's gonna give the keys to a young lad who was looking to open it up. Aren't ye Barry?

Barry hasn't turned to me da. He just watches me.

And I was showing the lads a green dress I'm after getting, but I'm throwing it out cause it's in bits, I say.

Never mind his barber's, my da says. Look what I'm after finding in the driveway.

Barry turns away finally and says to my da, I don't play football.

I didn't bring it in for you, ye thick, my da laughs.

Grand so. I'm going to bed, Barry mutters.

Drop the keys for the barber's out before ye go, I say.

Barry stops at the door, turns to say something, takes a breath and leaves.

Who's this? my da says.

He's my friend, Dean.

He one of those lads?

No. He's a different lad.

Da looks Dean up and down and shrugs, Alright our.

Chillin with my orange soda shorty

♫ Orange Soda – @Baby Keem

Tanya mouths the words to the song in selfie pov. There's a thin lad beside her on the couch. They laugh before she flips to front pov: a greying man, can of beer in hand, is across the room on the chair shaking his head and smiling.

>27

Bless

A Saturday morning in May. The sky is cloud-free and dazzling blue. Somewhere behind the silhouette of the viaduct, the sun is casting strong shadows over the beach.

Morning swimmers change out of their Dryrobes under the cover of the lifeguard's shack. Some are moaning about the rubbish, kicking coke bottles out onto the sand. There's a smell of petrol. They say it stinks. One lady nods to the shoreline and the scorched black skeleton of a small bonfire. Two pale men crouch in their swimming trunks and stretched swimming caps. The Irish Sea laps at their ankles as they try to remove a half-submerged shopping trolley before they go any deeper.

Up the canal, over the willow tree and beyond the back of the Budgie Bissett's Casino, at the monument for the slain locals, two middle-aged women in high-vis jackets scrub frantically at the dirty limestone. Others dressed like them are dispersed along the boarded-up buildings on one side of Mainstreet. They stoop and straighten as they clip stray wrappers in their pickers before shuffling them into Fingal-crested blue plastic bags.

Young lads in green Glebe North football shorts and socks, large gym bags slung over their shoulders like they're on their way to a day's work, bounce down Mainstreet. Cars settle at the traffic lights in the shadow of the hotel. The drivers and their young passengers in the back – O'Dwyers jerseys already on, gumshields in – watch two teenagers standing together in front of the barbershop window. The lights go green and the cars roll on.

The two teenagers hunch their shoulders in the shade. They check their phones, bite their lips. Princess raises her head, watches the hill. Angel makes signs with his hands, circles her almost on his toes, as if they're standing on lava and he doesn't want to get burnt.

—It's only a quarter past, Princess says, still peering towards Deli Burger.

—It's calm, Angel says, eyes on his runners, the gum stained, grey pavement.

The traffic lights go again, and the green man's insistent noise amplifies their silence.

Mainstreet is busy with life, but Angel looks sick.

—It's not that late, yet, Princess says.

—Calm, calm, Angel whispers.

He takes out his curl sponge and starts to massage his head.

A window opens above the barber's. Angel glances up. The sun, having cleared the hotel roof, softens the cigarette smoke streaming from the apartment window.

As the minutes ebb by, the shadow line fades and Angel and Princess squint and shield their eyes in the new light. Past the square, coming over the hill and through the scaffolding outside the library, two figures appear. They walk slowly, confidently, as if the streets are theirs. The shadows from the scaffolding ripple over the couple until they emerge, bright and smiling. The girl has a football under her arm.

Angel watches them and continues to sponge, slowly now. His stern, almost worried face doesn't change. Princess, chin raised, neck strained, continues to look towards Deli Burger and FLC where the blue-vested women with the pickers have stopped to chat.

The couple approach the traffic lights. Dean thumbs the grey button and Tanya bounces the football while they wait. Dean watches Angel across the road. When their eyes meet Dean nods. Angel doesn't reciprocate.

—Yo Princess, he says.

The tremolo zap from the green man fills the street.

Tanya and Dean cross quietly, their eyes only on the road before them.

Princess catches her bottom lip with her front teeth again.

The sponge stops circling, but remains on Angel's head, as if his hand is stuck there. His face is grave.

Tanya giggles as she unveils a silver set of keys from her tracksuit top. She holds them out to Angel.

—These are yours, she says.

Angel looks to Princess.

—They the barbershop keys? Princess asks Tanya.

Dean smiles.

—Yup, Tanya says.

—Bless, Angel exhales, his hand opening to Mainstreet.

In Memory of
Jack Kevitt
(2001–2018)

Acknowledgements

Thanks to the following readers and collaborators:

Dave Lordan for commissioning the story 'Saving Tanya' in 2015.

John Patrick McHugh for reading the early Tanya, Dean and Princess chapters.

Darine Abuniemh for her time and wise words on the Princess chapters.

Glory Agbator, Tommolina Tom-Irehovbude and Queen-Monica Yembet (the always smiling trio!) for their time, good humour and invaluable insights on the Princess chapters.

Yinka Adedokun for his time and advice on the Angel chapters.

Marissa Tshibangu for her time, Lingala knowledge and ideas on the Angel chapters.

Thanks to:

The Arts Council of Ireland and Fingal County Council Arts Office for providing financial support during the writing of this novel.

Everyone at the Lilliput Press, Ruth, Dana, Bridget, and especially Antony Farrell.

All of my students – past and present – at Balbriggan Community College for continuously setting an inspiring example for what a truly diverse, multi-cultural and tolerant society can look like.

Special thanks to:

My parents, John and Una.

Sebastien Curran and Fleur Curran.

Seán Farrell for his editorial expertise and incredible vision for what *Youth* could be.

And finally, Helena. Without her unwavering support, generosity and understanding, this book couldn't have been written.